PRAISE

SEA FEVER

"Inspired by on-the-ground research, Elsie Sze weaves and then untangles a series of knots in a plot worthy of its exotic locale: Kazakhstan! *Sea Fever* swept me away to a world of intrigue, a thrilling journey led by two characters whose unlikely pairing led me—in close pursuit—to the Aral Sea. It is a wonderful escape from the ordinary and a gateway to another part of the world."

—**Isabel Huggan**, author of *Belonging: Home Away From Home*

"Elsie Sze tells an unforgettable and riveting story about the interconnectedness of human and ecological health and sickness, and the negative consequences of human attempts to dominate nature and other people. In reading this book, we are invited to listen to the death cries of what was once a vibrant, life-sustaining sea. Sze raises poignant questions not only about the past but also about the biggest issues confronting the human species today. Can we really imagine that we can vaccinate ourselves against the very ecological sicknesses that our industrialized military and medical systems are creating?"

—**William F. Sullivan**, MD, CCFP, PhD (Philosophy); Family Physician, St. Michael's Hospital, University of Toronto; Incoming Joseph P. Kennedy Chair in Ethics, Kennedy Institute of Ethics, Georgetown University, Washington, DC

"Among the greatest environmental tragedies of our time, the death of the Aral Sea at the hands of man and a regime remains the main event of the region and the heartache of Kazakhstan to this day. Elsie Sze's personal experiences, her deep cultural and historical insight, lend extraordinary authenticity to this wistful, but gripping, mystery set in modern Kazakhstan."

—**Aidar Kazybayev**, CEO, AIFC Green Finance Centre, Nur-Sultan, Kazakhstan

SEA
FEVER

SEA FEVER

a novel

ELSIE SZE

RIVER GROVE
BOOKS

Published by River Grove Books
Austin, TX
www.rivergrovebooks.com

Distributed by River Grove Books

Design and composition by Greenleaf Book Group
Cover design by Greenleaf Book Group

Publisher's Cataloging-in-Publication data is available.

Print ISBN: 978-1-63299-588-9

eBook ISBN: 978-1-63299-589-6

First Edition

To Michael, with love

KAZAKHSTAN AND NEIGHBORS IN 2006

* As the Aral Sea continued to lose its water, Vozrozhdeniya Island (Voz Island in the novel) became a peninsula connected to the Uzbekistan mainland.

** The name of Kazakhstan's capital was changed from Astana to Nur-Sultan in 2019.

THE ARAL SEA IN 1960 AND 2006

* As the Aral Sea continued to lose its water, Vozrozhdeniya Island (Voz Island in the novel) became a peninsula connected to the Uzbekistan mainland.

CONTENTS

BOOK I

AYAN

1

A FRIEND FROM THE PAST

1991

To Ayan Kazbekov and the world, August 23, 1991, might well have made all the difference. As he drove his secondhand Zhiguli in the direction of his apartment, he knew nothing of the surprise visitor who awaited him that evening, nor the secrets their meeting would lead him to—secrets that might shake the world and change its course. That afternoon, Ayan left his office at the Institute of International Languages in Moscow for the last time, having cleared out his desk and shelves and packed two boxes of books to take home—to Kazakhstan and the Central Asian steppe, in the far reaches of the USSR. Looking back one last time at the office that had been his daytime quarters for the past six years, he felt that same heaviness in his chest as he had the first time he left his hometown of Aralsk by the Aral Sea fourteen years earlier. He had taken the 2,400 kilometer train journey to Moscow to attend university. Perhaps this time the anxiety of separation was more acute, for he could not foresee a reason to return to Moscow again in the predictable future, not with the disintegration of the USSR looming in the near distance. These days, the city was beset with discontent and unrest as its republics clamored for separation and independence. Ayan wanted to return to the safe haven of his home in Kazakhstan, even though it meant giving up a good teaching job in the mega capital.

He drove his beloved car along Moscow's wide and busy streets, one of the last times he would be driving the car before turning it over to a new buyer the next day. He purposefully took a longer route back to his apartment, like a sentimental fool bidding farewell to every familiar sight and sound in the fearsome, awe-inspiring city. Against the looming gray sky, Ayan noted through his windshield the gold domes of defunct cathedrals, the pointed red towers of the Kremlin, and the multicolored onion-tops of St. Basil's, that iconic symbol of Soviet Russia. He took a detour up Lenin Hills to Moscow State University, the incubator of the best minds within the Soviet Union, which had captured Ayan's esteem long before he was admitted into the establishment. The Main Building was still as intimidating to Ayan as it was the first moment he set eyes on it, its solid, somber symmetry and its dangerous, insurmountable height, so awesome, mystifying, and formidable. Ayan could only imagine what secrets it must have held in the two hundred some years since its formation.

Ayan had just stepped inside his apartment after hauling his two boxes of books up the stairs when the phone rang. He answered.

"Ayan Kazbekov?" asked an unrecognizable, muffled male voice.

"Yes," he answered somewhat warily.

"Victor Luganov here."

"What?" Ayan said in surprise. Had he really heard that right?

"Victor, your friend from Moscow State! Hey, I'm in town. Let's meet tonight for a drink at the Russian Bear by Sverdlov Station, like old days, okay? See you there at eight." A click. The caller had hung up, giving Ayan no time to respond.

Ayan sat down on one of the boxes he had taken home and tried to compose himself. He bit into his tongue and stabbed his index finger with his thumbnail. He felt the pinches. He wasn't dreaming.

—

One autumn afternoon in 1977, as Ayan was walking through Gorky Park from his hostel to the university's Main Building, he noticed that a man running in front of him had dropped his keys. Ayan called after him. The man turned back, thanked him, said he had had enough running for the day and decided to walk along with Ayan as he too was going that way. The man was Russian, apparently in his early twenties. He was good looking with suave manners, a wisp of light brown hair falling over the right side of his forehead and brushing his brow. He was tall, about ten centimeters above Ayan's meter seventy-five. The fellow said he was heading back to Zone B of the Main Building, where he resided, to take a shower before going to class.

"Oh, so you are one of the privileged few who never have to leave the Main Building for anything. You can walk right from your room to just about everywhere, even your classes, without ever going outside," Ayan said with a wink.

"That's right! Except I would suffocate if I didn't go outside, breathe fresh air, and see the sky every day."

They exchanged laughs and names. The fellow introduced himself as Victor Luganov. From his Russian, it seemed Victor was a Muscovite. Ayan was almost right. Victor said his family lived on the city's northern outskirts.

"And you? Where are you from?" Victor asked.

Ayan paused for a moment to mentally frame his answer. "Kazakhstan, on the eastern edge of the Union. It's basically the end of the world, depending on whom you ask."

"Nothing wrong with being from one of the Central Asian republics. Remember, we are all equal."

"But some are more equal than others." Ayan chuckled, looking over to Victor, who seemed to see no reason for amusement. Ayan continued, "Things are different where I come from—a town called Aralsk. My father was a fisherman there, back when there were fish in the Aral Sea."

"Are there no fish anymore? How come?"

"The Aral Sea is losing its water, a terrible environmental disaster. And with no water, there are no fish."

"Oh . . . Sorry to hear that," Victor said, then seemed unsure what more to say. After a few moments, he asked, "So what's your field of studies here, Ayan?"

"English is my specialty."

"Wow! I'm in fourth year biology, and I thought that was hard."

By the time they reached the Main Building that morning of their first encounter in Gorky Park, Victor had impressed Ayan as a disciplined person. He seemed to spend long hours in the lab or library every day and still managed to balance his studies with regular attendance at the gymnasium, plus jogging in Gorky Park. Ayan didn't know how he did it all; it seemed he had fifty hours in the day.

They found they enjoyed each other's company so much that they agreed to meet that weekend for a jog together in Gorky Park. It soon became a routine.

—

The night of Victor's unexpected phone call, Ayan entered the dimmed recess of the Russian Bear mere minutes before eight. He was more than curious about what had happened to Victor in the nine years since he'd last seen him, in June of 1982. He edged toward the bar, his eyes eagerly scanning the handful of men sitting or standing around it. Soon someone tapped him on the back. He turned. It was Victor. He was still good-looking but was an older version of the friend Ayan remembered, with a more rugged face, darker complexion, leaner build, and a noticeably receding hairline. They paused for a moment, scrutinizing each other, Ayan searching for clues of what his friend might have lost or gained in the years of his absence. Then they gave each other a firm handshake and slapped each other on the shoulders.

Victor was the first to speak. "You are the same, my friend, same boyish look from the first day I met you! And not a strand of gray in that black mop of yours! What's your secret formula for eternal youth?"

"No secret. Just got the least stressful job I could," Ayan said, laughing, and added, "I teach English."

"To Russians?" Victor rolled his eyes. "And you call that not stressful?"

They moved to find seats at the bar to order some drinks.

Victor suddenly turned around to face the middle-aged man standing behind him. Ayan hadn't noticed the short, rounded figure whom Victor now stiffly introduced, his mirth suddenly erased. "By the way, this is Andrei."

"*Zdravstvuyte!*" Ayan said, extending his hand to shake Andrei's. The guy nodded lightly, taking Ayan's hand at cue to give it a flimsy shake, something less than a smile twitching over his lips. He then took the seat on the far side of Victor at the bar.

Victor ordered draft beer and snacks. He had retained much of his Muscovite accent. His speech told Ayan nothing about where he could have lived the past nine years outside of Moscow.

"Victor, my friend, where've you been since leaving the university? I never heard from you after we had our last drink here."

"I have been busy with research work ever since. I'm very sorry I haven't been in touch. What matters is I'm now home!" Victor answered with a forced grin, his smile too spirited to be genuine. Then, with sincere interest in his voice, he asked, "Tell me what you've been doing while I was away."

"Well, I was an *aspirant* in English studies till 1985 and then got a job teaching English at the Institute of International Languages. This is my sixth year there." Ayan's eyes wandered over to Andrei, who was finishing his first beer and helping himself to the pickled cucumber and salted herring. He remained apparently disinterested in their conversation, yet to Ayan he was an uncomfortable presence.

—

"What are your plans after graduation, Victor?" Ayan had asked on one of their Saturday jogs through Gorky Park.

"Short term, I plan to stay on at Moscow State as an aspirant in microbiology after my diploma. Long term, I want to be one of the best in my field." Victor's face lit up as he spoke. "I want to make a mark as a scientist and make a difference. Maybe even discover something that will be a contribution to my country and to science." He looked into the distance as though he was seeing the future in which he lived up to those big dreams.

"Wow, those are some lofty goals! The world needs people like you. You've got the brains, ambition, and discipline to drive progress and make life better for all of us. I hope you get there, my friend."

"Thanks. That's the idea, anyway. Time will tell if I can pull it off. All I can do is try my best, work my hardest, and make the most of whatever opportunities come my way. What about you, Ayan?"

"My plans seem dull compared to yours. All I want is to be a good teacher of English, the most spoken language in the world."

"Your goal is higher than you think. We both want to make some impact on mankind. Your magic wand is the teacher's pointer, and mine is . . . well, all I can think of is the glass stirrer I use in the lab!"

Ayan laughed.

Not only did they jog together in Gorky Park on weekends for a good part of Victor's remaining years at Moscow State University, but they also shared fun nights in the city. Between the scholarship Ayan received for his good exam results and his part-time night job scrubbing floors in one of the campus buildings, he had enough money every month for more than a few beers with Victor at bars in the theater district around Sverdlov Square. For all of Victor's intent in the pursuit of academic excellence, he spent many evenings painting the town red in the company of Ayan and sometimes a few other friends.

The first time Ayan went with Victor to a bar at Sverdlov Square, after a few shots of something a little stronger than Russian stout, Victor started inventing perceptive names to call every female whose shape or assets caught his eye, names like hourglass, roly-poly, teapot, and double-trouble, but only for Ayan's ears. Victor's jokes drew hearty chuckles from Ayan, who was amazed to see a different persona in his highbrow scientist friend. There was obviously more to Victor than the bookish fellow with mighty ambitions.

Over drinks at the bar and meals in the university cafe, he and Victor had become firm friends. In spite of Victor's sky-high ambitions and Ayan's own down-to-earth goals—and the fact that the disciplines they pursued were as far apart as the opposite shores of an enormous sea—they understood and trusted each other. They could joke without qualms and make unguarded remarks, knowing their comments, fancies, and fantasies would go no further than the space between them.

—

The Russian Bear was filling up by the moment. "Hey, update me on your love life! What happened with Lady Godiva?" Victor had to raise his voice to be heard above the increasing din at the lively bar.

"Her name is Valeria," Ayan jokingly corrected his friend. "I'm surprised you remember her."

"How could I ever forget? You were quite enchanted with her. Remember when I moved out of the university, I rented an apartment in a house across from where she lived? Not intentional of course!" Victor chuckled.

"Of course I remember that. We dated for a good while after you were gone."

"And?"

"And then we went our separate ways."

"How could you? That's a pity." Victor heaved an audible sigh, and with a mischievous grin added, "If only I were still in Moscow, I would gladly have stepped in. Some pretty woman she was!" He picked up some salted herring and munched. "One of my docents at Moscow State once said, 'A man gets married twice: the first time for Moscow residence, the second time for love.' You should have at least married her for Moscow residence. Then there'd be no need to prove your own worth with hard work, although I see you've done it on your own. Besides, it seemed you really did love her, so you would be . . . how do the English say it? Killing two birds with one stone!"

"I had wanted to marry her for herself, but things didn't work out." Ayan looked away, regret in his eyes. Then recovering himself, he turned back to Victor and said with renewed interest, "Hey, let's not talk about me. I want to hear everything about you!"

"There's really nothing much to say," Victor said with finality. That answer told Ayan that whatever Victor had been doing, it must be classified—like many jobs in the Union—and he could not talk about it. There was an air of secrecy in Victor's behavior. Ayan darted another glance at Andrei. Now on his second beer, Victor's companion remained stone-faced, continuing to seem uninterested in their conversation, although he could clearly hear every word they spoke, unless he was stone deaf as well. Ayan shifted in his seat. Bodyguard or KGB, Andrei made him uneasy.

"Are you married?" Ayan asked, turning back to his friend. At least, his love life should be a safe topic.

"No." Victor slurped up some of his beer.

"How come?"

"Marriage demands a lot of sacrifice on both parties. I'm afraid I'm not cut out for that kind of commitment," Victor said very matter-of-factly. This was definitely not the Victor Ayan knew, the genuine and optimistic person with high hopes for the future and a ready joke for any woman who walked by. There was a boredom bordering on sadness in Victor's countenance, as though his life had not turned out the way he wanted it to, and he was burdened with disappointments and regrets.

At a loss for what to say next, Ayan looked around the bar. "Remember when we used to come here as students?" Ayan tried changing the subject again. With that, he seemed to have hit the right key.

"That was the best time of my life," Victor said, brightening up. "We'd come for a beer when we needed a break, and afterwards we'd go down to the metro stations late at night, singing and carousing as though we owned the place. Remember those nights?"

"How could I ever forget? You were the one who introduced me to night patrolling the metro stations, as you called it," Ayan said.

Ayan had been enthralled by Moscow's subterranean stations since the first time he took a metro train. Like a kid wanting to go on every ride at an amusement park, he hopped by train from station to station, soaking in the sights at each one. To him, every station was a museum in its own right. Each had a unique theme, be it the commemoration of a major historical event of the Soviet Union, a tribute to one of its republics, or an architectural extravaganza in the style of a historical period. He loved the varying environments of the stations, some grand and magnificent, others elegant and artistic, and a few chillingly spooky.

He and Victor would often take the metro out to Sverdlov Square to frequent the bars. By the time they descended down into their station again to head back home, the platforms would be almost deserted. They found the empty stations surreal, and soon they started venturing down into deserted stations all over the city shortly before their closing time of one in the morning. Late at night, they could have the stations to themselves, to discover and rediscover, to wallow and lose themselves in. Ayan liked the sounds of quietude, the shadows cast on the walls by glittering chandeliers or austere ceiling lights. He found the atmosphere at once fascinating and daunting, an escape from his daily grind of studies. There was a thrill to being the only souls in the huge stations through which thousands would pass as soon as day dawned.

"Remember the night you had the scare of your life at Ploschad Revolyutsii Station?" Victor asked, with a playful twinkle in his eye.

"Don't I remember! I thought you'd gone missing, and then you jumped out at me from behind the statue of the guard with the dog. I almost fell off the platform!"

"And your scream echoed through the entire terminal!" Victor laughed as they lived the moment again.

Ayan found Ploschad Revolyutsii Station to be the spookiest of all the metro stations. It was inhabited by tall life-sized bronze statues of different workers in uniform peeking at them from behind dark red and brown marble arches and pylons, the low-hanging pendant lights casting eerie shapes on the walls. Ayan's nerves tingled every time he wandered that haunting labyrinth of hallways at night, wary of the dark looming statues surrounding him from all sides.

"I was nervous about those statues, but we became pretty fond of the guard with his dog," Ayan reminisced. "We used to rub the dog's nose every time we passed. For luck."

"Yes! The dog's nose! That has to be the most polished piece of bronze in all of Moscow." Victor laughed. After a pause, he asked, "Remember Old Maid?"

Ayan had to think for some seconds, then the image came to mind. "Oh yes, the statue of the female sailor next to the guard and dog. You called her that because everyone would pet the dog but no one paid any attention to her. You were always good with nicknames," Ayan said with a half-smile, shaking his head.

"I was scared of those statues as a kid. They looked so much taller, and sort of sinister, and yet I loved going there with my father to take the train to the Georgian Market." Looking into the distance, Victor seemed to have lapsed into a more serious disposition again. "Sometimes I want to confront what I'm afraid of, as though in doing so, I'm conquering my inner enemy."

"Hey, you're getting to be very philosophical, my friend. I hope you are not troubled by something serious." Ayan fiddled uncomfortably in his seat, waiting for Victor's response. Seeing no reaction from him, Ayan continued, "You've changed, Victor. You are much more sober than before. I am very happy to see you though. I wish we had more time to catch up, but I'm leaving Moscow and going home."

"For the summer? When are you leaving?" Victor asked, taking another sip of his beer.

"In two days," Ayan paused. "And no, not just for the summer. I've resigned from my teaching job here. I'm going home for good."

Victor almost choked on his beer. "What? Why? But you had a good job here, and the city has everything, not like in Kazakhstan. And in two days! Are you crazy?" He shifted in his seat, looking somewhat thrown off balance, but recovered himself soon enough. Then looking fixedly at Ayan, he said emphatically, "I'm very glad I caught you in time." In that moment, Ayan sensed that his friend wanted to tell him something important but did not. Perhaps he could not.

Ayan said, "I am very sorry we have so little time before I leave. My parents are getting old. I should be with them. Even so, I'll be teaching in Kyzylorda, 450 kilometers from Aralsk and a bit farther still from our village, Balta. There are no good jobs for a teacher like me in Aralsk. But at least my parents and I will be in the same *oblast*. Kazakhstan is my home." Ayan stopped, hesitant, then added, "You know the Aral Sea is almost gone."

"Yes, I've heard. I'm very sorry," Victor said. "I remember well going with you to visit your parents that summer at their house by the draining sea."

"My parents enjoyed your visit very much. It was the summer of '79," Ayan reminisced.

"That was one of the happiest times of my life. I have often thought of it," Victor said, his words shaky. "How are your parents coping these days?"

"They're getting by. They raise camels and sheep and farm some produce, and it brings in just enough. Life is hard, but they manage."

"That's good. I wish them well," Victor said, a tremor in his voice. After a moment, he shot a quick glance at Andrei, then stood up and excused himself to go to the toilet, leaving the other two men to share an awkward silence between them. Ayan offered to get Andrei's empty mug refilled, but Andrei signaled with a wave of his hand that he had had enough. Stalemate resumed. No need to strike up a conversation for conversation's sake, if all this Andrei guy wanted was to be left alone. After a long ten minutes, Victor came back. Looking at his watch he said, his voice quivering, "I really wish we had more time, but I should be going, Ayan."

"So soon? I don't even know where you are staying! Are you back for good?" Ayan asked, almost begging for an answer.

"I'm staying for the time being at a friend's place. I don't have future plans yet," Victor replied, glancing askance at Andrei who sat expressionless but no doubt listening closely.

"So, you have quit your job, whatever and wherever it was," Ayan deduced. He pressed on, "I don't go home till the evening after next. Let's meet again tomorrow. There's so much more for us to catch up on."

"I'm not sure about my schedule, but I'll give you a call." With that, Victor stood up, fumbled in his pants pocket, and took out his wallet. "The drinks are on me. Please pay the bartender," he said, stuffing a few bills into Ayan's hand. Andrei also stood up, pulling a handkerchief out of his jacket pocket and pressing it to his face as if to wipe the sweat off his forehead.

"You'll call tomorrow, yes?" Ayan reminded his friend.

Victor nodded with hesitancy. He then gave Ayan a long and firm handshake, his free hand on Ayan's back. They looked at each other, sad intensity in both their eyes. Ayan could not find the right words to say. There was still so much Victor had to tell him, so much he wanted to know of his friend in those missing years. Yet time seemed to be running out. Victor let go of Ayan's hand and turned to go. As he headed toward the door, he looked back to Ayan once, waved and mouthed "*Do svidaniya!*" Then he walked out, with Mr. Grim-Face a step behind him. As Ayan watched him vanish into the darkness outside, his gut told him he might not be seeing Victor again.

Clutching the banknotes in his hand, Ayan waited at the busy bar counter for one of the bartenders to come by. He looked down to count the money and was surprised to find that there were two three-*ruble* banknotes and a folded piece of paper stacked in the middle of them. He took the paper out and unfolded it. It was a note scribbled as if in a hurry, not in Russian but in English.

> *Before you leave Moscow, be sure to pay one more visit to the young woman across the street from your best friend and give her a real good feel. If fortune permits, we will meet again.*

Ayan's first thought was Valeria, his former girlfriend who had lived across the street from Victor. But as much as Ayan felt flattered that Victor might call him his best friend, he could not take the note at face value. The urgency he'd seen in Victor's eyes, the fact that he'd written this in English, as if he feared it might fall into the wrong hands, and the secrecy with which he passed it to Ayan told him there was more to it than its surface meaning. And aside from the apparent raunchiness of Victor's message, Ayan detected an underlying uncertainty about the future. Perhaps Victor had a premonition of danger ahead for himself, a presentiment that he and Ayan might not be seeing each other again.

Ayan stuffed the note quickly into his shirt pocket, paid the bill, and left the bar.

Nonetheless, the next day, Ayan called Valeria, who had moved to Leningrad. They had kept up a friendly relationship since their parting and called each other occasionally. Valeria had known about Ayan's decision to return to Kazakhstan for some time. After a few pleasantries over the phone, Ayan asked, "Remember my friend Victor, the scientist?"

"Oh yes, I remember him. Why do you ask?"

"He called me yesterday, said he was in town, and we met up for drinks last night." After a short pause, Ayan asked, "Has he been in touch with you since he left Moscow?"

"No. Why?" Valeria sounded surprised, making Ayan feel suddenly embarrassed for bringing it up.

"Never mind. It's just that he remembered living across from you in his last year in Moscow."

"Oh . . . " Valeria sounded a bit disconcerted. "No, I haven't heard from him in almost ten years. I only knew him through you, so when he disappeared from your life, he also disappeared from mine."

—

Ayan was right; he did not hear from Victor the day after their meeting at the Russian Bear, or the one after that. No chance to ask him about the note. Victor had vanished from Ayan's life again as quickly and suddenly as he had reappeared. During those nine years of silence, Ayan had often wondered what happened to his friend, and now after their meeting at the bar, he had more cause to worry about Victor's well-being, especially after seeing him with Andrei, whose presence at their rendezvous Victor did not, or dared not, explain. He could only hope his friend was not in any immediate danger.

Uneasy as Ayan was about Victor's note, there was nothing more he could think of doing to unravel whatever deep secrets might be coded into it. With his imminent departure from Moscow and no plans to return there in the foreseeable future, he put the note in the cigar box where he kept other mementos—letters from his father, small notes from Valeria, photographs and such. Over time, whenever he thought of Victor, thoughts of the note would come back to haunt him. It seemed Ayan had some unfinished business he ought to tend to.

BOOK II

AYAN AND GRACE

THE ROOM AT THE TOP

April 18, 2007, Astana, Kazakhstan

T he elevator takes Ayan as far up as the greenhouse level filled
with luxuriant verdant climbers and large planters of radiant
multi-colored blooms. He has to climb the remaining few stories to
reach the pinnacle of the iconic glass and steel pyramid of the Palace of
Peace and Reconciliation. With hurried steps, he ascends the narrow
spiral staircase leading to the top. All is quiet. Not a soul is around, or
so it seems at that late hour near the closing time of 8:30 p.m. Ayan
has been wanting to visit the Palace and witness its unique architecture
since its inauguration over seven months ago. Above all, he wants to
experience the conference room at the top, designed for the Congress
of Leaders of World Religions that will be held there triennially, a tribute to humanity that befits the building's name.

As Ayan emerges into the illuminated room at the apex of the pyramid, he is immediately struck by the images of doves in flight covering
the four slanted faces of the stained-glass roof, their outlines visible

against the reddish twilight sky. With their outspread wings seeming to beat against the pyramid's glass exterior, they are forever outsiders trying to get in. The vermilion glow in the sky from the setting sun shines through the blue stained glass, bathing the entire space in a golden brilliance. The sight is mesmerizing and beautiful.

Ayan takes a moment to catch his breath, then looks around the room. It is larger than he imagined, with ample space to accommodate some 200 persons at a time. A huge round table with chairs occupies most of the floor space, and all the furniture is draped in banquet-white fabric. The table is shaped like a ring, its center a dark void.

Alone in that glowing room, as if afraid to disturb the celestial peace, Ayan walks lightly across the carpeted floor and looks out to the city below. The room commands a panoramic view of the Kazakh capital, the River Ishim dividing the city in two—the south bank a conglomeration of modern geometric architectural wonders, like a futuristic city out of a science fiction comic book, contrasting with the simple rectangular buildings on the north bank of the river. Except for the pyramidal structure Ayan stands in, the buildings on this side are more traditional and solemn.

Breathing deeply, Ayan feels the tranquility of being alone in the pinnacle space of the Palace of Peace and Reconciliation. He hears footsteps, followed by a bang as the door opens and quickly shuts. Instinctively he turns toward the doorway to see what unwelcome visitor is intruding on his quiet solitude. It is an Asian woman, looking trendy in jeans, a short brown jacket, and calf-high fashion boots. She appears a little frantic. Her eyes rest on Ayan. Quickly she walks around the huge round table to where he has perched by one of the stained-glass windows. She stops beside him, seeming out of breath.

"Zdravstvuyte!" In spite of his displeasure at being disturbed, he greets the stranger in Russian, out of politeness. Receiving no response, he repeats in English, "Hello!"

"Hi," the woman responds, taking a deep breath. The uneasy expression in her eyes softens, even though she and Ayan are total strangers. She looks to be in her mid-thirties, not tall, perhaps a meter six. She could be Kazakh, but for her tanned complexion, much darker than city women in his country. At the moment, she looks somewhat distracted, not impressed by the stained-glass doves or the panoramic view. "This place seems pretty deserted. I was a bit scared walking up from the elevator," she says to Ayan with a nervous laugh. Her English betrays she is not local, probably American.

"It's near closing time," Ayan explains. "I hear it's crowded on weekends. This is a new building, just opened last year, and quite an attraction for the city."

"That's what I heard," the woman nods. She starts to look around her, focusing for the first time on the unconventional stained-glass windows. "These are amazing!"

"The architecture is quite unique. The symbol of doves is fitting for the Congress of Leaders of World Religions planned to be held here every three years. In fact, one of these conferences was already held here last year." Ayan says as much as he knows.

"Oh!" She looks at him with raised eyebrows. "I suppose that's why this place is called the Palace of Peace and Reconciliation."

"Yes, this country has come a long way since the breakup of the Soviet Union. Just look at all the buildings across the river." Ayan points with his chin. Looking at her with inquiring eyes, he asks, "Where are you from?"

"Chicago."

"Chicago! I have a friend who lives in Milwaukee. He says he sometimes drives to Chicago, meets friends for lunch, and drives home the same day." He pauses for a few seconds. "Are you just visiting Kazakhstan?"

"You could say that," she replies after momentary hesitation. "And yes, you can drive from Chicago to Milwaukee and back the same day."

The double doors to the conference room open suddenly. They both instinctively turn to see a man entering, a blond fellow. Probably another tourist, Ayan turns his attention back to the view of the city beyond the river.

"How long are you staying?" he asks the woman beside him. She seems not to hear, her attention still turned in the direction of the man who has just entered. She looks troubled again, her face tense. "How long are you in Astana?" Ayan repeats.

"Oh, only a week," she answers, turning back toward Ayan absent-mindedly.

"You like Astana?" he asks.

Without responding, she looks back at the other man again. He is now standing only several glass panels over from them, apparently also looking out at the view. This man's presence seems to upset the woman, although the hall looks big enough that conversations wouldn't be overheard. "I'm sorry, what were you saying?" she asks Ayan.

"I was wondering what you think of Astana," Ayan says.

"Oh, I like it, especially the buildings across the river."

"This city is magical. It was built out of the steppes. And it's one of the coldest capitals in the world," he keeps on.

"You don't say! All these modern buildings on what used to be wild grasslands? And in such unfriendly climate!" He finally catches her attention for the moment, or so it seems.

"Not unfriendly," Ayan corrects her. He continues emphatically, "The steppes were good for our people for a long time. Before the Soviets came, Kazakhs were happy nomadic people. Our animals grazed on the steppes." Nostalgia for bygones seems to have taken over his countenance. He continues in a heavy voice, "Nowadays people like big cities and modern living. And I don't blame them."

"I didn't know there were nomads in Kazakhstan, but I've read about them in Mongolia. The city looks grand from here, but it's sad how modernization can change a way of life forever," the woman comments.

"I shouldn't grieve over the past that's gone," Ayan says with a sigh. "Modernization has its good. And it was not the main reason for the end of nomadic life." He frowns before he speaks again. "We have a very sad history under the Soviets. Collectivization killed two and a half million Kazakhs, while over six hundred thousand escaped to other countries."

Just then, the door behind them creaks. They both turn toward the entrance to see it closing. The blond man has left. The woman looks relieved.

"That's awful," she picks up on the conversation. "I'm sorry your country suffered so much during Soviet time." She pauses and continues, "I'm also sorry for being so distracted just now. That man that just came in—I don't have a good feeling about him. I was climbing the stairs up here alone, with no one in sight, until I saw him appear as if from nowhere! He was going down, so I moved to let him pass, and as our paths crossed, he gave me this chilling, scrutinizing glare, the kind you see from Cold War spies in the movies, if you know what I mean."

Ayan furrows his brow in confusion and concern. "Why would he do that?" he asks.

"I don't know. The guy looked too serious to be just enjoying the view. He looked like he was on some sort of mission. He disappeared down the stairs after that, and I came up as fast as I could."

Ayan listens attentively to her whole account. "I don't blame you for feeling nervous about that guy on the stairs. But are you sure it was the same man who just came in?"

"Absolutely!" Her voice is lowered to an urgent whisper. "And he seemed to be looking my way every time I glanced back at him."

Ayan ponders for a moment, searching for the right words. "Well, it'd be quite natural for him to look your way if he noticed you looking at him, don't you think?"

"True, but why would he come back up, assuming he had been in here before?"

"That does seem strange. If he had already been in here, though, it must have been before I walked up from the greenhouse level, because I saw no one all the way up and no one else in the room until you came in. But you say you saw him going down on your way up, and you came in after me. Maybe I missed him if he was in the toilets just as I was walking up? That's the only explanation I can think of for why I didn't see him earlier." Ayan pauses. Then with what he hopes is a reassuring smile, he says, "Don't worry. He might have just wanted to see the view closer to sunset even if he had been up here earlier."

"You are very reassuring," she smiles. She glances at her watch. "I'd really like to stay and learn more about the history of your country, but I'm supposed to meet my husband at our hotel in less than an hour."

Ayan looks at his watch. "I should be leaving too. They are closing soon. I'll go down with you."

"Thank you," the woman says, sounding relieved. "By the way, I am Grace Curran. And you are?"

"Ayan. Ayan Kazbekov." They shake hands.

By then, the sun has set, leaving a diminishing afterglow filtering into the conference room. They exit the room and walk down the spiral stairs leading to the greenhouse level. As they make their way down, Grace remarks, "By the way, your English is very good. Did you study English abroad?"

"Thank you. No, I didn't study abroad, unless you call Moscow in Soviet time a city abroad. I studied English at Moscow State University, and now I teach English at a university here in Kazakhstan."

At that instant, some faint pattering comes from the stairs above them, like someone tiptoeing. Grace starts. Ayan hears it too.

"Is someone still up there? I thought everyone had gone except for us. If this was an old Soviet building, I'd think it was haunted!" Grace gives a nervous laugh.

"Cleaners, probably."

"Yes, of course. You must think I'm really paranoid. I'm not crazy, I promise. It's just creepy being up here by ourselves." She pauses a moment and continues, "Anyway, your English is impressive. And so is the fact that you're an English professor at a university!"

"Well, not a professor. I'm a docent at the university, or what you might call a lecturer. Still, the road to becoming a docent, especially in the English language, has been a long and difficult one. I have been very fortunate," Ayan says, trying to sound modest.

They have reached the greenhouse level. From there they take the elevator down to the ground floor lobby. Other than a couple of women closing up the front desk and a male cleaner maneuvering a sweeping machine across the shiny marble floor, no one else is in sight. Ayan and Grace emerge from the Palace of Peace and Reconciliation into the crisp, cold air beneath the waning twilight.

"Which way are you going?" Ayan asks.

"I'm headed to the bridge, back to my hotel on the other side," Grace replies.

"I see. I'm staying with a friend while I'm in Astana, on this side of the river."

"You don't live here?"

"I'm a visitor here, like you. I live in Kyzylorda, where I teach, and my family home is near Aralsk, which used to be one of the biggest harbor towns of the Aral Sea," Ayan says.

"Sorry, I haven't heard of any of those places." She looks somewhat embarrassed.

"No need to feel bad. Not many visitors have," Ayan says. "They are not on the usual tourist route."

As they walk down the central pathway leading away from the Palace of Peace and Reconciliation, Ayan turns to gaze on the pyramid one more time. Under the dark but clear April sky, the building's silvery facades glow with gray silhouettes of more doves in flight, an awesome, incandescent, mystical spectacle. In that moment, against the delicate light illuminating the glass pinnacle room, he sees distinctly the outline of a still figure standing inside. The person could be gazing out to the city, but he could also be watching Ayan and Grace as they walk along the well-lit pathway away from the Palace. Ayan keeps his sighting of the figure to himself. No sense in alarming Grace, as if she hasn't already been nervous tonight. But to himself, Ayan wonders if the person he saw could be the same man she encountered earlier. Is he watching her? Or him? Or both of them?

They have reached the end of the central walkway leading from the Palace.

"Nice to have met you, Ayan." Grace extends her hand. "I guess this is hello and goodbye. I've enjoyed talking to you."

"I'm glad to have met you too, Grace. Welcome to Kazakhstan. I wish you and your husband a pleasant stay."

They part ways here, two strangers lately met whose paths, in all likelihood, will not cross again. As Ayan walks away, he cannot resist glancing up at the room at the top one more time. The mysterious figure is gone.

BOOK III
GRACE

3

RECEPTION IN ASTANA

April 19, 2007, Astana, Kazakhstan

The first time Grace accompanies Glen on a business trip away from Almaty, where he is stationed for work in Kazakhstan, they go to Astana. After all she has heard about Astana—the modern, futuristic capital of the young republic—she is curious to see this miracle city herself. The main social event on that trip is a formal reception held at the Rixos Hotel, hosted by a Kazakh oil prospector. Attending the reception are top Kazakh government officials, World Bank personnel, as well as USAID staff stationed in Kazakhstan. As Texcom's Senior Assistant to the Chief of Party for Kazakhstan, Glen's presence with his wife is appropriate and even desirable.

When Glen was assigned to work in Kazakhstan, that remote Central Asian country that had only recently awakened like a sleeping giant from the grip of the Soviet regime, Grace readily agreed to take a year off from her job teaching high school English on Chicago's North Side to accompany him. Glen's job in Kazakhstan is to seek out experts in various fields for Texcom's consulting projects and to procure funding from first-world financial and humanitarian sources, all for the worthy cause of providing aid to the fast-developing republic. Glen has an edge over many company managers in that part of the world: he speaks enough Russian to carry on a day-to-day conversation. He took Russian in college, believing with the breakup of the Soviet Union and ending of the Cold War in 1991 that Russian would only increase in popularity and business usage in days to come. His foresight seems to be paying off with this one-year assignment to Kazakhstan. As for Grace, she is hoping her year off to an exotic locale such as Kazakhstan will give her time and inspiration to finally write her novel, a passion she has shelved for many years, mainly due to the daily grind of teaching.

The grand reception at the Rixos takes place the second evening of their stay in Astana. For the occasion, Grace has on a beaded black sleeveless top with black dress pants, a dusty pink satin jacket with mandarin collar, and silver sandals with a low heel. She never dons much makeup, just a light lipstick and eyeliner coupled with a tint of eye shadow to accentuate her natural refined beauty. She has worn her hair short, page-boy style, ever since high school. While Glen has added a few forgivable pounds to his athletic physique since his best bachelor days, Grace has kept her figure trim, a consolation prize for not having borne a child after seven years of marriage in spite of her dream of motherhood.

The grand ballroom is a sparkling extravaganza of glamor. Glen introduces Grace to the host, a stocky middle-aged Kazakh man with a flat-topped crew cut. He is a jovial fellow whose cheeks seem to reach up to his eyes every time he laughs thunderously, like a lion clearing its throat. Whether his happy disposition is put on for his guests is hard to tell, but he certainly puts them at ease, including Grace. Cocktail in hand, she keeps close to Glen while they mingle with local and foreign guests.

Grace was born and raised in Chicago, but as the child of Chinese immigrants from Hong Kong, her Asian looks have caused her to be mistaken for a local since arriving in Kazakhstan. People often address her in Kazakh, and even more often in Russian, the language spoken by all Kazakhstanis whether of Kazakh, Russian, or other ethnic origin. Many people they meet at the Rixos reception make the same mistake until she and Glen set the record straight, at which point the conversation quickly shifts to English. There are lots of handshaking and sundry small talk, and soon Grace's cheeks hurt from putting on a smile for so long.

When Glen gets involved in shoptalk with a few work associates, Grace excuses herself and wanders away on her own. She comes across a bevy of expatriate wives spectating from a couch in the corner, their eyes following any outfit or action that warrants a not-so-subtle whisper. Grace has met a couple of the women on another occasion in Almaty, though she hasn't bothered to pursue their acquaintance further. Bypassing the group, she eases out to use the powder room to take a breather.

Coming out of the powder room into the hotel lobby, she passes a beautiful red wood cabinet carved with the traditional curved Kazakh motif, which to Grace looks like an artistic stylization of the male reproductive organs, with exaggerated scrota and a modest penis. She has never asked the real meaning of the motif since arriving in Almaty, not wanting to embarrass herself with her overactive imagination. Through the beveled glass door of the cabinet, she sees among other artifacts a miniature model, about six inches tall, of a two-stringed, lute-like instrument, carved beautifully from wood. She leans in for a better look.

"That's a *dombra*," a voice behind her explains.

Grace turns to find the warm, quiet smile of Ayan Kazbekov. He is wearing a blue suit jacket and gray trousers, and on his head a black and blue Kazakh *taqiya*. In the more comfortable ambience of the hotel lobby, Grace observes that he looks to be in his mid-forties, and rather striking in a reserved manner.

"Oh hello! What a small world!" Grace exclaims, failing to find a better expression of her surprise than the cliché.

Ayan nods. "Fancy meeting you here!" He looks pleased to see her, his countenance more relaxed than the day before. Pointing to the little replica of the dombra, he asks, "Have you ever heard the music of the dombra?"

"As a matter of fact, yes. I recently went with a friend to the Museum of Kazakh Musical Instruments, where there was a lovely dombra demonstration."

"And how did you like it?"

"It was captivating. The dombra is such an expressive instrument. As the musician played, I could almost hear the sound of horses galloping in the wind, wild and free."

Ayan nods. "Yes, the dombra preserves a way of life that is no more." Focusing on Grace, he asks, "And what brings you here?"

"I'm attending a reception with my husband who's on a business trip in Astana." Seeing Ayan's questioning look, Grace continues, "We are in Astana for the week. We are actually living in Almaty where my husband works at the moment."

"How do you like Almaty?"

"It's very different from Chicago, for sure!" She laughs. "And what brings *you* here tonight?"

"I am here to attend a fundraising dinner organized by a human rights organization I belong to. That's why you see me all dressed up! And tomorrow, I'm going on a bus tour with the group to Karlag. It's about two hundred and fifty kilometers south of here. Karlag was one of the largest Gulag labor camps in Stalin's time."

"I didn't realize there was a Gulag labor camp within driving distance from here!" Grace's eyes widen with interest.

"You should visit Karlag Museum if you have a chance."

"I think I should! The images of the Gulag stuck with me for so long after I read Alexander Solzhenitsyn's *One Day in the Life of Ivan Denisovich*. I was very sorry for the inmates, and I was totally inspired by the undefeatable spirit of the book's main character."

"You must visit Karlag then. This was the Gulag labor camp

described in Solzhenitsyn's book." Ayan looks thoughtful. "In fact, I will see if you can join us on our day trip tomorrow."

Grace can hardly hide her excitement. It is an opportunity she could never dream of having back in Chicago. "That's very kind of you. I'm so excited. My husband has meetings here all day tomorrow, but I have nothing scheduled. Let me discuss with him. If things work out, I would really like to join you on your trip."

"I'll ask the organizers at tonight's dinner if there is room on the bus for one more. What's your mobile number? I'll have an answer for you by the end of the evening."

—

Back in the ballroom, Grace finds Glen. Weaving through the many guests, they head for the buffet table where a sumptuous spread of salads, smoked horse meat, *manti*, Kazakh breads, and varieties of *shashlik* are served. Shocking as it would be to her friends back home, Grace has grown accustomed to eating horse meat, smoked or freshly cooked. Her favorite local food though is shashlik, the Russian version of shish kebab, especially the lamb variety, while the manti remind her of Shanghai dumplings. By now, Grace and Glen are quite famished. They pile their plates with food and settle down at one of the small tables at a far end of the room to indulge in what she considers the best part of the evening. As soon as they are seated, she tells Glen about her two chance meetings with Ayan Kazbekov and the possibility of joining the tour of the Gulag the next day.

"This Ayan sounds like a decent guy. And yes, I've heard the World Human Rights Organization is holding a fundraiser here tonight. The trip will be with a big group tomorrow. You should go. Make the most of it. You never know, the Gulag might just give you the kind of inspiration you need for your book."

"Oh I hope so," Grace says, smiling with anticipation. "I can just imagine the Gulag as the setting for my story." She ponders for a moment and says, "I have an idea, Glen. If you are not too tired, I'd like for you to meet this guy Ayan. What better opportunity than after dinner tonight, since he's here in the hotel?"

"That's a good idea, Grace, especially since my wife may be going with him to the Gulag tomorrow," Glen says with a teasing wink. "Let's go over to the banquet hall next door and ask him to meet us at the bar for a drink after dinner."

———

"Well?" Grace asks as she and Glen walk back to their hotel from the Rixos. "What do you think of Ayan?"

"Very decent fellow. I would trust my wife with him on an outing to the Gulag, even with his good looks!" Glen says teasingly. "Seriously, I am impressed not so much because he went to Moscow State University or he is a college teacher, but because he's involved with this human rights organization, and he told us a reason he left the good life in Moscow was to go home to his aging parents. I like his values." Squeezing Grace's hand as they walk along the magnificent tree-lined central boulevard, Glen continues, "I hope you have a good visit to the Gulag tomorrow. You know, Grace, I have a feeling you will find your story on this sabbatical."

4

THE GULAG

April 20, 2007, Dolinka, Kazakhstan

The bus bumps its way along the rough road to Karlag. The passengers are mostly donors from the previous evening's fundraiser, including some descendants of Karlag inmates. Grace is the outsider from America among them.

"How did you come to be involved with the fundraiser here?" Grace asks Ayan, who is sitting next to her on the bus.

"I have a personal reason to be. Let me first tell you a little about my family history. I am actually from a fishing village called Balta, which used to be on the shores of the Aral Sea," Ayan says. "My parents still live there. It's a small village, just twenty-three homes and a small mosque. The closest town is Aralsk, a harbor town in the old days."

"In the old days? But not anymore?"

"Correct. There is no harbor anymore."

Grace tilts her head in confusion.

Ayan continues, "You see, up until the early 1960s, the Aral Sea was the fourth largest inland sea in the world and fish were bountiful.

My father hauled in as much as three hundred kilograms of fish in a day. He and his fellow fishermen would take their fish to Aralsk to be cleaned and sorted. From there, it went to supply the locals and people all across Kazakhstan and many other parts of the Soviet Union. But by the mid-1970s, the Aral Sea stopped yielding fish."

"Why?"

"It's a long story. And one that ends sadly for my paternal grand-father, Aidar Kazbekov, who was an engineer in Soviet time. My grandfather was a great man, respected throughout the Aral District. Unfortunately, the State did not appreciate him," Ayan continues.

"You mean the Soviet government?"

"Yes. He was assigned to work with a team of engineers in the fifties in a project to divert the flow of the two main rivers, the Syr Darya and the Amu Darya, that had been feeding fresh water into the Aral Sea since time immemorial, to irrigate the cotton fields of Kazakhstan and Uzbekistan."

"I don't suppose your grandfather had a choice under the Soviets," Grace remarks.

"We all have a choice, no matter where our choice may lead us," Ayan asserts with adamance. "My grandfather warned the project committee that such a project would shrink the Aral Sea drastically, raise the salinity of the water to unimaginable height, and kill all the fish, effectively destroying the livelihood of entire fishing communities. He also predicted that the shrinking of the Aral Sea would bring about harmful changes to the entire ecosystem of the region." Ayan takes a deep breath. "Unfortunately his objections fell on deaf ears. He turned in his resignation. Then he went further by publishing an article in a local journal in Aralsk predicting the death of the Aral Sea and warn-ing of all the disastrous results to humans and the environment if the project was carried out. Soon after his resignation and the publication of the article, he was arrested by the Central Government and tried for insubordination and inciting dissidence. He was found guilty and sen-tenced to Karlag, where we are headed now."

Grace feels her eyes burning. "I am so sorry. What a brave sacrifice your grandfather made for the good of his people."

Ayan nods. "My grandfather gave up his freedom, his family, and his life to uphold his principles under the Soviet regime."

"It must have been very painful for your grandmother and the family too."

Ayan sighs. "Yes, my father said his mother was devastated. Luckily she had my father and three older children to give her comfort. But my father said she never really got over it."

"How old was your father when your grandfather was taken away?" Grace asks.

"Seventeen. As the youngest son in the family, he had the duty to remain home in Aralsk to care for his mother. He never wanted to take up engineering like his father, or study in university and be a teacher like my Uncle Birzhan. Right after he finished secondary school, he started working for a fisherman. He still tells stories of his early days as a crewman on another fisherman's boat, going out into the Aral Sea every morning at the break of dawn and learning all the skills of the trade. In 1956, he married my mother. They lived with my grandmother in the house my grandfather built by the harbor in Aralsk till her death a year later, then they moved to Balta, the fishing village where I was born."

"Is your mother also from the Aral Sea region?"

"My mother was born in Kyzylorda, where I now teach. It's the capital and biggest city in our oblast."

"Like our state capitals, I suppose."

"Yes, our oblasts are similar to your states." Ayan pauses and as an afterthought adds, "However, my mother's side of the family was originally nomadic, from eastern Kazakhstan."

"You have such a rich and interesting family history," Grace says. She continues after a pause, "So what happened to your grandfather in the Gulag?"

"As a member of the intelligentsia, my grandfather was given better treatment than most inmates at Karlag. They put him to work planning out the construction of canals in the Karaganda region. Unfortunately, a year after his internment at Karlag, in 1954, he contracted dysentery and died. As a privileged prisoner, he was given a gravesite in Dolinka Cemetery instead of being buried in an unmarked grave like most of the inmates who died there."

"I'm so sorry. What a terrible fate for such a great man. Have you been to his gravesite?"

"Only after Independence. I've gone there three times with my father since I came back home from Moscow. This is my fourth trip there. My father decided not to come with me this time because his gout was causing him a lot of pain just before I left for Astana."

"It's hard for us Westerners to imagine the hardships your people must have suffered under the Soviets. I would really like to read more about this period of your history, do some research, and what better time than now while I'm here." After a pause, Grace continues, "And then maybe I'll write a book about your country!"

"You are a writer? What do you write?" Ayan asks, staring at Grace with new interest.

Grace can't help smiling at his sudden change of tone. "So far I haven't published anything other than a few short stories for my university magazine. But I'm on sabbatical leave from my teaching job while my husband is working here for a year, so I just thought this might be a good time for me to indulge in my lifelong fantasy of writing a novel."

"A novel! I teach English but I could never write a novel." Ayan looks over to Grace with admiration.

"I don't know if I can either! Writing has always been a passion of mine, but I've never had the time to sit down and really focus on it with my teaching schedule and all."

"What kind of novel?" Ayan pursues.

"I don't know yet. Probably a story based on my experiences in Kazakhstan."

"You must have a very good imagination," Ayan says.

"I must confess my first few weeks in Almaty have produced no writing results. I'm suffering from a writer's block, you might say. I am looking for an intriguing story. Perhaps this trip to the Gulag will lead to some inspiration."

The bus pulls into Karaganda, a coal-mining center that has grown into a sprawling industrial city. Solemn-looking rectangular building blocks from the Soviet era along with smokestacks emitting polluting vapor make up the skyline. The bus winds its way through a labyrinth of wide, tree-lined boulevards, passing monuments, some impressive and awe-inspiring, others daunting and formidable. Another thirty minutes out of the city take them to the village of Dolinka and the Karlag Museum. There are only a few other cars parked along the winding driveway. It must be a slow day for the former prison camp.

As Grace alights from the bus, she takes in a deep breath of the mid-spring air, fresh but still cold. The sky is overcast, the atmosphere dismal. Grace finds herself at a wide-open cast-iron gate, through which she sees a long and broad walkway paved with interlocking bricks, leading to a circular three-tiered fountain. Beyond the fountain is a white neoclassic two-story mansion with four front columns on the upper-level façade.

"This mansion was built by the inmates of Karlag and was used as an administrative building for the Gulag during the 1930s," Ayan explains to Grace, as he reads the Russian on a plaque at the front gate.

"It certainly looks grand—fitting for a museum—but its history makes me feel like it's haunted or cursed," Grace comments, scanning the building's expansive width.

A local tour guide greets the group at the front entrance to the building. Following her into the lobby, Grace and Ayan find themselves facing a big broken wooden circular frame mounted on a wall partition.

"What you see here is a *shanyrak*, the wood framework on the roof of a *yurt*, a symbol of the family for Kazakh nomads. A broken shanyrak signifies the end of the Kazakh traditional way of life, the

nomadic life, the end of a world order for the Kazakh people," Ayan
translates for Grace what the guide says in Russian. They walk around
the partition, and what Grace sees on the back side of the wall makes
her cringe. It is a full-blown portrait of Joseph Stalin. Grace tries to
avoid the fearsome gaze of the larger-than-life dictator, but his fierce,
penetrating eyes beneath thick bushy eyebrows seem to follow her no
matter where she stands. Meanwhile, Ayan goes on translating the
guide's spiel to her, "Karlag was closed down in 1959, and the entire
Gulag work camp system was shut down in 1960."

The tour continues. Grace shudders and follows along.

The visitors are led down a long, spooky corridor into a photo
exhibit spanning several rooms, the walls hung with celluloid evidence
of some of humanity's most brutal and shameful moments. There are
photos and painted depictions of nomadic families being evicted from
their yurts, forced to migrate to unknown destinations—images of
the horrors of collectivization under Stalin. One of the most poignant
and gut-wrenching paintings in that collection depicts a group of
Kazakh nomads waving pitchforks, clubs, and axes, accompanied by
two snarling dogs on leashes, bravely confronting uniformed Soviet
soldiers holding rifles with bayonets, their captain behind them on
horseback, ready to give his signal to open fire.

Grace finds the painting heartrending, a cruel display of the dis-
parity of conditions between the two sides. The nomads look ready to
fight and die for a way of life they know they cannot protect, charging
headlong into a battle they have no hope of winning.

From there, the group is led to the exhibition halls dedicated to
the Great Famine of 1930–1933 that hit the Soviet Union, especially
Kazakhstan and Ukraine. Here the visitors encounter graphic, black-
and-white photos of death by hunger and starvation, fields of skeletal
corpses piled up in stacks, unattended orphans herded into crammed
facilities, breeding grounds for disease. In one photo, a little girl no
more than two years of age sits beside her mother who lies motionless

on the street. The dead woman's hand is touching the little girl's bare foot. Grace notices Ayan is deeply affected by this photo.

In response to the question in her eyes, Ayan translates the caption below the frame for her, his voice at a breaking point, "This picture was taken just a short time before the little girl was cannibalized."

"You mean eaten by humans?" Grace asks in shock.

Ayan nods. "Cannibalism was sometimes practiced during the Great Famine, mostly upon famine victims, those who were already dead." Here he pauses. With effort, he continues, "But in the case of this little girl, she was butchered alive."

As if they haven't seen enough human horrors for one day, the tour group continues to the basement level where they can look into replicas of the prison cells at Karlag. The cells are inhabited by life-sized mannequins playing prisoners in different situations in the camp—the new arrivals, the prisoners interrogated by Gulag officers in uniform, the condemned and about-to-be-executed. Victim and visitor are together in one space, crossing the barrier of time and place, causing shivers to run up Grace's spine. Especially disturbing is the replica of a prisoners' torture chamber, morbid and grisly with telltale instruments of torture, a stretcher with hand and foot restraints, concrete walls spattered with blood.

The next room is dressed to look like a laboratory, with a setting of shelves displaying test tubes, petri dishes, beakers, and models of human parts—the brain, the torso, and limbs. A mannequin of a scientist in a white lab coat stands in the far corner. He has his back to the group, his fair head stooped down over the counter such that his face is totally concealed from the visitors' view. Reminded of Ayan's grandfather, Grace imagines what life was like for the imprisoned intelligentsia confined to the Gulag. She lingers by the entrance of the lab, not noticing that the group has moved on until she is the only person left in the room. Ayan too has walked on with the guide. All is quiet as Grace stands there motionless, letting herself soak in for a moment the sensation that she is actually here, in what used to be one of the biggest and most notorious of the Gulag work camps.

Suddenly, in the dead of silence she hears breathing. Then she sees the white-coated, fair-haired dummy scientist move! Only a slight movement of the shoulders, but it draws her notice. Could her eyes be deceiving her? Grace keeps her stance, remaining motionless, her eyes focused on the figure diagonally across the room from her, about sixteen meters away. Ten seconds elapse. It moves again, and this time Grace is certain. His head turns slightly to the left, such that she sees a bit of his profile but not his whole face. Without a second thought, she turns and runs from the lab.

"You probably have had enough of this. Let's go upstairs," Ayan says as Grace joins him in the basement hallway. She nods emphatically, trying to catch her breath, shaken by what she has just experienced in the lab and at a loss for words.

Back on the first floor, Grace tells Ayan about her sighting. "I wouldn't be surprised if the building is haunted, after all the atrocities that were committed here," Ayan rationalizes.

"That's very comforting, thank you," Grace says, putting on a sardonic look. "But if it wasn't my imagination and that blond mannequin did move, then was it a ghost? Or was it really someone there?"

—

Across the unkempt burial ground in Dolinka are the worn and slanted old tombstones of Gulag victims, at least those more fortunate ones who were buried there instead of being dumped in unmarked, forgotten graves. The snow has long melted, but the ground is still soggy. Grace follows Ayan as he searches for his grandfather's gravesite. A sudden spring breeze swooshes through the landscape of disheveled grasses and unattended graves. Suddenly Grace hears the faint squish of slow, steady steps on the damp earth of the cemetery grounds. She turns to look all around her. She and Ayan are alone, the rest of their group having elected to see a cluster of old huts, once the living quarters of Karlag inmates, situated just outside the cemetery. Then, out of the corner of her eye, Grace detects a dark shadow flitting among the tombstones. She turns suddenly, studying the area about twenty meters away from where she and Ayan are standing. Perhaps someone is hiding behind one of the tombstones, she thinks. The cemetery is open to visitors. Or was it just her imagination? She looks over to Ayan who seems not to have heard or seen anything as he stoops to search among the gravesites for his grandfather's tombstone. Then again, there may well be an invisible presence trampling among the old tombstones, Grace considers. After all, this is unholy ground where the incarcerated, non-vindicated dead were laid to unrest. She decides to keep her thoughts to herself, especially after her episode with the figure in the white lab coat, lest Ayan wonder at her acute imagination.

After a bit more searching, Ayan points out a simple slab of concrete among the old, slanted, and darkened tombstones. It marks the burial site of Ayan's paternal grandfather. Below his name are words engraved in Kazakh, which Ayan translates for Grace:

Aidar Kazbekov 1906–1954

"What a wonderful world the Creator has given us!"

"The line is from the poem 'Spring' by the great Kazakh poet Abai," Ayan explains. "My father told me my grandfather loved Abai's poetry, and 'Spring' was one of his favorites. My grandfather loved nature, and he loved the Aral Sea. Naturally the inscription wasn't there when my grandfather was buried. This was a godless country then. Creator?" Ayan laughs. "I asked a stone mason to engrave it on my first trip here with my father after Independence."

"That line is so appropriate," Grace says. "God gave your people the Aral Sea. Your grandfather died trying to protect it."

—

"When are you going back home?" Grace asks Ayan as they eat sandwiches for supper on their bus ride back to Astana.

"I leave for Almaty tomorrow. I'll be in Almaty for a couple of days before going home on Tuesday. Like you, I'm on sabbatical from the university, but only this semester. I'll be spending some time with my parents in our village and in Aralsk."

"Well, we might run into each other again in Almaty then," Grace says. "Glen will love to see you again too."

"I'll contact you in Almaty," Ayan promises.

By the time the bus drops Grace off at her hotel, it is past 9:30 p.m. and pitch dark outside. Once inside the lobby, she fishes for her room key card in her purse, but no luck. Glen wouldn't be back yet from his business dinner. She stops at reception to get another key card to her room.

"An envelope was left for you, Mrs. Curran," the girl at the desk says.

"For me?" Grace is surprised. "Do you know who left it?"

"No. I just saw it on the front desk when I started my shift. It has your name on it." The girl hands her an envelope. Walking toward the elevator, Grace rips open the envelope. In it is a folded piece of scrap paper on which is scribbled one single sentence in English, unsigned.

Ask Ayan Kazbekov what he knows about Voz Island.

5

PANFILOV PARK

April 23, 2007, Almaty, Kazakhstan

By the time Grace and Glen return to Almaty from the business trip to Astana, they have been in Kazakhstan for about three months. Texcom has provided them with a fully renovated, well-furnished apartment on Gogol Street, in an old part of Almaty not far from Panfilov Park and the Green Bazaar. According to their landlady, they are just a few minutes' walk from the hotel where Trotsky, once Stalin's trusted right hand, had stayed briefly with his wife while in exile in Alma Ata, the old name for Almaty, after he fell from grace in 1928.

Grace is getting used to the infrastructure of the old part of town, its gray Soviet building blocks, overpowering and forbidding. The expansive boulevards are lined with extra-wide gutters separating the pedestrian pavements from the roadways. She has become accustomed to the sights which had awed her when she first set eyes on them, from the huge old trees whose lower trunks are painted white for protection against insects, to the disproportionately large uniform hats worn by policemen. These things are now just a part of everyday life, no longer warranting a second look.

Glen typically leaves for his office around 8:30 a.m. in a company car chauffeured by a Texcom driver, and with Panfilov Park close to their home, Grace has been spending many of her mornings walking. The park is quiet and peaceful at that hour. Mostly elderly men in baggy pants with taqiyas on their heads and women in calf-length floral-patterned dresses with tightly wrapped headscarves come out for their morning stroll. Occasionally, smartly dressed office workers whisk through the park with hurried step, utilizing the park as a shortcut on their way to work. Grace occasionally picks up the mouthwatering aroma of fresh baked *samsa,* and often she stops at the vendor's cart for a couple of those triangular pastries filled with meat, onion, and potato. Glen has not developed a taste for them, but Grace thinks they are heavenly, her favorite being the lamb.

Grace is happy the city streets in this mega city follow a strict grid system with the mountains to the south, making it easy for her to explore without getting lost. What strike her curiosity most are the pre-Independence sections of town, with shabby-looking housing no higher than three or four stories, old mosques and Orthodox churches functioning again after Independence, open markets and bazaars with labyrinths of lanes selling food and sundry items, ethnic or otherwise. On such afternoon outings, she always stops for a coffee and pastry, often bringing a novel and spending hours reading at a favorite cafe. And always, waiting for her flow of inspiration for a story . . .

By mid-April, the snow has all melted away from the city streets, leaving curb gutters gushing with water like little rapids. Spring is in the air. *"Dobroe utro,* Akma!" Each morning Grace greets the magazine vendor at the street corner by her apartment building as she heads toward the park. She feels comfortable with simple exchanges of greeting in Russian. Kazakh beyond "hello," "thank you," and "goodbye" will come later.

The Monday morning after she and Glen got back from Astana, Grace again steps out of her apartment building and heads in the direction of Panfilov Park. That day she has a special purpose: Ayan Kazbekov, who is stopping over in Almaty for a couple days before he heads home to Aralsk, is meeting her at Panfilov Park to give her a copy of the English version of a novel set in the Central Asian steppes in Soviet time, *The Day Lasts More Than a Hundred Years*, by the Kyrgyz writer Chinghiz Aitmatov. Grace is glad to have a chance to see Ayan again, not only for the book he is lending her but also to ask him about the anonymous note she received the night she returned to her hotel in Astana after visiting Karlag.

Their rendezvous spot is on the main path of the park. As Grace waits, she studies the twenty-eight stone markers that line the path, each commemorating a soldier of an Almaty infantry unit who perished defending Moscow from a Nazi attack in 1941 on the Eastern Front of the Second World War, or what the Soviets called the Great Patriotic War. Grace stoops at several of the stone memorials to read their inscriptions. The ages of the fallen soldiers range from late teens to early thirties, the younger ones the ages of the seniors Grace teaches, the older ones a few years younger than Glen. Yet, their lives were prematurely cut short fighting and dying for a federation to which their homeland belonged, of which they knew little about except for the fact that Big Brother who controlled and owned their lives and destiny lived in the capital, Moscow. Grace cannot help empathizing with them, their fathers and mothers, their wives.

Ayan soon arrives. He looks cheery. Perhaps the few days' getaway from home has refreshed him.

"This will be my reading material for the next few days," Grace says, beaming with anticipation as Ayan hands her the book.

"It's become a classic in our part of the world, great historical fiction of the twentieth century set against the beauty of the Central Asian steppes," Ayan says. "You'll find in it a bit of myth and legend, a bit of science fiction, and a moving love story."

As Grace flips the pages, a bookmark falls onto the ground. She picks it up.

"*Shevchenko's Aral Sea* at the Kasteev State Museum, Almaty. April 15 to May 30, 2007," she reads.

"Oh yes, that was a reminder for me to tell you. The Kasteev Museum here is hosting a special exhibit called *Shevchenko's Aral Sea*," Ayan says.

"Who's this Shevchenko?"

"He was a famous Ukrainian artist and poet of the nineteenth century in the time of Russia's Czar Nicholas I. This is an exhibit of his Aral Sea paintings."

"Back when the Aral Sea was big and bountiful!" Grace comments.

"And beautiful. I think the exhibit will mean more to you now that I've told you about the demise of the Aral Sea," says Ayan.

"Yes, I would love to see it, especially since it's right here in Almaty," Grace says. "I am just curious why a Ukrainian artist would be painting the Aral Sea."

"Well, the circumstances were interesting. Shevchenko was also a political activist and was arrested for his anti-Czarist poetry. As punishment, he was sent to a remote part of the Caspian Sea for military service. During the time he was serving his sentence, the Czar ordered an expedition to survey the Aral Sea," Ayan says as they walk toward the south exit of the park. "The leader of the expedition, a scientist and explorer named Butakoff, had heard about Shevchenko's talent as an artist and poet and asked the Czar for permission to have him accompany them. The request was granted. So, for a short time during his exile, Shevchenko was part of this mapping expedition as an illustrator of the sea and surrounding landscapes."

"Like a present-day photojournalist," Grace concludes.

"More or less. These paintings on exhibit are some of Shevchenko's works from this expedition. They depicted what the Aral Sea looked like back in the mid-nineteenth century. When I heard this special collection was on loan in Almaty, I wanted you to see it."

"I could spend hours at the art gallery." Grace pauses. "I suppose I can get there easily by taxi."

Ayan ponders for a moment. "I'm in Almaty these couple of days, basically trying to find some distractions here before going back to Aralsk tomorrow. I'd had some rough time back home before coming out, which I'd rather not talk about," he says. "Anyhow, I have no special plans the rest of the day and haven't been to the museum in years. If you have time today, I'd be happy to take you there."

"I'm sorry to hear you've been going through rough times," Grace says, trying to be sympathetic without overstepping into Ayan's personal life. "But sure, I have no plans for today. You can take me to the museum, and I'll buy lunch. After our Karlag trip, I know you'll make a good guide for me."

Passing the beautiful historic triple-domed Holy Ascension Cathedral located within Panfilov Park, they walk out of the park's gate onto Gogol Street. Ayan puts out an arm by the curbside to hail an "unofficial taxi," as he calls it.

"It's quite common and safe to get a ride this way in Kazakhstan, and in Moscow too," Ayan assures his companion. "Gives ordinary drivers a chance to make a few extra *tenges*. It's also cheaper and faster than an official cab."

What he doesn't know is that Grace has ridden in several unofficial taxis on her own before. So, when a driver rolls down his window and stops beside them to ask where they are headed, she steps forward and pipes up in her limited Russian to settle on a price before they hop into the car, which is cranky, beaten, with a cracked windshield.

Ayan looks impressed.

As the car is about to drive away in the direction of the Kasteev Museum, Grace spots the samsa vendor with his cart at the crosswalk— too late to pick up any of those delicious pastries. At that moment, in front of the samsa vendor, Grace's eyes fall on a blond Caucasian man of medium height hailing a ride by the curb. Something about him seems familiar. Then she remembers where she has seen him, or at least the like of him: the Palace of Peace and Reconciliation in Astana several days before.

6

KASTEEV MUSEUM

April 23, 2007, Almaty, Kazakhstan

"Ayan, what do you know about Voz Island?" Grace probes with the question apparently out of the blue as they sit in the back seat of the unofficial taxi on the way to the Kasteev Museum.

"Why do you ask?" Ayan turns to face Grace, looking surprised and disturbed.

"Some anonymous person left me an unsigned one-line note at our hotel front desk the night I returned from Karlag. It said, 'Ask Ayan Kazbekov about Voz Island.'"

"Did the hotel staff know who left it there for you?" Ayan looks grim.

"No."

Ayan is silent for a good long moment, as if pondering what to tell her, eventually settling for the facts: "It's an island in the Aral Sea. There was a military base on the island during Soviet time. Since Independence, it has become openly known that the island was also used as a site for biological weapon research and testing. The project was shut down in 1991 when the Soviet Union broke up, and the island is now abandoned. But it's very strange you should get a note asking you to ask me about Voz Island."

"I searched for Voz Island on the internet after getting that note. What the internet tells me is pretty much what you just said. I read about biological weapons being produced there during Soviet time, and that the United States and Russia had sent decontamination teams to clean up the island after the breakup of the Soviet Union," Grace says. "But it seems the sender of the note thinks you know something more about the island than what the internet says."

"I don't know anything about it beyond what everyone knows." Ayan looks troubled. "Strange someone sent you that note," he reiterates, shifting uncomfortably several times in his seat. Grace says no more, seeing that Ayan is visibly disturbed by the message she has received.

—

Ayan and Grace enter the special exhibits gallery at the Kasteev Museum. The first exhibit of the Shevchenko Aral Sea special collection consists of two maps of the sea. One shows a full, healthy body of water in western Kazakhstan, plotted by Commander A. Butakoff of the Russian Imperial Navy in 1849. In the other, an aerial image dated 2006, the once vast, majestic sea has shrunk to three segments, one in the north within the boundary of Kazakhstan, and two pitiful patches of water shaped like strips of fried bacon in the south, in the Republic of Uzbekistan. Ayan excuses himself to go to the washroom, leaving Grace to study the maps of the Aral Sea, its past and present.

"Sad, isn't it?" remarks a man as he comes to stand beside Grace. He gestures toward the two maps, apparently addressing her as there is no one else nearby.

Grace looks over to the speaker beside her. She freezes. It is the flaxen-haired man she encountered at the Palace of Peace and Reconciliation in Astana. So she was right about seeing him earlier outside Panfilov Park. He has obviously followed them from there to the museum. Looking fortyish, he is somewhat stocky, with his blond hair in a neat crew cut. Clad in a blue t-shirt, dark pants, and a beige windbreaker, he looks quite decent. The cold, scrutinizing gaze of a spy has been replaced by a harmless, innocent look, affected though it seems to Grace, who has seen him in his chilling element during their first encounter.

Bypassing the stranger's question, she shoots her own question at him without rhetoric: "Were you at the Palace of Peace and Reconciliation in Astana a few days ago?"

He seems taken aback, perhaps more by her unexpected directness than the fact that she recognizes him. "Well, yes! Were you there too?"

"Yes! I believe I saw you there," Grace says assertively, continuing her line of verbal attack.

"Small world!" he comments, looking astonished.

"Funny we're at the same places spanning two cities, and at the same time," Grace remarks in a sarcastic tone, eyeing him warily.

"True. I must say coincidences do happen," he says, still wearing a look of feigned surprise. Focusing on the maps again, he points to the one from 2006. "See this peninsula joined to the mainland of Uzbekistan on this recent map? It was once an island surrounded by water." He points to an island on the older map. "Voz Island. Have you heard of it?" He looks intently at Grace. He speaks decent English but with an accent much like Glen's Russian coworkers' in Almaty.

"No, I've never heard of the island," she snaps. Better not mention the note she received the night she returned to her hotel in Astana. It may be a coincidence that he is calling her attention to the island . . . unless he was the sender of the anonymous note. She continues, "I bet much of the ecosystem there has been affected as a result of the disappearing sea."

"Yes, everything is affected," he says and nods slowly, deliberately, while studying Grace's facial expression so much as to make her wince.

"Have you been there?" she asks, looking over at him boldly as if to prove she is not intimidated by his scrutiny.

"No, not the island, but I've been to the shores of the Aral Sea. I'd like to go back someday, maybe to the island next time."

"It should be interesting," she comments. At that moment she is greatly relieved to see Ayan through a window to an inner courtyard.

The stranger looks quickly at his watch and says, "Well, I have to run. Enjoy your visit." With a slight nod, he abruptly exits through an inner door into the next gallery.

The man has barely left the gallery when Ayan approaches. Grace wastes no time blurting out, "That creepy guy I saw twice at the Palace of Peace and Reconciliation is here. Remember, the man I saw on the stairs going up to the apex who gave me that look? He came up to me just now while you were gone. I'm worried he's following me. Why?"

"He's here? How strange . . . What did he say to you?"

"I jogged his memory, asked if he was at the Palace of Peace and Reconciliation a short time ago. He admitted he was there, but he didn't remember seeing me. Or at least that's what he claimed. He called my attention to these two maps of the Aral Sea and mentioned the island that has become a part of the mainland."

"Voz Island?"

"Yes, he said that name. Strange that he should mention that same island we were just talking about." Grace contemplates for a moment. "Do you think he wrote that note?"

"It's possible. But this may well be just a coincidence." Grace can tell from Ayan's tense expression that he too thinks there is more to it than being a coincidence.

"It's too many coincidences, Ayan. But if he was the one who sent me that note, he must know your name. Perhaps he knows about you. Yet he didn't seem to recognize you when he walked into the top of the pyramid." Grace voices her thoughts aloud.

Ayan looks uncertain. "To tell you the truth, I don't think I would recognize the man from the pyramid if I ran into him again. I hardly glanced at him that day." Looking at Grace with a more relaxed demeanor, he continues, "Coincidence or not, don't let that man's presence or what he said upset you and spoil your enjoyment of Shevchenko's exhibits. They are very beautiful and unique."

For the next hour, Grace allows herself to be transported back in time to the Aral Sea of the mid-nineteenth century, depicted in dream-like monochromatic tones. She finds herself absorbed into the poetic sense of Taras Shevchenko, the Ukrainian artist who viewed life through sadness and disillusion while in love with its beauty.

"I love this one, *Kazakh station on Kos-Aral*, with yurts and fish-ermen's families and even cattle right on the seashore!" Grace's voice resonates with appreciation and enthusiasm in the quiet gallery. "And look at this one, *Moonlit night at Kos-Aral*, that yellow full moon just above the marshes and its golden reflection in the water. So roman-tic!" Strolling from one frame to the next, Grace's eyes drink in the serenity and calm of the sea, the stillness amid the motion expressed in the people, boats, and water, and the tranquility of identical scenes at varying times of day and night, all in pastel monotones of gold and brown, green and gray, burnt orange and tan. It is the first time she actually sets eyes on the Aral, or the representation of it through the vision and experience of an artist who had loved it with his heart and soul. Her unnerving encounters with the blond man—and the subject of Voz Island—are driven into the back of her mind.

"It's good to see you enjoying the collection so much, appreciating the Aral Sea at its finest. The Aral has always meant a lot to me. I grew up on its shores, and the sea was my teacher and loyal friend."

"Your nanny too perhaps. My mom used to tell me the person she loved most as a child next to her own parents was her nanny who took care of her in Hong Kong since she was three months old. The nanny died three years ago in Hong Kong. My mom, who long ago immigrated to the United States, still misses her very much," Grace says. "The Aral must be like a nanny to you, nurturing and caring, but unfortunately dying."

Ayan nods appreciatively at Grace's analogy. He looks gravely at a golden watercolor entitled *Steep Coast of the Aral Sea*, of perpendicular cliffs rising from the water's edge. "One of my earliest childhood memories was standing at the top of one of those cliffs by our village, picking berries from trees that grew there and looking out to the sea beyond. My older brother Arsen would go up there with me, and sometimes my two best childhood friends Aldiyar and Darkhan." He pauses, swallowing a lump, and takes a full minute to find his words again. "On rough days, I loved to watch the waves rushing to the shore below me and hear the howl of the wind. I remember imagining the white waves to be faceless ghosts and the wind the sound of their groaning and moaning."

"How close were you to the sea when you were a child?" Grace asks.

"My earliest memory was of the Aral Sea coming right up to our backyard in Balta. My mother told me one of my first baby words was '*Avay*' which was as close to 'Aral' as I could manage." He pauses again. "One of the main reasons I left Moscow and went home, other than being closer to my parents, was to be close to the Aral Sea again, especially in its current condition."

"It is so sad." Grace shakes her head slowly.

After walking through the Shevchenko exhibits, they stop at the museum café for a late lunch.

"Do you have a family, Ayan?" Grace asks, while digging into her omelet.

"You mean am I married? No. I guess I'm married to my work."

Grace smiles. "I'm sure your parents are happy every time you are home. I know mine are, though I guess I won't be seeing them for quite some time since they are far away, back in Chicago."

"Yes, my parents are always happy I'm home, especially for the summer. And my maternal grandparents are happy when I'm teaching because they live in the same city where I teach!"

"Your nomadic grandparents!"

"That's right!"

By the time they walk out of the museum, it is past three in the afternoon. The mid-April air is crisp and fresh. For once Grace sees some blue sky between white clouds, unusual at that time of day in a city clouded by pollution, the exhaust fumes from the dense traffic entrapped in the valley at the foot of the Alatau mountains. Before Grace catches an unofficial taxi back to her apartment, she turns to Ayan, shakes his hand firmly, and says, "Ayan, I guess I won't be seeing you again. I'm sorry Glen is busy tonight, else we could have dinner with you. Have a safe journey home. Goodbye and good luck. After learning about your rich heritage and the demise of the Aral Sea, I have no excuse not to come up with a story to write."

"Good luck with your book. Now that you've learned about the dying Aral Sea, maybe you can make up a story about it."

Grace laughs. "I need to fish one out of the sea, but all your fish are gone."

"The more likely you may find a story at the bottom," Ayan replies with a grin.

———

The morning after Grace's visit to the Kasteev Museum with Ayan, she steps out of her apartment building soon after Glen has left for work to do her weekly shopping at the Green Bazaar, just across the street from the southern exit of Panfilov Park. As she heads toward the magazine vendor's stall at the street corner, she waves to the old woman. "Dobroe utro!" she utters her usual morning greeting. By the time Grace has finished her shopping, it is eleven thirty in the morning. She crosses the street toward the magazine stand on her walk home, carrying two cloth bags of groceries. The vendor sees her coming and waves with excitement, signaling for her to stop by the stand. As soon as Grace gets close, the vendor grabs Grace's lower arm with one hand while she fumbles in her apron pocket with the other, producing a white envelope that she stuffs into Grace's hand. The envelope has no writing on it. The old woman points at Grace implying it's for her. Grace rips open the envelope. It is a newspaper clipping in Kazakh, showing just the headline of a news article without the content. She shows the clipping to the curious vendor. A lot of jabbering on the latter's part follows. Frustrated, Grace looks around for a passer-by who can translate for her.

She doesn't have long to wait. A young woman carrying a backpack and looking like a college student comes up.

"Speak English?" Grace immediately asks.

"Yes," the young woman says confidently.

"Can you please tell me what this says?"

The woman glances at the article heading, then raises her eyebrows with an expression bordering on consternation. "It says 'Bodies of Two Missing Aralsk Residents Found in Aral Sea Near Voz Island.' The paper is dated April 12, 2007."

Grace feels her heart catch in her throat. Voz Island again! Looking at the young woman, she says in an excited voice, "Can you ask the magazine lady who gave this to her, and why she shows it to me?"

Some chattering in Kazakh ensues between the young woman and the magazine vendor. Then the young woman turns back to Grace.

"She says a man gave her the envelope this morning soon after you passed her stand and asked her to give it to the foreign Asian woman who just walked by."

In spite of her pounding heart, Grace's instinct tells her not to show her nervousness in public, lest people wonder at her connection to the two drowned victims, or, worse, to Voz Island. "Someone must be playing a joke on me," Grace says, sounding undisturbed, and brushing it off as a prank. Then as an apparent afterthought, she asks her translator, "Can you ask her what the man looked like?"

More Kazakh jabber, then the young woman turns to Grace. "She says she was busy with a few customers at the time and barely looked at him, but she has an impression he was a white man, middle-aged, medium height."

—

That evening soon after Glen returns home, Grace wastes no time showing him the newspaper clipping. She has already told him of her previous run-ins with the blond man over the last few days. "The sender cut off the rest of the article, leaving only the headline, as if to scare me. It was also strange that both the note I got at the hotel in Astana and this headline note have to do with Voz Island. You think the sender was the same person?"

"It's possible." Glen ponders for a while, looking at the headline clipping, then says, "The dead bodies were recovered in the sea near that island which produced biological weapons during Soviet time. They might have been thrown into the sea after the victims died on the island."

"Ayan said the island was abandoned after the Soviet Union broke up. If those two Aralsk residents were really killed on the island, I don't see why they were there to begin with. And why would someone send this clipping to me? Glen, you think that's a warning? A threat? What does the sender want from me?"

BOOK IV

AYAN

7

A MYSTERY ISLAND AND A HORSE

1958–1970

Ayan knew of Voz Island from his childhood growing up in Balta, a fishing village on the northern shore of the Aral Sea, although at the time he did not have a name for the island. To him and his childhood friends, it was just the mystery island out in the sea where a monster lived.

One of Ayan's earliest impressions was of his father's fishing boat, *Kari qaiyk*. She was smaller than most of the other fishing boats working the Aral, but Nurzhan took her out to sea each morning to bring home fish, lots of fish. *Kari qaiyk* became a household name. Nurzhan told his family that she was so named not because she was an old boat as the words implied, but because he considered her a good old friend.

Nurzhan and his helper, Kanat, would go out to sea early in the morning, before the first glow of dawn. Each day they would drive their daily catch in Nurzhan's truck to a fish receiving station in Aralsk, where the fish were sorted, washed, and cleaned for transport to different destinations across the Soviet Union, with some left for the local markets. Ayan and his brother Arsen would look forward to the fish their father brought home for the family every day, hoping it would include their favorites, pike, carp, and bream. The family had meanwhile expanded with the birth of two daughters, Karlygash born in 1962, Aigerim in 1964. The Aral Sea not only provided Nurzhan with a living; Ayan sensed that it was also his father's best friend, his calling, and, next to his family, his greatest love.

From his childhood, Ayan remembered fishing as a year-round occupation. Before the Aral Sea lost most of its water and its salinity rose to unprecedented heights, it froze at the beginning of December and thawed at the end of March. To the young Ayan, the Sea was like an endless magic skating rink. He loved the winter. His father and fellow fishermen used to go out onto the frozen sea in dog sleds. Ayan and Arsen loved hearing their father tell of how the fishermen hewed out ice to make openings into the water below, then threw seine nets through the openings, leaving them in the water. A week later, Nurzhan and his fishing companions would go back to haul the nets out. They were always full of fish. After emptying the nets, they would comb them and throw them in again. When Ayan was seven, he asked his father if he could go out with him on a winter fishing trip one time. His father said, "It is not safe for a young child to go fishing on the frozen sea." Ayan was disappointed, but knew better than to press the matter.

Ayan had inherited his father's love of the Aral Sea and had felt a kinship with it for as long as he could remember. He loved being by it, particularly in the summer, not only on calm days when the water was a beautiful sparkling azure, but also when mighty winds and forceful gales rocked the fishing boats and white, foamy surfs rose to towering heights. On such days, he imagined a mighty giant blowing enormous puffs of wind to whip up the tall waves. To him, the giant was a good and benevolent one for he also brought rain, and his father said they needed the rain for the sea, the earth, and the air. On clear days, Ayan would follow Arsen up a jagged trail to a bluff called Sea Cliff, so named because its top extended over the coastline. Once at the top, Ayan would sit on a big rock looking out, his eyes fixed on where the sea met the sky. Even at the age of five, he loved watching the waves rushing ashore, constant and unfailing. That image of the Aral Sea had remained vivid in Ayan's mind long after he left for university. It gave him peace, tranquility, and a sense of nostalgia. The Aral Sea of his childhood was the center of his world then. Life was good.

Before Ayan started school, he played with other children in their village every day. His two best friends, Aldiyar and Darkhan, were the same age as he, and their fathers were also fishermen. While their fathers were out to sea, the three of them played on the beachfront of Balta, games like tag and a rudimentary version of soccer. And whenever Aldiyar and Darkhan saw Ayan going up Sea Cliff with his brother, they would follow, to watch the waves, and on their way downhill, the three friends would race to the bottom, tumbling at times, mindless of the scrapes and scratches they would pick up along the steep and sandy slopes. Occasionally a fourth boy joined them, a boy named Mukhtar from Alty qudyq, the next village over. It was from Mukhtar that they heard one day about a mysterious island in the Aral Sea where a frightful monster lived.

"Yesterday, my mother's cousin came to visit from Moynaq in Uzbekistan. He told us about an angry monster living on an island in the sea. You can't see the island from here, but it's out there," Mukhtar told a bunch of the village kids. "The monster captures animals from the mainland, takes them back to the island, and eats them."

"I don't believe in monsters," Darkhan said. "They're just made up to scare us."

"You want to bet? My mother's cousin lives in Moynaq, and he said he could see the island occupied by the monster." Mukhtar looked annoyed at Darkhan's comment.

"Did he see the monster there?" Darkhan challenged.

"It's too far to see the monster!" Mukhtar said. "Nobody would dare go near the island anyway."

But Ayan was greatly troubled by Mukhtar's words. When he asked his father about the island, Nurzhan said, "There are a number of islands in the Aral Sea, but none has a monster that eats animals. Don't worry. It's just a tale to frighten children."

Still, the story disturbed young Ayan a lot and gave him nightmares. Ever since he heard about the island, whenever he and Arsen hiked up Sea Cliff on sunny days, he would strain his eyes from the top of the bluff, searching the wide horizon for any sign of an island. He could see no island from the northern shore of the Aral Sea. However, his mind was not at ease. What was invisible to him was all the more frightening, leaving his imagination to run wild. It seemed some evil creature was out there hiding from him, watching him, ready to pounce and devour him at any unguarded moment.

Ayan started school in 1967 at the age of seven. He loved school. He'd walk with Aldiyar and Darkhan to the one elementary school located within the village. The three friends were quite inseparable. Of the three, Darkhan was the tallest for his age, muscular and stocky. Aldiyar, on the other hand, was skinny and pale in complexion. Ayan was a little taller than Aldiyar and had a more robust look. With Darkhan as their champion, Ayan felt safe from village bullies, as did Aldiyar.

Ayan enjoyed middle school even more because that's when he started learning English as a foreign language, at the age of ten, starting with the alphabet, phonetics, basic conversation, and grammar. Gradually he learned to read children's story books in English, then progressed to extracts from abridged versions of English classic novels in his English study book. While Aldiyar and Darkhan found English a big hurdle that they could not overcome, Ayan thought differently. For him, English opened up a whole new realm of stories, tales different from those he grew up with in Kazakh or Russian. His favorites were the tales of adventure—*Gulliver's Travels, Robinson Crusoe, Treasure Island.* He longed for the day when he would master the language well enough to read the original classics. His middle school English teacher was a caring, patient woman named Kuralay Akhmetova, from Kyzylorda. She told her class she was educated in Moscow. As Ayan grew to like English and to excel at it more and more, he wondered if he might one day study in the big city too.

———

Around 1970, the Aral Sea was receding further and further away from Aralsk and the fishing villages on its northern shores. Balta was not spared that fate. What used to be the bottom of the sea along the coast had become the new seashore, covered with seashells, sand, and salt. Ayan noticed his father looking worried most of the time. A few evenings, Ayan had heard his parents talking in low earnest voices after he and his siblings had gone to bed, and although he could not hear their conversation, it seemed they were discussing a grave and worrisome matter. Not only was the sea losing its water, but also the water that was left tasted much saltier than before. When Ayan asked his father the reason for it, he explained, "Son, the less water there is in the sea because the rivers are no longer flowing into it, the faster the hot sun evaporates the water that's left. As a result, the salt that's in the sea is dissolved in a smaller volume of water, and so the water tastes saltier."

"That's not good for the fish, my teacher says," Arsen chimed in.

"Right. The salty water is killing many of our fish. Not only that, but also the salt deposited on the shores is killing plants on the land, and we need the plants to break up dust storms," their father said.

Ayan remembered the dust storms becoming more frequent, blowing sand and salt everywhere. Rain became scarce. Summers were much hotter than before, and winters were becoming unbearably cold. The winter fishing season became shorter. His father said that the high salt content in the sea lowered its freezing temperature, making it difficult and unsafe for fishermen to venture out for a good part of the winter. Fishermen were bringing in fewer fish by the late sixties, while their anxiety was rising. Ayan understood his father's concern.

In spite of the trouble his family was facing, Ayan had the grandest surprise when he turned ten on March 28, 1970. When he arrived home from school that day, his mother greeted him with a secretive smile. His father had not yet returned from his day trip to Aralsk. It was Aigerim who broke the news to him. "Ayan, *Ake* and *Apa* got you a horse!"

It had been Ayan's dearest dream to own a horse from the time he was six, when one of their neighbors brought home a colt. The neighbor's son had let Ayan sit in the saddle many times as he walked the horse along the beach. At the time, it seemed having his own horse was just a fantasy never to come true. So when Aigerim told him he was really getting one, Ayan could not believe his ears. Perhaps it was still a dream. But his mother soon set it right when she took him around the far side of their single-story home, and there, tied to a pole, was a stout brown horse with an unusual orange-brown mane.

"He is a six-and-a-half-year-old male," his mother said in Kazakh, the only language spoken in their house when Ayan and his siblings were growing up, as their mother said they must never forget their roots and mother tongue. She continued, "Very good steppe horse. Take care of him. He will give you a lot of joy and companionship for many years."

"Where did you get him, Apa?"

"Ake's good friend from Alty qudyq is moving with his family to the east, where there is lake and river fishing and relatives can help him and his son find other work too. He asked if we would take their horse. They cannot take him to where they are going, and he knows you like horses. His son Ali will help you train him and teach you to ride before they leave." Akzharkyn looked as excited as Ayan himself, and he knew his mother was happy because he was happy. "His name is Sarzhal, because of his orange mane," she added.

In the next two weeks, Ali came over to Balta a few times to help Ayan with Sarzhal, showing him how he had trained the horse and secured his respect, so that Ayan too could earn Sarzhal's respect as his new master, managing him and giving him commands as Ali did. They rode Sarzhal along the four-kilometer stretch of sandy flats between Balta and Alty qudyq and brought Sarzhal up to the low plateaus where there were scattered coverings of grass for him and a few other horses to graze. Though not exactly handsome with his short neck, jagged head, and muscular rump, Sarzhal was an intelligent and energetic horse, obedient and good-natured. On the last day before Ali and his family left for East Kazakhstan, Ayan could tell Ali was sad to be leaving the Aral District, and particularly his beloved horse. Ayan saw him actually crying into Sarzhal's mane as he embraced his rugged head. Not knowing how to comfort him, and even though Sarzhal was really his horse now, Ayan said to the other boy, "I will take good care of him in your absence. I promise."

From that day on, Ayan and Sarzhal were inseparable, much to the envy of Aldiyar and Darkhan, whose dreams for their own horses would never be realized. Ayan knew the horse was happy to be with him, for when he sidled up to him, his nostrils were relaxed and his ears perked forward. Sometimes when they were together, Sarzhal looked at his new young master directly in the face, his ears up, as if to say, "I love you." And Ayan loved him back. Occasionally, on clear sunny days, Ayan rode Sarzhal up the slope to the top of Sea Cliff. From there, he would sit on his rock a short distance from the edge, Sarzhal leaning against him, nuzzling him at times. Ayan hadn't forgotten the mystery island where an animal-eating monster lived. But no matter how hard he strained his eyes to look into the distant horizon, he could not detect the outline of land. Still, it remained a haunting presence at the back of his mind.

Sarzhal meant the world to Ayan. His only fear was he would have to give him away if his family were to move to East Kazakhstan too. Horse and boy had developed a close bond that nothing could break, or so it seemed. In spite of the shrinking sea, life was still good.

8

EPIDEMIC AND DEATH IN THE SEA

1971–1972

Nurzhan continued to go out to sea daily before the break of dawn in *Kari qaiyk*. His helper Kanat left at the end of 1970, when Ayan was ten. Like many of the fishermen of the Aral Sea, he decided to look for better waters in East Kazakhstan. Much as Nurzhan appreciated Kanat, his leaving was also a relief, as the Aral was no longer yielding enough fish for him to hire a helper.

Among all the fishermen in Balta, only three of them had trucks, Nurzhan being one of the lucky ones. His was an old cranky 4x4 that he had purchased in Aralsk from a retired shopkeeper. It did its job well, bumping and thumping across non-marked steppe country, arid grassland, and sandy shores. The three truck owners took turns driving to Aralsk, transporting all the village fishermen's daily catch to the town receiving station. Since the late sixties, with the alarming decrease in the quantity of fish harvested each day, their village's catch could be loaded into a single truck for transport to Aralsk. And so, each truck owner would drive to Aralsk every third day, accompanied by one of the fishermen who did not own a truck to help with the unloading once they got there. In the summer, Arsen would accompany his father out to sea, and sometimes he would ride with him into town to help with the unloading. He told Ayan about Aralsk's colorful thoroughfares, the townsfolk going by, and all the action at the former waterfront from which the distant sea could still be seen. Whatever fish the sea yielded, their father always held back enough for his family's supper, but he usually had the better ones taken to town to sell. The family could no longer be choosers.

When Nurzhan moved his family from Aralsk to Balta in 1958, Nurzhan offered his house on March 8th Street by the harbor in Aralsk to his wife's cousin Kairat, who was moving with his family to Aralsk to work in the fish canning factory there. They could stay in the house for as long as they were in Aralsk. Kairat happily accepted and had been living there ever since. Early in August 1971, they got some bad news from Kairat. Their house in Aralsk had been partially damaged by a kitchen fire. Nurzhan decided to go to Aralsk with Arsen to help Kairat with the repairs, staying at the house until the job was done. In the second week of August, they drove into Aralsk.

While Nurzhan and Arsen were away in Aralsk, the job of transporting fish every day to Aralsk fell entirely on the other two fishermen with trucks. The villagers in Balta took care of one another. In the absence of his father, neighbors gave Ayan and his family some of their daily catch. His mother had fish salted for rainy days, and the family ate that as well, and drank camel milk from the few camels they were keeping. Ayan liked camel milk a lot for its rich creamy flavor and could live on it alone with its high nutrition.

The week went by fast. Nurzhan and Arsen had been away for several days, and the family was expecting them home soon. On the fifth day after they left for Aralsk, a neighbor named Bakhyt, who owned one of the trucks, drove with another fisherman into town to deliver the fish caught earlier that morning. An hour after they left Balta, Bakhyt's creaky old truck returned and soon jolted to a halt in front of Nurzhan's home. Bakhyt jumped out of the truck, looking agitated, and ran over to Ayan and his mother, who had come out of the house on seeing his truck back so soon after he left.

"Back so soon? What happened?" his mother asked. Ayan didn't know how to interpret Bakhyt's frantic look.

Out of breath, Bakhyt blurted out, "We got to the outskirts of Aralsk but were stopped by guards. All the roads into Aralsk have been blocked. We were told to turn around and leave. There has been an outbreak of smallpox in Aralsk. The whole town is locked down. No one can go in, and no one can come out."

"How could that happen? Impossible!" Akzharkyn looked desperate, as though the sky was falling.

"When can my father and brother come home?" Ayan asked, as if Bakhyt knew.

"We don't know. I guess it depends on how many people have been exposed. I heard from the people at the blockade that so far there is only one diagnosed case, a woman scientist. We don't know the details, but smallpox is very contagious. She could have passed it on to others," Bakhyt said, looking grave.

Akzharkyn broke into tears. "Yesterday there was no quarantine! If only they had come home yesterday! They've both had the smallpox vaccination. They won't get infected, and they won't infect others! Why won't they let them leave?" Her sobs turned to ranting.

The rest of the day and in the days that followed, villagers came over to offer food, comfort, and support for Akzharkyn and her children, but she could not be consoled. Reports came out from Aralsk that the scientist had gone with a crew on a vessel into the Aral Sea on a fisheries research expedition. She was most likely exposed to smallpox at one of the ports of call along the Uzbek coast. She became ill with fever and was diagnosed with smallpox after arriving home to Aralsk. Immediately, the city was placed under lockdown. It was just bad timing that Nurzhan and Arsen were in Aralsk when lockdown was imposed.

Within days, the public health authorities in Kyzylorda ordered everyone in Aralsk to be vaccinated against smallpox. The days and nights were long and hard while Ayan and his sisters waited with their mother for their father and brother to return home. "At least they won't catch it," his mother kept saying, trying to convince herself. "They were vaccinated against smallpox long ago. We all were."

The incubation period of smallpox is around two weeks. The boat transporting the research team returned to Aralsk waters, and by the end of two weeks, no other crew member had contracted smallpox. However, the scientist had infected her younger brother, who in turn had infected others. The lockdown was eternal agony, or so it seemed, for no one could tell when it would be lifted. Ayan and his sisters woke every morning hoping that it would be the day their father and brother would come home. Meanwhile, their mother was a constant portrait of anxiety and despair. Weeks came and went. August turned into September. Still no sign of their father and brother. During that trying time, Aldiyar and Darkhan would spend all their free time from school with Ayan, playing ball with him or hiking up Sea Cliff with him, with Sarzhal in tow. While Ayan was very anxious about his father and brother, he found distraction and comfort being with his two best friends.

It was not until the middle of October that Nurzhan and Arsen were allowed to leave Aralsk and return to their home, more than two months after they'd left. When Akzharkyn saw them, she embraced them and cried all the harder. During their quarantine, Nurzhan and Arsen had stayed in their former house with Kairat, his wife, and their two daughters. All residents of the city were ordered not to leave their homes except for necessities. Fortunately, as a result of the mass vaccination and enforced quarantine, only a total of ten persons were infected, of whom three died. The scientist who started it all and her younger brother both survived.

The evening of Nurzhan and Arsen's return to Balta, the villagers gathered on the open village square to hear Nurzhan talk about his ordeal. Akzharkyn and the whole family were naturally there.

"The strange thing is that the woman scientist was the only one on the boat to be infected, no other members of the crew," Ayan heard his father tell the villagers. "Our cousin Kairat was at the harbor and heard a man saying he was on the boat with the scientist who caught smallpox. He said the boat stopped at three ports at the end of July and early August, but she never left the boat, never went ashore at any of the three ports, while he and the other crew members did. So she couldn't have been exposed there. And since no other crew member was infected, she couldn't have gotten it from any of them who went ashore either. *It's a mystery that she was the only one infected!*" Nurzhan said the last sentence emphatically.

"How else could she have caught the disease then?" one of the villagers asked.

"Good question. Other than the three ports of call, the only place the vessel even got close to was Voz Island, according to that crew member. The vessel anchored maybe fifteen kilometers from that island one night, but he said no one went ashore since there is a military base there and the only people allowed are the military, their families, and people authorized to work there. Nobody on the *Lev Berg* landed on the island, so it's unlikely she could have caught smallpox there!"

Standing behind his father in the public square, that was the first time eleven-year-old Ayan heard the name Voz Island. In that moment, his thoughts spontaneously went back to the mystery island from his childhood where supposedly an animal-eating monster lived. Just because he couldn't see it, even from the top of Sea Cliff, didn't mean it wasn't somewhere out there in the Aral Sea. Ayan wondered if that fearsome island Mukhtar had told him about might actually exist, and if Voz Island was its name.

—

An increasing number of dead fish were turning up in fishermen's nets. As the daily catch diminished in size and quality, Nurzhan's family began to raise some sheep as supplementary income, in addition to the few camels they already had. In spite of their struggles, Ayan was glad his father had decided to stay in Balta and continued to sail out in his faithful *Kari qaiyk*, even though more and more fishermen had left in hopes of finding better fishing in the lakes and rivers of East Kazakhstan, or other kinds of work in the big city of Almaty. Ayan had spent his childhood listening to the Aral Sea lapping on their village shores. It was painful to watch the sea shrinking and drifting away, but like a loyal friend, he didn't want to leave it in its moment of distress. He didn't want to leave Aldiyar and Darkhan with whom he had played ever since they could walk. He also loved attending his middle school, where his English teacher Kuralay Akhmetova never failed to inspire him. Above all, he did not want to leave Sarzhal, his horse and brother.

As Ayan grew older, his father would alternate taking him or Arsen into town. Ayan had always regarded a trip to Aralsk as a big treat. By then, the sea had already receded to about seven kilometers away from Aralsk, except for a man-made canal channeling water from the sea to the harbor front—an expensive project that was keeping the port alive for the time being, but just barely. In the dried-up parts of the harbor, the seabed was littered with broken pipes, rusty old cans, glass fragments, and all kinds of garbage, the only water left being the occasional muddy puddle. Ayan would stare in awe at the two giant cranes above the Aralsk harbor, imagining they were dragons with long necks that snatched up cargoes from the boats to devour them.

On a late summer day in 1972 before he started sixth grade, Ayan accompanied his father into Aralsk to deliver the day's catch to the fish sorting station. As they were eating *belyashi* by the old harbor, they heard some loud commotion by the harbor front close to the canal. Ayan was curious. His father asked a passer-by coming from that direction what the excitement was all about.

"A police boat patrolling the sea earlier found a dead body in a boat adrift in the water," the man said.

"How did he die?" Ayan asked immediately, a tremor in his voice.

"Don't know yet, but his death sure seems suspicious. The police are taking care of the corpse. But they didn't tow the boat to Aralsk. Don't know where they took it."

As Nurzhan drove home with Ayan to Balta that afternoon, neither spoke much. Nurzhan seemed absorbed in his own thoughts. As for Ayan, a dead man in a boat adrift in the Aral Sea added to his suspicion that something mysterious, something strange, was going on out there beyond the horizon. He could not dismiss his subconscious fear that the man's death was also related to activities on the mystery island of his childhood, the island he had somehow associated with Voz Island ever since the crew member on the *Lev Berg* mentioned its name.

One evening about two weeks after the discovery of the corpse adrift in a boat in the Aral Sea, Nurzhan came home from his trip into town and told his family, "That man found in the boat—even though there is no official report to confirm the cause of death, rumor says that he had died of the plague."

The whole family looked stricken.

9

DUST STORM AND GREATEST LOSS

1974–1975

In September 1974, Ayan started eighth grade in Balta. He continued to do well in all subjects, particularly in English. The next year, he would be going on to secondary school. Balta shared a secondary school with the neighboring village, Alty qudyq. It would be easy to walk to school if Ayan was to attend his village secondary school. However, Kuralay Akhmetova, his middle school English teacher, had been encouraging him to take the entrance examination for a secondary school in Kyzylorda, which had a special program for talented and promising students in English that was taught by a very proficient teacher from Leningrad. Much as he wanted to pursue his studies in English language and literature, Ayan was not sure if he wanted to study in Kyzylorda, away from his family and home, away from Aldiyar and Darkhan, and from Sarzhal.

Sarzhal had become a constant and true companion and a member of the family. Sometimes Ayan rode him on the beach, his flaming mane dancing in the wind, although in the summer it was a hot wind that brought no relief. Sarzhal spent most days and nights on the grassy plateau with the other horses of the village, enjoying the open field and the cool night air. The ten horses had formed a herd of their own, and one of them would stay awake keeping watch while the other horses slept. When not on the plateau, Sarzhal stayed in an enclosed shed Nurzhan had built for him by their house, especially for shelter from the dust storms that razed Balta with blinding sand, dust, and salt about ten times a year.

And not only sand, dust, and salt—at the time, Ayan, his family, and the villagers did not know that the worst elements in the dust storms were what they could not see or feel: the poisonous chemicals from the pesticides and fertilizers used in the cotton fields that were drained into the sea and then deposited on the former seabed when the water evaporated. When dust storms blew, the toxic chemicals that had mixed in with salt and sand were blown all over the region, contaminating the air and drinking water. It was some years later that they finally learned about those chemicals. But even before they knew about the danger they were exposed to, Akzharkyn had made her family wear face masks during storms "to keep the bad stuff in the dust away."

As to his dilemma of whether or not to attend secondary school in Kyzylorda, Ayan knew his family would take care of Sarzhal in his absence, but he hated the idea of not spending time with his beloved horse except on holidays. His hesitation about attending secondary school in Kyzylorda was resolved by a tragic happening one Sunday morning in April of 1975.

That morning, the sun was present though no more than a muted glow, coloring the sky in a dull yellow. The wind pitched to a chilling, threatening whine, sending desert shrubs and trees wildly thrashing left and right. Out of the dusky air, the villagers of Balta and Alty qudyq saw what seemed like a threatening, dark, looming curtain across the faraway horizon. It grew more prominent and closer by the minute as it moved toward them.

"Dust storm! Dust storm!" Nurzhan hollered to his family and neighbors. "Everybody, gather your things, to cover!"

Ayan's first thought was Sarzhal. He ran out of the house to the base of the plateau and clambered up the slope as fast as his legs would let him, his heart thumping till he felt his chest would explode at any moment. But he could not pause to rest, not until he had brought Sarzhal downhill and put him safely in his covered shed as he had done every time a dust storm was about to hit. He reached the top, panting wildly, his eyes scanning the field of battering shrubs and scattered grass patches where Sarzhal had spent the night with the other horses, as was his usual custom. But that April morning, there was no Sarzhal in sight. In fact, there were no horses at all.

"Sarzhal! Sarzhal!" Ayan shouted as loud as he could, blaming himself for not getting him sooner, his call competing with the now howling wind, hoping his horse would appear. No Sarzhal.

The other horses had probably been rounded up and taken down to their sheds and stables, Ayan thought. Could Sarzhal have followed them and their owners down? Was he already back at the house and waiting outside his shed?

Ayan ran down the slope, half tumbling, scraping his knees and hands. When he reached his house, Arsen had already put all the sheep in the covered pen. The girls had gathered the washings. His parents were anxiously calling for him to get into the house. But still, no Sarzhal.

"I can't find Sarzhal!" he cried like one deranged. "Where is he? Have you seen him?"

"Don't worry, he must have come down with the other horses!" his father shouted. "Come inside!"

"Don't worry, son," his mother assured more calmly. "Horses don't get lost. Come inside. Hurry. We need to seal all the doors and windows. No time to look for him now."

The faint but threatening dark curtain Ayan had seen on the horizon moments earlier had now become an advancing wall of sand and dust, a thousand meters or more high. Soon the dust storm was directly upon Balta, like gigantic and powerful waves covering and smashing everything in their paths. All the families had locked themselves indoors. Even though their houses were mostly brick, the shattering sounds of blowing sand beating against wooden shutters and the heavy pounding of raging wind on shingled roofs sounded like an army of ogres trying to break in. Ayan closed his eyes and saw Sarzhal trapped in the flood of blinding, suffocating sand and dust. In the frenzy of his mind, he saw Sarzhal bound and dragged into an unknown darkness from which there was no escape. Ayan shuddered and cried as no fourteen-year-old boy would.

"Apa," he said, tears streaming down his face, "I am scared for Sarzhal. Not that he is caught in the dust storm out there, but that something really bad has happened to him, and he is not coming back ever again." His mother held him close, as she had not for a long time, ever since he had become taller than she. Her silent embrace seemed to tell him she too was worried about Sarzhal.

Within minutes, the dust storm was over. Villagers emerged from their homes. First, Ayan checked with neighbors who owned horses too. Their horses likewise had not returned and were nowhere to be found. They had all vanished as if into the dusty void. Ayan's fear was well grounded. Ever since the evening before the dust storm, when he said goodnight to Sarzhal and patted him on his back before leaving him with his fellow horses in the grass-scattered field, his horse had not returned.

Ayan blamed himself for whatever had happened to his beloved friend. He had failed to protect him and had broken his promise to Ali. Scenarios ran through his mind of what might have happened. Had Sarzhal been stolen by horse thieves? Would he be sold out of greed? Or killed out of malice? These questions filled Ayan's days with anguish and his nights with restless sleep and disturbing night-mares. The shores and cliffs around Balta, once so comforting to him, now only reminded Ayan of happier times with Sarzhal there. After weeks of mourning, Ayan knew he had to escape, or else he would be smothered by his grief. In a rational moment of discernment, Ayan resolved to take the entrance examination for the prestigious Manshuk Mametova Secondary School in Kyzylorda.

Ayan passed the entrance examination, much to the pride of his former English teacher, Kuralay Akhmetova, who had recommended the school and had been a constant pillar of confidence and source of encouragement for Ayan through his middle school years. To Ayan, she had been a shining star that guided him on, no matter how many language hurdles he faced. In the late summer of 1975, Ayan left home for Kyzylorda to begin his secondary school education that autumn. Saying goodbye to his parents and sisters was a weepy affair. His brother Arsen was already in Kyzylorda, attending the Pedagogical Institute and staying with their maternal grandparents. His mother wept like she was losing her second son as well, even though Ayan assured her he would be home for the summer, as Arsen had been every year. Saying goodbye to his best friends was hard too. A couple days before he left for Kyzylorda, Nurzhan drove Ayan, Aldiyar, and Darkhan to Aralsk, so the three childhood friends could spend the day in the town. With middle school behind them, both Aldiyar and Darkhan had no intention of continuing their education in the local secondary school. They had been helping their fathers out at sea all summer but would be looking for work in town when autumn came. Aldiyar had actually considered apprenticing with a cobbler in Aralsk.

"At least I know I won't miss going to secondary school with you," Ayan said. "You guys do well in your jobs, okay? Good luck. I will see you both every summer I'm home. We will be friends forever," Ayan assured.

"Friends forever!" echoed Aldiyar and Darkhan.

—

The big city gave Ayan a healthy change of scenery. Kyzylorda was exciting and colorful, especially through the eyes of a sixteen-year-old from a small fishing village that was dwindling as the Aral's yield of fish decreased by the day. Ayan was totally in awe of the huge building blocks, three, four, and five stories high, that lined the wide and spacious city streets. Some newer buildings even rose to eight stories; to Ayan, they seemed to touch the sky. The lifeblood of Kyzylorda—and of the entire oblast—the majestic Syr Darya meandered through the city in all its grandeur and dignity.

For the two years he attended Manshuk Mametova Secondary School, he lived in his maternal grandparents' house. Grandpa Arystan and Grandma Aliya were more than delighted to have him with them. Since childhood, Ayan had looked forward to his annual visits with his maternal grandparents, loving especially Grandpa Arystan's stories of his early childhood years as a nomad on the steppes of Eastern Kazakhstan before collectivization changed his life. He admired his grandfather's resilience, diligence, and discipline, which had eventually led him to success as a student of music and later a college teacher of music in Kyzylorda. He also looked up to Grandpa Arystan's wisdom and insight regarding the state of affairs in the Soviet Union at the time.

Living in his grandparents' house in Kyzylorda, Ayan was free from cares except the responsibility to live up to expectations at school and the self-imposed pressure to be top in his studies to gain admittance to one of the best universities within the Soviet Union. Excelling in English, in particular, was important to him, not only because he appreciated the literature, but also because he wanted to have a skilled command of the most widely spoken language in the world—an asset not many scholars in the Soviet Union had. His English teacher, Ivan Sergeyevich, a man of letters educated at Moscow State University, thought highly of him and often spent extra time with him after school to help him improve his English. "Ayan, you can make it to the moon if you set your mind to it!" he liked to say. Under his guidance, Ayan began to read English classics in their original versions, beginning with *A Tale of Two Cities* and then his first Shakespearean play, *Julius Caesar*.

Ayan still blamed himself for leaving Sarzhal on the plateau the night before that ominous dust storm, for failing to protect him. The memory of Sarzhal filled Ayan with profound pain and regret long after. He might never know what had happened to Sarzhal, but whatever happened, he hoped his beloved horse had not suffered.

10

THE SHIP GRAVEYARD

1976

For the two years that Ayan attended secondary school in Kyzylorda, he went home in the summer, staying with his parents in Balta and making some day trips to Aralsk. By the mid-seventies, Aralsk had suffered a drastic downturn from its heyday, when it hosted a fancy hotel and nice restaurants and an active harbor. The defunct harbor town, despite having lost its former busy traffic, still afforded little pleasures for Ayan, who always enjoyed a bowl of *pelmeni* or some fresh grilled lamb shashlik in the local eateries.

By 1976, Aralsk's former harbor was about ten kilometers away from the sea. With the death of the fishing industry, its canning factory also closed. As a result, Ayan's Uncle Kairat lost his job. With his former experience in construction, he took work repairing old houses, since there were no new buildings going up in Aralsk. He and his family continued to live in the house Ayan's paternal grandfather had built on March 8th Street.

As Ayan grew into his teenage years, he became more conscious

of Voz Island. It was no secret that a Soviet military base was stationed there. Ayan had observed military planes flying southbound
over the diminishing sea, apparently in the direction of Voz Island,
that invisible but commanding presence for those on the northern
shores of the once great sea. As well, from the old harbor quays Ayan
had observed cargoes loaded onto barges bound presumably for the
island's military base. In the mid-seventies, it was getting harder for
boats to maneuver along the dug canal, which had to be constantly
extended to reach the receding sea. Like all Aralsk locals, Ayan knew
little about what was really happening on the island. The unspoken
awareness of military personnel and cargoes being transported to
the island—and of soldiers and civilians coming back to Aralsk from
the island on their way to mainland destinations—was mystifying to
him. That no one in Aralsk seemed to be asking questions or talking
about Voz Island in public added to the cloud of secrecy surrounding
it. No unauthorized person was allowed near the island, which was
continually well guarded by speed boats, yet at the same time, no one
seemed to want to be near it.

—

The summer of 1976, at the end of his ninth grade, Ayan went home
to Balta with Arsen, who had just finished his second year at the
Pedagogical Institute in Kyzylorda. Their father picked them up from
the train station in his truck. As soon as Ayan saw his father, he noticed
he had a few more age lines on his forehead, and his eyes were baggy
and tired. His smile on seeing his two sons was genuine, but the cor-
ners of his mouth seemed weighed down by worry. On the way back to
Balta, he asked about their studies, their lives in Kyzylorda, and about
Grandpa Arystan and Grandma Aliya and how their health was. But
in spite of his interest, Ayan sensed that something was not right, that
his father's mind was deeply troubled.

"Ake, you look tired," Ayan said. "What's wrong?"

Nurzhan was silent for a moment. Then he said, "There has been mass death of fish in the Aral Sea. The last few days, all I hauled up were whole nets of dead fish." He paused and swallowed hard. "Not a single live fish for days." Ayan knew then that his father's life as a fisherman was over. His sister Karlygash later told him and Arsen that their father was just waiting for them to return home, so that they could all sail with *Kari qaiyk* on her last journey and bid her a proper goodbye.

On July 17, 1976, Nurzhan Kazbekov sailed *Kari qaiyk* into a lagoon in the Bay of Beket, some thirty kilometers to the east of their village, until the boat hit muddy bottom and could go no further. There, he left his old and loyal friend in the company of six other abandoned fishing boats. Ayan, his mother, brother, and sisters were all present to accompany *Kari qaiyk* to her final resting place. That was the first time Ayan saw his father cry. Tears ran down his furrowed cheeks like rivulets of rainwater gushing through gutters. He wiped them off with a rough and callused hand. Ayan's mother was crying, and so were both his sisters, as his father steered *Kari qaiyk* into the lagoon. Ayan was no exception. Arsen probably had tears in his eyes too, though he kept his sunglasses on the whole time.

Before they disembarked from *Kari qaiyk*, they walked the deck from bow to stern and back again. She was still a beauty after nineteen years of seafaring life with Nurzhan, the two of them braving high winds, tall waves, and rough swirls every time a storm struck while they were at sea. Then there were those good days when they sailed with the calming breeze just before dawn, under a gradually lightening sky when the moon was down and the sun had not peeked above the horizon but was already staining the eastern sky.

Nurzhan had kept her always cleaned and polished, maintaining her in the best condition possible. Kanat had helped the years he was on the boat, and Ayan and Arsen too in the summers. But the day they left *Kari qaiyk* grounded in the slushy mud of the Bay of Beket, they were leaving her to the mercy of the blind, raging elements and merciless looters who would rip her to pieces scrounging for parts.

Ayan's heart was heavy as a millstone as he climbed down from *Kari qaiyk* with his family into the ankle-deep water of the mushy damp shore. His father was the last to leave her. Before they walked away to the waiting truck of a fisherman friend who would drive them home to Balta, Nurzhan took one more lingering look at his *Kari qaiyk* and called out at the top of his voice, his face drenched with tears, "When the sea comes back, *Kari qaiyk*, I will come back for you! We will go out together again to deep waters every day and catch one or two or three hundred kilograms of the finest fish the Aral has ever yielded. Wait for me and take care of yourself for me, my good old friend!" His shaking voice reverberated across the muddy, slushy shore, a hollow cry from a broken heart that could make the Heavens weep. In that moment, the sky darkened, portending rain. That was a scene, a memory, that had been etched into the inner recess of Ayan's soul.

In the years that Ayan was in Kyzylorda and then in Moscow when he attended university and later worked there, he returned home every July and accompanied his father, his mother, and sisters to pay an annual visit to *Kari qaiyk* on July 17, the anniversary of the day on which his father bade farewell to his boat. To them, it was a sacred mission, paying respects to the beloved dead. Most summers, Arsen too would come home and join the family on their pilgrimage to the ship graveyard. He graduated from the Pedagogical Institute in 1979, married an Uzbek girl named Kamilla that same year, and had moved to Tashkent in Uzbekistan to teach in a secondary school.

Kari qaiyk looked a little worse for wear every time Ayan saw her, more rusted and broken parts, more missing pieces as scrap metal collectors and souvenir hunters unscrupulously wrenched off her various parts. Every year they cleaned up the ground on which *Kari qaiyk* rested as best they could, clearing away empty beer cans and bottles, cigarette butts, and all kinds of unspeakable trash. To Ayan, it seemed every time his father visited *Kari qaiyk*, another piece of his heart died with her.

Nurzhan never left the Aral, even when most of his fisherman friends had gone. In his stubborn ways, he was determined to stay on.

He was born by the Aral Sea, he grew up with the Aral Sea, and when his eyes dimmed with age, he said, he would look out to where the Aral Sea had once been even though he could see it no more. For a living, he and Akzharkyn continued sheep rearing and added more camels to their camel farm, selling their milk for some added income. Every time Ayan came home, he hurt to see his father struggling hard for a living, and his mother with him, but he was proud of them—proud that they would not desert the Aral in its moments of dire distress.

"History tells us the Aral had lost most of its water twice and come back. I believe it will return for the third time. We must be patient and wait," Nurzhan said. "When I have touched the dry bed of the Aral and can go no lower, all I can do is to gaze up at the sky and hope the sea will come back some day. I will not stop hoping, nor will I rest, till I've seen that day."

11

THE TRAIN TO HELL

1976

On August 29, 1976, Nurzhan drove Ayan to the railway station in Aralsk for his train journey back to Kyzylorda, a few days before school would reopen on the first of September. Ayan got there some ninety minutes early and told his father just to drop him off at the station, as his father had errands to run in town before driving the fifty plus kilometers back to Balta.

"Study hard, son, and make me and your mother proud." Ayan remembered well his father's parting words and the fond fatherly slap on the back every time he dropped him off at the railway station.

"I will do my best, Ake," Ayan promised as in times past. "I won't disappoint you and Apa."

The Aralsk train station was a broad, white, two-level concrete building with a big clock embedded in the center of the mansard roof—an impressive construction in contrast to the simple, boxy, often dilapidated structures all around. The station's waiting room, though small, was roomy enough for the moderate traffic going into and out of Aralsk. White-washed walls, arched windows at opposite ends, a high ceiling, and rows of metal linked chairs completed the bare and plain interior, creating a cold and gloomy atmosphere. The only adornment was a huge mosaic extending the entire width of the center wall. It depicted Aralsk's fishing labor force, all facing a full-length profile figure in soldier's uniform with outstretched arms, holding a letter. A facial profile of Lenin was inset above the uniformed officer who was presumably an emissary of his. Across the top of the mural were the words in Russian: *In Response to Lenin's Letter, We Will Send Out 14 Wagons of Fish*.

—

The waiting room was only thinly occupied when Ayan arrived, but the interior was very hot so he went upstairs to the platform where he might get some air. It was about noon. Except for a woman holding a baby and sitting on a bench on the opposite platform, no one was around as no train was scheduled to leave in the next hour. At first, he paid little attention to the woman, trying to tune out the baby's restless wail. The child eventually stopped crying as the woman held it close to her breast, draping her scarf over its head. After a while, she stood up, carried the baby in one arm, and walked slowly to the edge of the platform directly across from where Ayan was standing, leaving her suitcase by the bench. She looked over to Ayan across the tracks. She was probably Kazakh by the look of her Asian features, in her mid-twenties, and most likely not a woman of poverty, going by her fashionable floral dress and leather ankle boots. At first Ayan thought she was staring right at him. He looked down at himself, self-conscious. But no, she was not focusing on him, nor did she seem to be looking at any object in particular. She seemed to be staring into an emptiness past him with a still, vacant look in her eyes, like one distraught. Ayan was afraid she might, in an unguarded moment, drop the baby onto the tracks. He thought to engage her in conversation to call her back to reality.

"Are you waiting for a train, ma'am?" he asked in Kazakh. No response. She might not have heard him. He yelled across the tracks, louder and more clearly, "Where are you going?"

She heard him that time, and directing her tired eyes toward him, said slowly and clearly, "To hell."

Her words sent a chilling jolt through Ayan, but pretending he wasn't disturbed, he changed the topic altogether to draw her thoughts away from whatever had caused her to give such a troubling answer. He called across the tracks, "Your baby is very cute. How old?"

"Three months," she said curtly.

"A boy?"

"Girl."

Ayan began to wonder if brevity was just her nature. "Girls are good. I have two sisters," Ayan said, trying to be friendly. "Where is your home?"

She ignored his question and said in an agitated gush of words, "I am not going back! I am not going back!" She broke into tears. "My baby will *die* if we go back."

"Please, don't be so upset," Ayan called over. He was at a loss as to how to comfort her, especially since they were two train tracks apart. He looked at his watch. It was 12:45 p.m. A few more people had arrived on her side of the station as their departure time drew closer. But they were mostly at the center section of the platform, while the woman and her baby were at the very front end.

"I cannot bring up my baby there! I cannot!" She sounded frantic by then. Ayan needed to call for help.

"Please, calm down, madam. I will ask someone to help you. Please go back to the bench and sit down to rest. Think of the baby. Go sit down, please!" She was silent for a moment, then turned and proceeded to walk slowly toward her bench, like one in a trance. Ayan waited till she had sat down again, her baby in her arms, then immediately left his platform and walked down to the main hall, his knapsack on his back and suitcase in hand. He went up to the ticket window. There was a long queue, but he bypassed everyone in line, ignoring their angry glares, and spoke urgently to the ticket agent through the window. He asked the ticket agent where he could find the officer in charge of the station as there was a lady in great distress. The girl at the window directed him to the manager's office inside the station. Ayan made his way to the office, but found no one there. By the time he asked his way to where the manager was talking to some workers outside the main entrance of the station, more than fifteen minutes had elapsed since he left the woman and baby to themselves. He told the station manager that there was a very sick woman with a baby on Platform 2. Without much delay, the station manager went in with him. Ayan was relieved to see the woman still sitting there on the bench with her child in her arms when they got to her boarding platform. By then, the platform was filling up. When the station manager approached her, she looked up at him, her eyes red and puffy, but she wasn't crying. She appeared to have calmed down somewhat.

"Excuse me, madam, where are you traveling to?" the station manager asked in Kazakh.

She answered, "Guryev."

"May I see your ticket please?"

She produced it from her coat pocket. He checked it and returning it to her with a polite nod said, "That train is arriving in twenty minutes. Are you feeling unwell?"

She answered in a steady voice, "I am fine."

"This young man here told me you didn't seem to be well."

She shook her head. "I am fine," she insisted, looking up at the station manager assertively.

"I'm sorry for disturbing you, madam. Have a good trip," the station manager said to her. He then turned to Ayan and said, "She seems fine to me. I have to get back to my work." Looking somewhat frustrated, he left them.

Alone with the woman, Ayan said, stooping over her, "Madam, my train will not be arriving for quite some time. I can stay with you and help you get on the train before I go back to my platform."

She looked up at him. "I don't need any help. I can manage," she snapped, bordering on rudeness. Perhaps she was upset with Ayan for calling the station manager to her. However, her earlier desperation seemed to have abated. Ayan remained hesitantly in front of her, and she added more courteously, "She is small. I can carry her on one arm and lift the suitcase with the other hand." She seemed adamant that Ayan should leave her.

"If you insist, I'll leave you alone. But I'm just across the tracks and you can call me over if you need help."

"Thank you."

He was about to walk away when she surprised him by saying, "My name is Kulyash Krylova. My daughter is Dina. I lived for the past four years with my husband who works on Voz Island."

Ayan looked at her with concern. When she said earlier that she was not going back, did she mean to Voz Island? If her husband was with the military there, she wouldn't be able to say much about his work. Better not ask her about Voz Island. Perhaps she was going to Guryev to visit family. After an awkward pause, he said, "I am Ayan Kazbekov from Balta, a village about fifty kilometers west of here."

To his amazement, she took his hand and gave it a firm squeeze. "Thank you for your concern, Ayan. You are a good young man. Now go back to your platform to wait for your train. I'll be fine." Her words sounded reassuring.

"Safe journey then, and good luck!" With that, he started walking toward the stairs at the center of the platform where more people were waiting for their train. He turned and saw her looking in his direction. He waved but she did not wave back. Perhaps she wasn't looking at him. He walked down the center stairs to the ground level of the station, crossed the hall, and went up the stairs to his own platform. He proceeded toward where he saw Kulyash earlier, about two carriage lengths from the front end of her platform. She was still sitting there.

He waved to her again. She did not wave back. She seemed lost in thought, not looking over to him.

It was now 1:30. A train was turning a bend in the distance and coming into view, headed toward the station. *It must be Kulyash's train*, Ayan thought. The train blew its whistle and slowed as it approached the opposite platform. From where he stood, Ayan could see Kulyash getting up, her baby in her arms, and proceeding toward the edge of the platform, ready to board the train. Soon the train would come between them, once it filled the length of the platform, blocking his view of her. Ayan suddenly noticed Kulyash's suitcase was not with her; she had left it by the bench! What followed was horror beyond comprehension. Kulyash approached the edge of the platform, with no uncertain step, like one possessed. Without a second's pause, she stepped over the platform edge, plunging herself and her baby down onto the tracks, in front of the oncoming train. There was no chance the train could stop before it hit Kulyash and Dina, crushing them beneath its weight and grinding wheels.

Ayan gave out a piercing, bloodcurdling, long-drawn-out cry, a full eight-second delayed reaction. He was shaking all over. Hugging himself with crossed arms, he crouched down, gagged, and vomited on the platform.

—

For days, Ayan could not eat or sleep. His first week of school was lost time, as thoughts of Kulyash in her final moments played over and over in his head. What could have gone through her mind? What desperation could have driven her to kill herself and her baby in such a grotesque manner? If only he had stayed with them until they boarded their train, Ayan kept telling himself, he could have prevented the tragedy. How foolish and naive he was to believe Kulyash's light assurance that she was fine when he had seen for himself how distraught she was, heard her say plain as day that she was taking a train to hell. He could not

forgive himself for not having done more. As guilt gnawed at his consciousness, he had a recurring dream that the horrific happening had all
been a nightmare and that he woke to see Kulyash getting on the train
to Guryev with baby Dina happily gurgling in her arms.

"Do not blame yourself," Grandpa Arystan said. "Even if you had
prevented her from jumping that day, she would have found another
way to end her life and her baby's. She was deeply depressed. Whatever
drove her to such madness was what killed her."

"*Ata*, when I asked her where she lived, she said she was not going
back, and although she did not say to where, I think she meant Voz
Island. She said her husband was working there. I knew there was
something evil about that island!"

At Ayan's mention of Voz Island, Grandpa Arystan raised his head
abruptly. His eyes capturing Ayan's full attention, he said, "Promise
me you will not talk about Voz Island with anyone outside these walls.
No one, understand?" Grandpa Arystan sounded firm and severe.

"Okay, Ata," Ayan replied faintly. "But what do you think is actually happening there?"

Arystan gave a heavy sigh. "People in Kyzylorda and the Aral
region know there is a military base on the island, where Soviet
troops are trained. However, among the academic circle here, there
has been some speculation that the Soviet government is doing top-se-
cret research on biological weapons there. If our guess is correct, we
just hope whatever they are researching and developing is for national
defense only, not a weapon they will use against their enemies in any
act of aggression." His words sent a tremor through Ayan.

"Ata, do you suppose the smallpox epidemic a few years ago could
have come from the island?"

"It's possible. But there is no proof."

"And then there was that corpse they found in a boat of a man
rumored to have died of the plague. No one knows where they took
the body after the police took over the case, and no one's heard anything more about the case since."

"We will never know what actually killed him, Ayan. The government is keeping a lot of secrets from the people. Best to keep silent. Speculating too much will not do us any good."

"Why couldn't Kulyash Krylova just raise her baby somewhere else? Like Guryev, where she told the station manager she was going?" Ayan asked, as if his Grandpa Arystan knew why. He simply couldn't let the thought of her go.

"Ayan, she was very depressed," Grandpa rationalized again. "A person suffering from depression oftentimes cannot think logically."

"Clearly not . . . It seems she felt her only options were to return to the island or to kill herself and her baby. What on Voz Island could be so terrible that she would rather choose death, Grandpa?"

———

In the second week of classes, Ayan began to gradually ease back into the rhythm of school. Regarding the tragedy of Kulyash Krylova, he was starting to accept his grandfather's position that even if he had been able to prevent her from jumping onto the railway tracks that day, she would have found other means to end her life once she had set her mind to it.

One afternoon, about ten days after the tragedy at the train station, Ayan returned home after class to find two officers from the Soviet Administration Center in Kyzylorda waiting for him. They wanted to question him about the death of Kulyash Krylova and her baby. Grandpa Arystan and Grandma Aliya were asked to leave the parlor. Even though the two officers were ethnic Kazakhs, the interrogation was conducted in Russian, the official language of the government. Mainly they wanted to know how much he knew about Kulyash and what she had told him before she jumped.

"I saw her for the first time from the opposite platform about an hour before her death. Seeing her alone with a baby, I called to her to start a casual conversation. She told me her daughter was three months old. She looked sick, like she was about to vomit, so I went to the station manager for help. When we got to the platform, we found her sitting on the bench holding her baby, and her color seemed to have come back somewhat. She told the station manager she was fine, and she really seemed better. The station manager asked her where she was going, and she said 'Guryev.' After the station manager left, I offered to stay with her to help her get on the train, but she told me she could manage on her own and told me to go back to my platform across the tracks, so I left her. Those were all my dealings with her."

One of the officers said, "This woman killed herself and her baby because she was suffering from depression, which often afflicts a woman soon after giving birth. Did she tell you where she lived?"

"She did not, and I didn't ask her. I assume she lived in Guryev, since she was headed there."

"Did she tell you anything about the baby's father?"

"No, she didn't."

"So, you knew nothing about her except what you told us?"

"That's correct," Ayan said, nodding his head with certainty and looking at the questioning officer with wide-eyed innocence. Then he added, "I hope you locate the baby's father soon."

—

Over the years, Ayan had thought often of Kulyash Krylova and her little Dina. Every time he waited for a train at the railway station in Aralsk, he could not help but be pulled back to that day. Whenever he heard the name Voz Island mentioned, it struck a jarring note of ugly discord in him, sending shivers down his spine. He could never erase from his psyche what had happened that fateful day of August 29, 1976.

BOOK V

GRACE

12

DINING WITH THE BEATLES ON KOK TOBE

May 2, 2007, Almaty, Kazakhstan

On a rare Wednesday afternoon, Glen takes a half day off work to go with Grace up to Kok Tobe, that popular hill and lookout point in Almaty. Standing at eleven hundred feet and capped with a television tower, Kok Tobe is the highest elevation within the city limits, breaking the monotonous landscape of rigid building blocks. However, its height is dwarfed by the Alatau mountain range that forms the natural border separating Kazakhstan from Kyrgyzstan, its neighbor to the south.

Glen and Grace take a cable car to the top, glad to have avoided the weekend crowds. Coming out of the cable car station upon reaching the peak, they walk down some concrete steps to an open square paved in brick and dominated by a fountain in the center, a gigantic rose-colored granite apple that gushes forth water. Grace circles the fountain, her hand brushing the cool, smooth surface of the apple, the symbol of Almaty as *alma* means apple in Kazakh.

The view is not exactly breathtaking. A haze enshrouds the boring, gloomy parts of old Almaty as well as the modern glass-and-steel constructions toward the south of the city, where it extends to the foot of the Alatau.

As they stroll through a mini children's zoo with huge cages for goats, deer, roosters, and exotic birds of many varieties, Glen says, "My coworker here told me just a few years ago, this area used to have outdoor food stalls serving delicious shashlik. But now they have done away with those and turned the whole place into a children's playground and amusement park."

"And lots of souvenir shops!" Grace observes. "Wish those food stalls were still here."

Beyond a line of shops, a beautiful and well-maintained garden, complete with a small bridge forming an archway over a gurgling streamlet, takes up a vast area of Kok Tobe. Halfway along the serpentine main path that cuts through the garden, Glen and Grace come to a clearing occupied by four bronze life-sized statues of the Beatles. John is seated on a park bench with his guitar, George, Paul, and Ringo standing in different poses behind him.

"What are the Beatles doing on Kok Tobe? I never dreamed I'd see them here!" Grace exclaims.

"Me neither!" Glen agrees. Seeing a young woman walking in their direction, he asks her to take a picture of them with the famous four. They pose for the picture, Grace cozying up to John on the bench, Glen standing between Paul and Ringo with his arms draped over their shoulders.

"A photo is the best souvenir, much better than those foreign-made knickknacks from the souvenir shops," Glen says, thanking the young woman. Turning to Grace, he says, "Hey, I'm getting hungry. I saw a pizza stand back the way we came. Want me to go grab some pizza and drinks while you wait here with the Beatles? We can eat here in their company."

"Sounds good to me! I'm going to rest my feet."

Glen walks back in the direction of the cable car terminal, while Grace remains sitting on the bench, enjoying the refreshing balmy breeze that hasn't blown her way since her arrival in Almaty. Less than five minutes later, a man comes up and sits down at the far end of the bench, John Lennon between them. Grace looks over to him out of curiosity. Her heart immediately jumps into her throat. The man is looking at Grace. He nods when they make eye contact, twitching his lips to indicate a smile.

"I believe we met before at the Kasteev Art Museum," he opens the conversation.

She has to get to the bottom of what's going on, and better now than later, she decides. She says, "Yes, we did. And prior to that, I saw you at the Palace of Peace and Reconciliation in Astana!"

"Yes, you did," the fellow nods.

"What strange coincidences that we keep meeting at different places," she remarks.

"Yes. Coincidences do happen," he says.

"You know, these coincidences could be construed as stalking, which is illegal," Grace says clearly, in no uncertain terms.

He looks surprised. "Stalking? I wouldn't worry about that, as that is not my intention at all. I'm visiting some friends here." He eyes her for a moment. "You live in Almaty?"

"That's not your business," Grace says sharply, surprising herself.

"I'm sorry. Didn't mean to pry," the man says. A pause, and he continues, "Speaking of the Shevchenko collection the other day, I must say it's worth visiting the Aral Sea region while you are here."

"I don't suppose it is the same as in the paintings."

The fellow nods emphatically. "So, you have an idea of what's happening there. But to really understand the tragedy, you need to go out there to see it for yourself," the fellow says, not taking his eyes off Grace, which makes her uncomfortable and mad. "Do you have any connection, any friend there who can show you around?"

"I can always get a guide if I go." As an afterthought, she adds, "If I go, I will go with my husband." The truth is Glen will not be able to take time off for a while, and if she makes the trip, she will have to go alone.

"Was the guy with you at the museum the other day your husband?" the fellow asks.

Grace's gut clenches but she keeps her face neutral. "You saw me with someone at the museum?" she asks lightly.

"Yes."

"He's not my husband." Ayan wasn't around when this man came up to talk to her that day at the museum. So he must have been following her, most likely since they were at Panfilov Park, for she thought she saw him at the park entrance trying to flag down a taxi as she and Ayan were leaving in one. Blood rises to her head at the unnerving surmise that he is following her and perhaps Ayan for some unknown reason. "My husband is here with me today. He's just gone to grab us some lunch," Grace says, emphasizing the fact that her husband is around, so he'd better not pull anything funny.

"So that was your friend I saw at the museum?" he pursues.

"That's also none of your business. You're very inquisitive." She shifts with discomfort at his interrogation.

In that instant, the guy sidles up closer to John Lennon, who has been sitting patiently as a statue would. "By the way, what was in the book that friend gave you the day you met him at Panfilov Park?"

"Why are you following us? And what do you care about what he gave me at the park?"

He shrugs. "I'm a very curious person."

A moment of pondering, then Grace challenges again. "So you knew he wasn't my husband, or else why would he meet me at the park to give me a book? Even your questions are lies."

All congenialities gone, the man replies in a harsh tone, "You want the truth? I think this friend of yours has given you not only a book but also some important information. I need to get that information he was passing to you." His words sound threatening. Grace is seeing the spy in him again. Her pulse races.

"I don't know what you're talking about. He gave me nothing but a book," Grace says, trying to sound composed, confident, and not defensive.

"Was there something in the book? Some writing inside? A note? What did he ask you to do with the book?"

"There was nothing in the book!" Grace answers, her voice becoming sharp and snappy. "There was a harmless bookmark with printed information about the Shevchenko art exhibit, that's all! The book was a novel he loaned me to read, an English translation of a bestseller by a famous Kyrgyz author. If you think he has information you want, why haven't you asked him yourself? You saw him the same day you saw me at Panfilov Park and the art museum, and before that at the Palace of Peace and Reconciliation. Are you following him to get some information you think he has? I met him totally by chance. There is no reason he would tell me anything!" Grace feels flushed with the volley of words she shoots at him.

"He would never give me what I am looking for. I am a stranger to him. He wouldn't trust me, but I think he trusts you." His manner of speech is terse.

"I have no idea what you're looking for, and he has not given me anything important as far as I'm concerned. I would appreciate your leaving me alone. My husband will be back at any moment. He will not be happy to know you are harassing me."

As if on cue, Glen appears from around a corner of the garden path with a box of food and bottled beverages in hand. He cuts across a patch of grass toward where Grace and the Beatles are waiting. As he closes the few meters between them, Grace calls to him, her expression spelling out annoyance and agitation. "This man here has been harassing me!"

Glen closes in. "What's going on?" he asks, looking wary.

"I first saw this man at the Palace of Peace and Reconciliation in Astana, then at the entrance to Panfilov Park the other day, and he approached me later at the art museum. And here he is now, asking me ridiculous questions."

If ever Glen had wanted to play a knight in shining armor defending his damsel in distress, this is the moment. "Can I help you?" His question comes out more as an interrogation than a genuine offer to assist.

"I'm a tourist myself. I just met your wife a couple of times by coincidence, and she imagines I'm following her. No problem, I will leave now." With his hands raised in innocence, the man stands up, looking perturbed by Grace's groundless accusation.

"Yes, leaving would be a good idea. My wife's well-being is my first concern. I'm commissioned by the United States foreign aid services to consult the Government of Kazakhstan, and they will not be pleased if my wife feels her safety is threatened in this country. All I have to do is report you to the authorities."

At Glen's words, the fellow betrays a momentary mien of consternation, which almost immediately gives way to an expression of contrived politeness as he says, "I assure you, your wife has no cause for alarm. Have a good day." So saying, he turns from them and heads in the direction of the cable car depot.

Grace wastes no time in telling Glen about the conversation that just transpired between her and the flaxen-haired stranger, particularly his pressing her for information he thinks Ayan has given her.

"You've told him point blank you know nothing of what he's looking for. After my warning to him, I don't think he will bother you again," Glen assures Grace. "Besides, I don't think he wants to get into trouble with the police, and least the Kazakh Government, or the United States Consulate here."

"I hope so. Whatever he told you, I'm sure he's following me. He might want information from Ayan, but he didn't ask me where he was just now even though Ayan left the city days ago."

"Well, he thought he could get the information from you," Glen says.

"Exactly. He thinks I have that information, whatever it is." Grace bites her lip, feeling very uncomfortable. "Now I know why I keep running into him. He was following Ayan, and then he saw him talking to me at the top of the pyramid and giving me a book in Panfilov Park, and thought Ayan was passing me the information he was after. So then, he changed focus. And ever since, he's been stalking me hoping to get it from me."

"Spoken like a fiction writer," Glen says with a wink. Then more seriously he continues, "Maybe the information he is seeking is linked to the two dead bodies in the Aral Sea, from that newspaper headline, which he probably left you. He must want that information badly."

"He most likely left me the first note too, the one I got in Astana after the Gulag trip, asking me to ask Ayan about Voz Island!" Grace is silent for a moment, and continues, "I just had another troubling thought. He showed up at the museum when Ayan had gone to the washroom, and just now he showed up while you were gone to buy food. It makes me nervous to be alone in public."

"I don't think he'll bother you anymore after what I said to him, but you should always be careful not to be alone in deserted places from now on." Then, taking Grace by the hand, Glen says with a comforting smile, "Come, forget about him. Let's enjoy the afternoon. You've wanted to come up for a long while."

"I'm okay now with you around," Grace murmurs.

After lunch with the Beatles, they walk toward the cable car station, stopping at a lookout, hoping for a panoramic view of Almaty. All they get is a nothingness in the valley below, which is enveloped in smog and haze. "On a clear day, I was told we should be able to see Panfilov Park, the Orthodox Cathedral, and the Central Mosque," Glen says. He hugs Grace from behind. She rests her back against his chest, shutting her eyes for a few moments to drink in the comfort and sense of security she can always find in Glen's arms.

"I am happy you brought me here," Grace whispers. "I don't mean just Koke Tobe, but to Kazakhstan."

"I'm glad to hear that," Glen says, brushing his bristly chin against her soft, smooth cheek. "You are not bored, are you, with me working long hours all the time?"

"Bored? Not at all. I'm excited and happy to be here with you. I wouldn't want you to come out here alone. Certainly don't want some Kazakh girl to steal you away!" It is Grace's turn to wink. "Wherever you go, I go. Besides, other than keeping you company, I have a weird feeling, almost like an intuition, that I am here for a reason. Not just to get ideas for my novel, but for another purpose, if you know what I mean. I don't know what it is, not yet anyway."

BOOK VI

AYAN

13

MOSCOW, HERE I COME!

1977

A yan scored high on the entrance examination to Moscow State University, and he would be enrolled there beginning in September of 1977. He would be studying English language and literature. The university boasted of academic excellence, and tuition and lodging there would be free, as in any university in the Soviet Union for its citizens in the pursuit of a higher education. Grandpa Arystan and Grandma Aliya were sorry he was leaving Kyzylorda, and his parents were sad their younger son was going some twenty-seven hundred kilometers away from home, but they had always believed in a good education, and most of all in giving their children wings to fly wherever in life they could reach. Ayan felt the Kazakh spirit of freedom was ingrained in him. After all, his mother was of nomadic roots.

The first time Ayan explored Moscow, he was overwhelmed by all the sights and sounds of the capital, the biggest and busiest city in all the Soviet Union. He had never seen any building like the GUM

Department Store that spanned a great length of Red Square, with its many levels of shops under a breathtaking arched roof made up of thousands of glass pieces. He was completely spellbound by Saint Basil's Cathedral. The interior of that church museum was a dream for a curious mind like Ayan's, and he happily lost himself in the labyrinth of passages rich and busy with painted frescoes and beautiful icons. And then there were the museums, concert halls, theaters, and art galleries; food markets selling abundant meats, fruits, and vegetables, some he'd never even seen before; clothing stores displaying garments in styles more modern than anything people wore in Kazakhstan. Moscow seemed endowed with wonders one would never find in Kyzylorda, much less Aralsk. Muscovites could indulge in all the luxuries Ayan knew little or nothing of back home. He was fascinated—and perhaps a little envious.

Among his early impressions of Moscow, one thing bothered him though. More than once when he asked directions from local Muscovites, many of whom were well dressed, with briefcase in hand, walking with confidant steps as if to work or to keep an appointment, he got a brief and abrupt "*Ya ne znayu*" for an answer. Surely the locals must know their city. Why would they say they didn't know? His spoken Russian was impeccable. Why would they rebuff him so rudely?

In the first three years he was studying at Moscow State University, he stayed in *Filial Doma studenta*, or FDS for short, a micro village of student hostels for first to third-year students. The hostels were four floors each, and Ayan shared a spacious room on the third floor with three other first-year diploma students. One of his roommates, Anvar, was from Almaty. He was studying computational mathematics and cybernetics. Even though they were in very different disciplines and from different cities in Kazakhstan, Ayan was grateful for their friendship and camaraderie.

The first day of the semester was September 1, 1977. After a quick breakfast of fried eggs and pancake in his hostel canteen, Ayan left at about 7:30 a.m. for the Main Building where classes would be held. Classes would normally start at nine, but that day being the first day and orientation day for new students, Ayan was all too eager to get there early.

The Main Building was conveniently a brisk, fifteen-minute walk through Gorky Park from his hostel. It was a pleasant morning, the air being fresh and crisp from rain in the night. Ayan's heartbeat raced as he approached the Main Building, although he had seen its exterior from a short distance soon after his arrival a few days earlier. A magnificent establishment it was, with symmetrical sets of pointed towers of varying levels on each side of a spired center tower that rose high to the sky. Ayan was totally flabbergasted by the elegance and immensity of the entrance hall as he stepped foot into the Main Building, the polished marble floors, white walls and pylons, sparkling chandeliers, overwhelming dome.

All new students were assembled in the main auditorium on the first floor for a welcome ceremony, after which they were given a tour of the Main Building. Classes would be held in the central section called Zone A, which had thirty floors, the tallest tower of the building. In addition to large auditoriums, meeting rooms, laboratories, and offices, Zone A contained a concert hall, a cinema, and a professors' canteen, all too incredibly amazing to Ayan from Kyzylorda and Aralsk in faraway Kazakhstan.

The orientation tour also took him and other new students to the two sections immediately bordering Zone A. Those were Zones B and C, identical and situated like bookends on either side of Zone A. These had nineteen stories each, much lower than Zone A. These two sections contained hostels for fourth-year diploma students and higher, including aspirants. Students in Zones B or C could walk along the corridor on the nineteenth floor of either zone to reach Zone A for their classes. In principle, students living in Zones B or C wouldn't need to leave the Main Building all the years they stayed there because everything they needed was inside the building, including access to classes! Totally impressed, Ayan set his mind that day that he would move into one of those two zones when he advanced to fourth year.

Attached to Zones B or C on the far sides away from the central sections were four more sections, two on each side, giving the Main Building complete symmetry. The whole structure was grand, imposing, solemn, and somewhat intimidating. Moscow State University was to Ayan a brave new world, untraversed ground into an exciting and promising unknown. He was bracing himself to face whatever challenges that might be awaiting him.

Ayan's first year as a diploma student went by faster than he had envisioned. The tough demands and challenges of his program of studies and uncompromising expectations from his teachers stimulated him to work his best to reach his highest scholastic goals. Much of his first year at Moscow State was spent in auditoriums, lecture halls, seminar rooms, libraries, but not without dutiful jogging sessions in Gorky Park on weekends and some evenings. Meals were usually taken in the student canteens. Although he missed his family back home very much, he had no time to let himself flounder in homesickness. But he kept his promise to his parents: he sent home a letter every month, and that was all his father expected from him.

Two months after the first semester started, Ayan's roommate Anvar got a night job scrubbing floors in the Computational Mathematics and Cybernetics building. He asked if Ayan wanted to work there with him. The job didn't pay much, but every ruble earned meant an extra beer in the student canteen. So two evenings a week, he left their hostel with Anvar at 10 p.m. to mop floors. On account of his good first semester exam results, he received a scholarship of forty rubles a month that spring. With that and his earnings from the night job, he counted himself a rich man. Right after he received his first scholarship stipend, Ayan took pride in sending thirty rubles home for his mother's birthday.

And, as fate would have it, that autumn of 1977, Ayan met Victor Luganov in Gorky Park.

14

VICTOR, ALDIYAR, AND DARKHAN

1977–1979

Ayan and Victor hit it off well from the start. Not only did they jog together in Gorky Park on Saturday mornings after their first chance meeting there, but they would also frequently share meals in the university canteen whenever they bumped into each other at the food line.

"So what's it like staying in a dorm in Zone B? I bet you are spoiled getting up just thirty minutes before class and still making it in time," Ayan said one time they were eating lunch together in the canteen.

"Fifteen minutes," Victor corrected. "I've made it in fifteen minutes, and not skipping breakfast, though it wouldn't be a nice hot one in the café. I have a fridge in my room. I usually make a kolbassa sandwich and eat while walking to class!"

"You amaze me, Victor!"

"I can show you my room sometime, so you know what you are moving into when your turn comes."

Victor did show Ayan his room on the nineteenth floor in Zone B one weekend after their jog.

"What's this biohazard symbol doing here?" Ayan asked, looking at a big sticker of four daunting black circles strategically positioned in a triangle on a bright red background on his door.

"So nobody would dare come into my room!" Victor said, snickering.

"Smart!" Ayan laughed. "Bet your room is full of girlie magazines!"

Once inside, Ayan was surprised and impressed with how neatly Victor kept his room after all the stories he had heard of dorm rooms being in terrible states of unimaginable disarray. Victor's turned out to be an efficient, cozy, and tidy haven furnished not only with a mini fridge but also a microwave oven for those midnight snacks. Shelves were stacked with books of science foreign to Ayan as a student of language and literature.

At the end of Ayan's second year at Moscow State, in the summer of '79, he invited Victor to go home with him to meet his family and experience life on the former shores of the Aral Sea. Victor accepted his invitation, planning to spend a week there before returning to Moscow to get ready for his *aspiranture* program that autumn.

Upon their arrival at Aralsk train station, Ayan showed Victor the commemorative mural depicting the 1921 event of Aralsk fishermen answering to Lenin's request as though it was the most outstanding episode in the history of the dying harbor town. Perhaps it was. Victor studied the mural with great interest for the longest time, from one end to the other.

"I hope Lenin showed his appreciation back then," he commented.

"He did," Ayan said. "To show gratitude, Lenin had lathes and milling machines sent to Aralsk for the town to build a workshop for a ship repair plant."

That week, Victor stayed in Balta with Ayan and his family. Nurzhan and Akzharkyn were at first uneasy when Ayan told them he was bringing home a Russian friend from the university, but they took to their polite and congenial guest from the first day he arrived. They were also delighted with the two bottles of premium vodka Victor brought them from Moscow. Naturally they conversed in Russian in their home that week, since Kazakh was totally foreign to Victor. It was the first time the Kazakh-only household rule was allowed to be broken.

When Ayan first told Victor about the environmental calamity confronting the Aral Sea, how its shrinking had ruined the lives of all whose work and livelihood depended on it, Victor was shocked and totally sympathetic. Apparently, the Aral Sea's demise was not an item generally known to the people of Moscow.

The first evening over dinner at Ayan's home in Balta, Victor said to Nurzhan and Akzharkyn, "It's very unfortunate that the government's decision to boost cotton growth has done such damage to the Aral Sea and affected all the people living around it. I wish Moscow would do something to remedy the situation."

"I appreciate your kind words. I am sure the government is aware of the harm that engineering project has caused. So much depended on that sea . . . " Nurzhan's voice broke with bitterness.

"Many people around here are suffering," Akzharkyn spoke up in her rarely used Russian. "Not just from loss of work, but breathing problems, anemia, and cancers from exposure to the pesticides and contaminated water. There have been more miscarriages, stillbirths, and babies born with birth defects. All because of the drying of the Aral!" She was about to continue but held herself back from saying more, remembering she was in the company of Ayan's Russian guest. Ayan had never heard his mother so verbally expressive.

"I agree, it's awful. But who was to argue with Moscow back then?" Victor asked quietly, looking down.

"If you argued with Moscow, you'd go to the Gulag, like my grandfather the engineer," Ayan responded to Victor's rhetorical question.

Then putting on a more cheerful demeanor, he said, "There's nothing you or I can do, Victor my friend, so let's just drop that subject and enjoy your visit here."

"Ayan, take the truck for the week. Drive around with Victor. Go into Aralsk, show him the old harbor, where the Aral used to be, and our house there." Turning to Victor, Nurzhan continued, "We want you to have a good time here. You are our guest, and we want you to take home with you happy memories of your visit. As for me, I'm going to open one of those nice bottles of vodka."

—

On a day trip to Aralsk with Victor, Ayan ran into Aldiyar and Darkhan along the old waterfront. It was their first meeting that summer. After Ayan started secondary school in Kyzylorda, he saw little of them, but every summer when he was home, he would look them up several times. Since they finished middle school, Aldiyar and Darkhan had gotten jobs in Aralsk, Aldiyar apprenticed to a cobbler and Darkhan loading at the train station. When the Aral Sea yielded no more fish, they stayed on in Aralsk while their families moved east to Almaty to be with relatives. With no higher education and no specialized skills, they would have a hard time finding work in Almaty where the competition for jobs was high. Although Ayan could not get together with Aldiyar and Darkhan as much as he wanted since they finished middle school, as their paths and interests had turned out to be very different, he was determined that their bond of friendship from childhood should never break. Ayan had a deep feeling of camaraderie with his closest childhood friends every time they met. At the same time, he was sensitive to his friends' pride and self-respect, and he would never offer to pick up their checks when he met them at their meal breaks. Only occasionally, he would treat them, citing an extra bonus he had received from his school for good exam results.

The day Ayan and Victor met Aldiyar and Darkhan by chance, they were about to buy some samsa and *bulochka* at a vendor food stand by the old waterfront. At nineteen, Darkhan had grown up tall and muscular, about a meter eighty in height, always with a ready smile, friendly and outgoing as Ayan remembered him to be when they were kids. Aldiyar, on the other hand, had remained skinny and pale-faced as he was, and seemed to lack the self-confidence that Darkhan exuded. He had retained his cautious and mindful attitude, as if to counteract Darkhan's impulsiveness at times.

"So our famous brother has come home for the summer!" Darkhan said in Kazakh after their initial hearty handshakes. Then more genuinely, he added, "We've in fact been expecting you. It's that time of the year."

"First of all, I'm far from famous," Ayan laughed modestly, switching to Russian for Victor's sake. "Yes, I just got home for the summer and have been looking forward to seeing you guys again. But I'm glad I bumped into you today. I want you to meet a friend of mine from Moscow, Victor Luganov."

Aldiyar and Darkhan nodded to Victor guardedly, regarding him with expressions of awe and wariness. Ayan was thankful, however, that they switched to Russian to continue their conversation.

"How long are you staying this time?" Darkhan asked, addressing the question to Ayan without looking at Victor.

"Till the end of August. I have to be back in Moscow first day of September, but Victor is here only for a week." Immediately Ayan detected a look of relief on Darkhan's face. "How come you guys are not working today?"

"I have the day off, and this is Aldiyar's lunch hour," Darkhan explained.

"In that case, let's have some lunch together at the Float. We have lots to talk about." Noticing their hesitation, Ayan added, "I want to treat you all today in honor of Victor's visit and having you two with us will make it seem more like a welcome party."

Ayan had selected the Float Restaurant because he wanted his Muscovite friend to try their local food at that popular café, which had miraculously outlived the fishing industry in Aralsk.

"I'm dying for a good bowl of pelmeni," Ayan said, after they had ordered. "They are not the same in Moscow."

"So how has Moscow treated you since we met last summer, other than not having the best pelmeni?" Darkhan asked.

"Well enough. I stay at the university most of the time. I don't go into the main part of the city much, except with Victor here when we want to take a break from studies."

"What do you do to take a break?" Aldiyar asked innocently.

"Whenever we need to get away from our grueling books, we either jog in the park or go into the city for beers. Victor here was the one who showed me where we could get good beers."

"I hope you won't think I'm corrupting your friend here!" Victor laughed, putting on a guilty look that brought forth laughter from Aldiyar and Darkhan.

"I don't think you can corrupt him," Darkhan said with continued mirth. "He was already a beer drinker before he went to Moscow."

"Well, it's true Aldiyar and Darkhan were the ones who started me on beers," Ayan said. Everybody laughed.

The tension was broken.

For the rest of the lunch hour, Darkhan and Aldiyar warmed up to Victor, and the atmosphere became quite relaxed.

"Want to hear the biggest news around here? Aldiyar got married!" Darkhan was all too eager to share.

"Congratulations! When did this happen?" Ayan asked, surprised and happy.

"Five months ago," Aldiyar said, beaming.

"Who's the girl? Do I know her?"

"Her name's Raushan. I don't think you know her. She and her family had their shoes repaired at our shop."

"Was that how you met?" Ayan asked, laughing. "I think I'm in the wrong business!"

"And they have a kid on the way," Darkhan interjected with more good news.

"You'll be a papa soon? Imagine, our buddy Aldiyar is going to be a father!" Ayan exclaimed.

"I'm not earning much as a cobbler's apprentice right now, but I hope one day I'll have my own shop. I have a family to support now," Aldiyar said. "Luckily for us here though, we don't need much to survive."

"True. This is all such great news, Aldiyar! What about you, Darkhan?" Ayan asked.

"No love life. Can't afford a wife. My job at the railway station has no prospects, unlike Aldiyar's," Darkhan sighed audibly.

"Give it time," Ayan said.

"What about you, Ayan?" Darkhan asked.

"You want to know?" Victor asked, putting on an all-knowing look.

"Don't make things up, Victor." Ayan pulled a chiding face at his visiting friend.

They chatted and joked till Aldiyar had to return to work. "Don't forget I will mend the holes in your soles free of charge, Ayan. And Victor's too if you come back again!"

"Thank you, Aldiyar," said Victor with a thumbs-up. "I'll remember that. And congratulations on your marriage and child!" Then he added, looking from Aldiyar to Darkhan, "I'm glad we bumped into you two. Any friend of Ayan's is a friend of mine."

All the years Ayan was in Moscow, he had thought of Aldiyar and Darkhan. He missed them; he missed their carefree days together as kids. In his heart, he wished them well and hoped they would get a break someday. But without a good higher education in Soviet times, it would be hard, unless they got really lucky.

As for Victor, he had a very good week-long visit to Ayan's home that summer. When Ayan and his father saw him off at the train station in Aralsk at the end of his week with them, he said he would return some day. Knowing him, Ayan believed he would.

15

MOSCOW DOES
NOT BELIEVE IN TEARS

1979–1980

Ayan and Victor got on a metro train at Bibliotek Imeni Lenina Station, heading in the direction of Universitet Station and Moscow State University, at the end of a day of reading and research at the Lenin Library for their respective papers.

The train was tightly packed with passengers, mostly standing, the time being 7 p.m. on a Monday evening. Those who could reach up hung on to the hand bars for dear life; those who couldn't grabbed anything or anyone close by as the train turned a bend or lurched to a halt. Standing passengers tried to keep to the spaces their shoes occupied, swaying and tottering but never falling, as they were guarded by human barriers on all sides.

"I'm sorry I have to hang on to your shoulder bag," Ayan apologized to the gray-haired man in front of him as the train rolled to an unsteady standstill.

"No problem. I'm just hanging on to her!" the man called back, tilting his chin upward to indicate the towering, buxom, blonde woman standing right in front of him, her back to them. How he was hanging on to her Ayan could not imagine, although he was curious to know.

At that moment, an old woman got up from a seat near Ayan to alight at Park Kultury Station. He took the vacated seat, while scanning the passengers getting on, looking for someone elderly or handicapped to whom he could offer his seat.

The person his eyes finally rested on was neither. Holding her purse under one arm, she was shuffled by the crowd into the congested train car. She was beautiful, glowing with freshness and youth, yet grounded by an air of sophistication, her loose golden hair falling below her shoulders. She was squeezed to the center of the car, apparently stranded with nothing sturdy to hold on to. Her eyes fell on Ayan wiggling uncomfortably in his seat as though he had no right to be sitting down. She was about to move on in her search for a handhold when he caught her attention by standing up, looking at her and pointing to his seat. Before she had a chance to move over to where he was, a middle-aged woman with a huge shopping bag pushed her way into the seat he'd just vacated. The girl with the golden hair smiled at Ayan, and he smiled back, not knowing how else to react in that moment. Just then, the train started with a jolt and, losing her balance, she was thrust forward toward him. He caught both her elbows to steady her and was luckily able to stand his ground. It all happened in a split second, and Ayan was thrilled to the bone. That was the closest he'd ever been to holding a girl in his arms.

The rest of the way to Universitet Station, he was bold enough to strike up a casual conversation with the girl. He could hardly believe his good luck. She too was getting off at Universitet; she too was a student at Moscow State University and had just finished her first year of studies in the Faculty of History. She was staying with her aunt on Vernadsky Avenue, and her family lived in Leningrad. They even exchanged names before the train reached their shared destination.

Meanwhile, Victor tactfully kept his distance while witnessing the whole episode with glee. He hung back too when they got off the train, letting Ayan escort the girl with the golden hair up the stairs to the station exit. Above ground again, the girl and Ayan parted with a simple "do svidaniya," as they headed in opposite directions.

"So how was it, Don Juan?" Victor caught up with Ayan soon after on the way back to their respective residences.

"What?" Ayan asked, looking sheepish.

"You and Lady Godiva."

"What'd you mean, Lady Godiva?" Ayan sounded annoyed.

"Doesn't she remind you of the lady with the long blonde hair on the Godiva box?"

"Lady Godiva rides a horse," Ayan said.

"Yes, naked." Victor nodded, pulling a serious face, obviously enjoying the exchange.

"We just chatted because she also goes to Moscow State University," Ayan said, for want of a better response, ignoring Victor's last remark, and being defensive although he had no reason to be.

"You got her name, I suppose," Victor said, "and did you get her phone number too?"

"I didn't get her phone number." Ayan paused a moment, and said, "I'm leaving in the morning for the *sovkhoz* anyway."

"So? She's worth a follow-up when you come back! What's Lady Godiva's real name?"

"Valeria." Ayan sounded short, not exactly approving of the nickname Victor gave her.

The next day, Ayan left for the sovkhoz, thoughts of Valeria still on his mind. As part of their diploma program, students were required during some years to work for a month at harvest time in the fields before classes began. In his third year at Moscow State University, Ayan was assigned to gather potatoes in a sovkhoz, a state farm in the village of Yurlovo in the Mozhaysky district. It was already icy cold by early September, especially in the open fields. The students were given accommodation in cottages used for kindergarten classes. Even with the blankets given them, Ayan and his roommates slept wearing their winter coats and were still shivering in the night. Every student was given an extra warm quilted jacket and rubber boots for the fields. The items looked and smelled filthy, as if they had been passed from one field worker to another over the years without ever being cleaned. At first, Ayan was reluctant to wear them, but his only winter coat was too good to be worn harvesting crops and his winter boots were not suitable for soil and dirt, so he begrudgingly put on the old jacket and boots. He was glad to have them after a while, as the temperatures continued to drop. To him, picking potatoes was fun, especially in the company of friends he'd known for a couple of years at university.

Ayan was getting used to Moscow, and he felt quite at home after two years there. When newcomers to the city approached to ask for directions, he had learned to say, at times, "Ya ne znayu," when in fact he did know but had no time to explain. Moscow was big, and he needed to hurry to get from point A to point B.

Ayan's third year went by in a blur of books and papers, punctuated by beers with friends. Consumed by his studies, he hardly gave Valeria another thought for months, until he ran into her by chance on campus the day before he was due to take the train home to Aralsk at the end of the third year. That time, he got her phone number and said he would call her to "get together" when he returned from Kazakhstan. It cost Ayan no effort to keep that promise. In the autumn of 1980, soon after he returned to Moscow, he gathered his courage, took a deep breath, and dialed Valeria's number. Her aunt with whom she stayed while attending university in Moscow answered, then Valeria came to the phone. Surely she remembered Ayan and said she would be delighted to see him again. They agreed on meeting the following Saturday, October 11. Ayan could not believe his good luck. He was thinking about taking her to the Bolshoi ballet, but Victor suggested a movie.

"A movie lets you get close to her in the dark, hold hands, maybe even steal a kiss, get intimate!"

"On the first date?" Ayan asked in shock.

"Why waste time, if she likes you?" Victor rationalized.

"I think a ballet would be nicer. We can still hold hands on the way home if things go well."

"Definitely not a theater where everyone is dressed up and acting respectable! That's not the best place for making advances on the girl of your dreams."

"Who said anything about making advances? I like her and I want to be respectful."

"Very well, do as you please!" Victor said, throwing his hands up in defeat.

The following Saturday, Ayan took Valeria to a movie. They got tickets to *Moscow Does Not Believe in Tears,* a new release about three young women from small towns who became close friends while working in Moscow from the '50s to'70s, their lives, loves and heartaches, trials and triumphs. Nothing happened at the movie, only tears from Valeria who was deeply moved by the story.

"Of the three girls in the movie, which one do you like the most?" Ayan asked afterwards over coffee and cake.

Valeria pondered a moment, then said, "Katerina's life is too tragic. An illegitimate child, the father abandoning them, although in the end she met the love of her life, so I suppose it's not all sad. Lyudmila's life isn't much better, with her giving everything to her marriage only to have it end in divorce. I think I like Antonina's life best, happily married to a kind and good man. His parents even owned a *dacha*!" She laughed.

That evening, Ayan and Valeria took the metro again and then he walked her back to her aunt's house by the university. They held hands the whole way.

16

THE NINETEENTH FLOOR

1980–1982

In the autumn of 1980, Ayan moved into Zone B of the Main Building, as was his prerogative as a fourth-year diploma student. The comfortable ambience made him feel right at home, with amenities including a swimming pool, concert hall, cinema, and, in addition to two students' canteens, a formal dining room for teachers and students where meals were served by attendants. Living in Zone B on the eighteenth floor, Ayan felt privileged: he had moved up to a higher level of living, literally and figuratively.

Meanwhile, Victor, who had graduated from his diploma program in biology in the spring of 1979, was staying on in Zone B as an aspirant. In the first year of Ayan's residence in the Main Building, he met Victor for meals at times in the canteen, but gone were their nights in Sverdlov Square, staying out late and painting the town red. Since Victor started his aspiranture in microbiology, he had been so busy with his studies and research that they rarely jogged in Gorky Park and never had a free night to laugh over beers together. In fact, Ayan saw less of his friend now even though they stayed in the same residence. Ayan missed the fun and carefree times they had as diploma students.

As the year rolled on, Victor became more removed, and when Ayan met him whether over a meal in the canteen or by chance in a corridor usually of Zone A or Zone B, Victor seemed to have put on a more serious persona. He was no longer lively and full of good humor, rarely joked, and not a bit as silly as he used to be. Ayan consoled himself that Victor was just busy and stressed, that at Moscow State, the pinnacle of academia in Russia and the entire Soviet Union, the atmosphere was especially intense at the research level, no matter the discipline. As time wore on, Victor seemed moody and reserved, as though he always had a lot on his mind. If the change in him was not due to the pressures of academia, then Victor himself had changed—his outlook on life, his vision for the future. Ayan was concerned.

"Is something wrong, Victor?" Ayan finally asked during one of their rare strolls through Gorky Park one February day in 1981. It had snowed the day before, and the ground was slushy and wet.

"No, why?"

"You seem . . . different. You don't joke much anymore; you don't blabber comments about every girl that passes by. You are just too serious."

Victor laughed, but his laugh was not the carefree, spontaneous guffaw that he often let loose in the past; it sounded contrived. "I guess I'm just overloaded with research and studies. No time to relax or have fun." He sighed. After a moment, he added, "Ayan, you know my moodiness has nothing to do with you, right? No matter what, you are my good friend. I trust you with all my heart." Ayan knew at that moment Victor was telling the truth.

A month later, in March of 1981, Ayan stayed up late one night to complete an assignment due the next day. By the time he finished, it was past two in the morning. He came out of his room on the eighteenth floor of Zone B with the intention of getting a soda, but there wasn't any in the kitchenette of his floor. So he took the stairs one floor up hoping to get one from the refrigerator on the nineteenth floor. As he emerged from the stairway into the main corridor on that floor, he saw the elevator door a short distance down the corridor open. Seconds later, Victor came out. Without looking over to the stairway exit where Ayan was, Victor walked toward the double doors at the end of the Zone B corridor that opened into a short interior bridge leading to Zone A, the center section of the Main Building. Curious as to what would drive Victor to head toward Zone A in the dead of night, when that area should in principle be locked until morning, Ayan followed softly from a good distance. The lights were dimmed at this time of night, and the shadows hid Ayan easily. At the double doors to the bridge, Victor stopped, fumbled apparently for a key, and unlocked the doors. The fact that he had a key surprised Ayan; only the chief building caretaker and certain administrative personnel had keys from Zones B and C to Zone A. Victor entered through the doors and Ayan heard them being locked again. What could Victor be doing in Zone A at such a late hour? Disturbed but nonetheless still thirsty for a soda, Ayan walked back to the kitchenette of the nineteenth floor and got his soda. Instead of returning immediately to his room below, he sat on the floor in a corner of the kitchenette, sipping his drink, taking a moment to rest after a long day's mental exertion.

Sometime in the silence of the night, Ayan woke. He was still in the corner of the nineteenth-floor kitchenette, his sitting position modified into a semi-reclining one. He checked his watch. It was five in the morning. He had dozed off in the kitchenette for almost three hours. Gathering himself up, he was about to leave when he heard voices outside, then saw through the broad window that opened into the main corridor Victor walking past the kitchenette in the direction of the Zone B elevator. With him was an unfamiliar man wearing a winter jacket with a furry collar. They were deep in conversation. The kitchenette being unlit, they had no notion of anyone in there at that hour and made little effort to lower their voices. An odd reference caught Ayan's ears: A-7. Ayan had no idea what it meant, but the way they said it made the reference stick in his mind. To be conducting business in the middle of the night behind locked doors, it was obvious to Ayan that Victor and his companion did not want their rendezvous known. Whatever Victor was up to that night in Zone A and whoever his companion was, the tone struck Ayan as secretive and aroused his suspicion, but he kept what he saw that night to himself. He had to protect Victor.

In the autumn of 1981, Victor's last year of aspiranture, he moved out of the Main Building into an apartment by the university, which happened to be across the street from where Valeria was staying with her aunt. Ayan thought when Victor told him where he was moving to that he might run into him at times when he walked Valeria home, but he never did see him. As well, Ayan seldom saw him at meals in Zone B anymore. They had stopped their weekend jogs at Gorky Park, not to mention their barhopping outings in the city. On the rare occasions when they met on campus that year, Victor looked forlorn and thoughtful, though always pleased to see Ayan and have a chance to chat with him, brief though their meetings were.

The spring of 1982 when Victor completed his three years of aspiranture was also the spring Ayan graduated with his diploma. As that academic year drew close to an end, Ayan called Victor with the intention of celebrating together and asking about his future plans. Victor did not answer the phone, so Ayan left a message. He never returned his call. Then by chance, Ayan ran into him in Gorky Park one warm early summer evening in late June, just a few days before he was to leave Moscow for home, taking Valeria with him to visit his family. Victor looked genuinely happy to see Ayan, although he didn't mention the phone message Ayan left him. They sat down at the riverfront.

"So, what's next? I suppose you are going to continue research and work toward your candidate degree?" Ayan wanted to know.

"I got a job related to my research," Victor said somewhat hesitantly. "I'm leaving in a few days. It will contribute toward my candidate degree eventually."

"Congratulations! What kind of job, and where?"

"Top secret!" He sounded impish, a glimmer of his former playful self shining through. Then he said more seriously, "Actually it's too complicated and technical to describe to someone outside the field. I don't want to bore you. I'll be going all over the country doing field-work." Victor sounded evasive. There was a pause. Then as if to fill in the lull, he said, "By the way, my father is retiring in a couple of months, and my family will be moving back to Novosibirsk, to the old house my grandfather built long ago. It's about four hundred kilometers east of Moscow."

"So, from now on you'll be going to Novosibirsk instead of staying in Moscow for the summer?"

"I'm afraid so." Victor paused. "Hey, let's make the most of this evening. What do you say we go into the city center for beers, for old times' sake?"

Ayan could hardly believe his ears. They took the metro to Sverdlov Station.

"So, Victor, tell me, who are you seeing these days?" Ayan asked soon after they sat down at the Russian Bear.

"You mean to ask if I have a girlfriend? No time for that." Victor answered. He quickly switched the subject to Ayan. "And you? Are you still seeing Lady Godiva?"

"No, I am not seeing any 'Lady Godiva,' but yes, I'm dating Valeria." Ayan might have sounded annoyed, which indeed he was, although he couldn't be for long with Victor. "You know, I've never run into you even though you are just across the street from her. Do you ever go back to sleep?"

"I keep such late hours in the lab. I go home around two or three in the morning sometimes. But you must be serious about her," Victor surmised, squinting his eyes to study Ayan intently, until they both laughed. Another hint of the old Victor, Ayan thought, trying hard to recapture the past.

"She is coming with me to Kazakhstan to meet my family in a few days," Ayan said. "She's never been to Kazakhstan."

"Most people haven't. Why would she, if it weren't because of you? No offense toward Kazakhstan, but I mean she must really like you," Victor said, looking insightful.

"I hope so, because I really like her."

"Really?"

"Yes!"

"I knew it! You were infatuated from the moment you saw her on the metro three years ago."

"Maybe it was infatuation then. But I am in love with her now," Ayan admitted.

They spent over two hours at the bar that night, joking and laughing, for old times' sake, as Victor said. It was almost as if they were carefree students again, before Victor's research work stole him from Ayan. Yet there seemed an unspoken sadness between them, as though they were dreading the unavoidable moment of farewell. Before they parted, Ayan made one daring attempt at probing into Victor's plans for his future.

"Victor, what is A-7?"

Victor's color drained from his face. Immediately switching from Russian to English, he asked in a low, tense voice, "Where did you hear that?"

"About a year and a half ago, I was up late working one night and went to the nineteenth floor of Zone B to get a soda. I saw you getting out of the elevator and walking to Zone A," Ayan answered in English, in a low voice. "I fell asleep in the kitchenette. Later when I woke just before dawn, I saw you walking past the kitchenette window with a man I didn't know, and you two were talking about something called A-7." Then lowering his voice further, he continued, "Is it some secret project you were on? Was that man an outsider of the university? What's going on?"

"Ayan, I trust you have not mentioned this to anyone. I entreat you not to, for your own good," Victor paused, and as an afterthought, added, "and for mine."

"You have my word, Victor. I have not mentioned that night to anyone. I would never breathe a word of it to anyone. I knew somehow it was a very sensitive, classified matter."

The tension on Victor's countenance eased. "I know you are my trusted friend and will never betray me."

"Knowing I am to be trusted, can you tell me what that term means?" Ayan pursued.

"I can't tell you. Not now. Just remember, my dear Ayan, everything I do, I don't just do for myself, but, with good intentions, for my country."

"Great words come from great minds!" Ayan said, hoping to part on a happier note. From Victor's vague responses about his new job and where he was going, Ayan knew that evening would probably be their last time together for a long, long while.

Victor must have suspected the same, for he looked genuinely emotional as he laid a firm hand on Ayan's shoulder and said, his voice breaking, "Ayan, I want you to remember I trust you more than anyone else I know. Someday, you will understand."

BOOK VII

GRACE

17

THE GIRL ON THE PLANE

May 13, 2007

A few days before May 13, when Glen will be flying out to Baku, capital of Azerbaijan, for a weeklong conference, Grace has an idea.

"I'm listening," Glen responds as he sips his morning coffee.

"Since you will be in Baku for a week, what if I go to the Aral Sea region during that time? I've searched on the internet. There are flights from Almaty to Kyzylorda, the main city in the Aral region, and from there I can take the train to Aralsk, the former harbor town by the Aral Sea. It's a super quick plane ride, just an hour and forty-five minutes, and seven hours by train from Kyzylorda to Aralsk. I can cope with that."

"Why so keen on going there?"

"I told you, I am very curious to see the Aral Sea after all I've heard about it." Grace takes his hand as he reaches to pick up the day's *Times of Central Asia*. "It's for my book. I need new scenery for inspiration! And Ayan can probably be my guide since he's home on sabbatical this semester." Glen is silent for a long moment, probably weighing the pros and cons of Grace's proposal. She adds, "Besides, I'll be alone here for a whole week while you're gone if I stay in Almaty."

"Grace, I know you want to go. And you're right, you'd be here by yourself that week. My main concern is your safety." Glen pauses, looking thoughtful. Then he says slowly, "If you fly out to Kyzylorda and take a train from there to Aralsk, and if Ayan can meet you when you get there and be your guide the whole time you're there, I think it could work."

—

Grace and Glen leave the same day, May 13, Grace on a 7 a.m. flight to Kyzylorda and Glen an hour and a half later to Baku. Glen's office assistant has booked a first-class train ticket from Kyzylorda to Aralsk for Grace, paying for both beds in the wagon so Grace would have her privacy.

"We'll update each other every evening," Glen reminds Grace as he kisses her goodbye at her departure gate, holding her for the longest time, as if hesitant to let her go on her solo adventure to a remote place in the heart of Central Asia.

"We will," Grace says reassuringly. "I'll call you every evening, and be very careful." Putting on a light demeanor, she quips, "And stay out of trouble, dearest, and don't you dare look at those Azerbaijani girls!"

The aisle seat beside Grace was vacant when she booked her flight, but soon after she settles in her seat, a pretty Asian girl, presumably Kazakh and in her early twenties, sits down beside her, giving her a friendly nod that Grace reciprocates with a smile. The girl looks sociable, but Grace isn't too keen to strike up a conversation. She's been looking forward to a much-needed nap after not sleeping much the night before due to the excitement of the trip. The hum of the plane quickly lulls her to sleep. Next thing she knows, Grace awakens to the captain's announcement that they will be landing in fifteen minutes. The captain's voice likewise wakes the girl beside her from her snooze.

"What brings you to Kyzylorda?" the girl asks, turning toward Grace.

"I'm actually going to Aralsk," Grace says, taken aback that the girl speaks very good English.

"So am I! I'm taking the train there from Kyzylorda. What about you?"

"Me too!" Grace replies.

"The ten o'clock from Kyzylorda?"

"Yes!" Grace says.

"It's about a twenty-five-minute drive from the airport to the train station," the girl says, then adds, "Maybe we can share a taxi!"

"Good idea! You can direct the driver better than I can!" Grace laughs.

"I hope so!" the girl laughs too. "By the way, I'm Ainur."

"Pretty name! And I'm Grace."

"As in the song 'Amazing Grace'?"

Grace raises her brows in surprise that she is even familiar with the English hymn. "Why yes!"

Grace and Ainur arrive by taxi at Kyzylorda train station well ahead of their 10 a.m. departure time. Each with two carry-ons, they decide to sit on a bench at their boarding platform to wait for their train.

"So is Aralsk your home?" Grace asks.

"I live in Araltuz, a town just eighteen kilometers north of Aralsk, and that's where I'm going. My brother will pick me up from the Aralsk train station. I'm now on break from university."

"You speak very good English," Grace says, then adds with a smile, "That's saying a lot coming from an English teacher!"

The girl looks flattered. "You teach English? I am studying English at the university. I want to be an English teacher too. Where do you teach?"

"Chicago. I'm on sabbatical right now to accompany my husband, who's working here for a year." Grace thinks for a moment and continues, "Living in the Kyzylorda region, you must know a lot about the Aral Sea and its drying up. One of the main reasons I'm traveling this way is to see the Aral Sea and the old harbors."

"That's surprising! I mean, not many tourists go there. Lucky you, to have such great opportunity and interest to travel across Kazakhstan," Ainur says with admiration.

"Well, I'm looking for a story for my book. I thought Aralsk and the Aral Sea might give me some inspiration."

"You are writing a story about the Aral Sea? Wow! I agree that to really know the sea and understand the environmental tragedy in that region, you need to go see it for yourself. What kind of story is it?"

"I haven't nailed it down to one genre. I suppose I'll know when I am truly inspired," Grace says with a smile.

Ainur thinks for a moment and says, "I should tell you about the island."

"Island? You mean Voz Island?"

"You know about that too?" Ainur looks flabbergasted.

"I've heard about it."

"You keep amazing me!" Ainur is thoughtful for a few good seconds, then continues, "Actually, I know a true story you might want to hear. It's one my mother told me, a tragedy that happened to her best friend's sister. It's a terrible story, but I can tell you, so you know how evil that island was, or still is."

"We have seven hours on the train. Let's talk then," Grace says with great interest.

"Tell you what, let's chat at the restaurant wagon after the train is on its way," Ainur suggests. "Tell me your wagon number, and I'll come get you."

—

About thirty minutes into their train journey, Ainur and Grace are seated in the restaurant wagon, sipping tea while Ainur tells the story she heard from her mother.

"My mother grew up in the town Tuzdyzhar, thirty kilometers north of Aralsk, not far from Araltuz. She and her best friend Anel attended elementary and secondary school together. For years, their families lived in the same apartment building, just different units. Anel had a sister ten years older whose name was Kulyash. As a young girl, my mother had talked to her many times when she went over to their apartment to study or play with Anel. My mother used to admire Kulyash because she was very beautiful. After secondary school, Kulyash decided to go to Moscow to live with some distant relatives. She wanted to see the world. She worked as a waitress at a café in the big city. There she met a handsome young Russian student from Moscow State University by the name of Vladimir Krylov. He went a lot to the café where she worked when he was a student. And they fell in love." Ainur pauses, as if hoping to freeze them in this happy moment.

"How romantic!" Grace is engrossed.

"Yes, for the moment," Ainur nods. "After graduation, Vladimir was assigned to work on Voz Island by the Soviet government. This was in the early 1970s. Kulyash was very proud of him. Anel often boasted about her sister's boyfriend, how smart and wonderful and kind he was. Their parents highly approved of Vladimir for a son-in-law. Before he began his work on the island, Vladmir and Kulyash were married in Moscow, where his parents lived. Then they stopped in Tuzdyzhar, her hometown, and held a banquet there on their way to Voz Island. As a close friend of the bride's sister, my mother was also invited to the wedding celebration."

"When was this?" Grace asks.

"The wedding was in 1972, when my mother was twelve. The couple left for Voz Island soon after the celebration."

"Did Vladimir talk about what he would be doing on Voz Island?" Grace is more than curious.

"According to Anel, Vladimir never talked about his work. I understand back then there were so many government secrets common people wouldn't know."

"Did Anel know anything about the island from her sister?"

"She said there was a very nice town on the island for the scientists and other workers and their families. At first, they were happy on the island. Anel told my mother that her sister wrote home and said she and Vladimir were living well, with luxuries they never had in Tuzdyzhar or Aralsk. They had a movie theater, library, shops selling expensive and fashionable clothes, even furs, expensive wines, even caviar! Anel showed my mother what her sister brought back for her the summer after their wedding, a beautiful scarf made from the wool of karakul sheep. My mother said Anel was frustrated though that even her sister Kulyash would not breathe a word about Vladimir's job, not even to the family, but everyone knew he must make good money to bring back the expensive gifts from Voz Island. Those items they brought back were imported from all over the Union, the best of all the republics."

"I suppose Kulyash wasn't sure what her husband was doing on Voz Island either, though she might have had some notion of it," Grace says. "But she couldn't talk about it to anyone even if she knew."

"True. And then, about two years after they were married, they stopped coming home in the summer, and there was no news of them for a whole year. Mother said Anel and her family were very worried about Kulyash. Then, I think it was 1975, Anel told my mother Kulyash was pregnant!"

"The family must have been thrilled!" Grace says.

"Everyone at home was very happy. They had a baby girl the following spring. I believe the baby's name was Dina. In July that year, the whole family saw the baby for the first time when Kulyash brought her home to Tuzdyzhar. Anel was over the moon when she held her little niece in her arms! My mother saw the baby too. Vladimir did not come that time. Kulyash said he was too busy with his work and could not leave. My mother said the baby was a darling, very sweet and cute, and she gurgled and smiled a lot. But Kulyash was not herself that visit."

"How so?"

"She seemed very depressed at times. My mother was still living in the apartment in the same building as Anel and her family and one night she heard a lot of commotion in Anel's apartment. The next day, Anel told my mother that Kulyash lost control and screamed in the night, 'I can't go back! I won't go back! My baby will die if I bring her back there!' Anel was very sorry for the little baby. Sometimes when she needed her mother to nurse her, Kulyash would just ignore her, Anel said. They stayed with Kulyash's parents for a month."

"Did Kulyash go back to the island with her baby after her visit that summer?" Grace asks.

At Grace's question, Ainur shakes her head. She looks at Grace sadly and says, "They never made it back to Voz Island."

"What? Why?"

Not addressing Grace's questions directly, Ainur says, "The day Kulyash was to leave Tuzdyzhar and go home to Vladimir on the island, her parents drove her and her baby to the military airport in Aralsk. They went with her as far as they could, then said goodbye to her and the baby at the entrance to the airport. But for some reason, she did not board the plane to the island. After her parents left the airport, she must have taken a taxi to the Aralsk train station. According to the manager at the train station, she bought a ticket going to Guryev. But they didn't get on the train." Ainur pauses, then says slowly and softly, "There was an accident. Both mother and child were killed by an oncoming train."

"No . . ." Grace is in total shock. "What happened?"

"My mother told me Kulyash jumped in front of a moving train, her baby with her. They were both crushed."

Grace chokes over Ainur's words. "I can't believe it . . . That's so heartbreaking! And Vladimir? How did he take it?"

"According to my mother, Vladimir went back to Tuzdyzhar from Voz Island for his wife and baby's funeral. My mom attended the funeral too. She said Vladimir was like a robot the whole time at the funeral, not saying a word to anyone, not even crying. He left soon after the funeral to go back to the island."

"I can't imagine what the whole family must have gone through. What a shocking tragedy," Grace murmurs, shaking her head.

Ainur continues. "Anel told my mother Vladimir showed up at Tuzdyzhar a year after the tragedy, on his way to Russia to see his own family, and told her parents that he had decided to put his heart and soul into his work. He stayed for only a couple days that time. For the next twelve years, he would call Anel's parents once a year. He never visited them again. Anel told my mother Vladimir called her parents on New Year's Day, 1989, to tell them he was leaving Voz Island to return to Russia for good."

"Was that the last they heard from him?" Grace is apprehensive.

"Yes, and no. In late 1989, the family got a letter from Vladimir's parents informing them that Vladimir had hung himself in his apartment in Moscow. Anel called my mother, crying." Grace gasps. Ainur continues, "With the letter was a short note from Vladimir before he committed suicide, addressed to Anel's parents. It said, 'I want you to know the happiest time of my life was with Kulyash. When she died with our baby girl, I had nothing worth living for.' He died on August 29, 1989, thirteen years to the day after the death of his wife and their baby daughter."

Grace remains silent for a good while, trying to process the senseless tragedy Ainur has just related. She is left with overwhelming sadness, and the sense of a looming arch villain in this story: Voz.

BOOK VIII

18

BOMBSHELLS

1987–1988

Ayan drove his father's truck out of Aralsk along the highway in the direction of Balta one summer day in 1987, two years after he finished his aspiranture and started teaching at the Institute of International Languages in Moscow. But he wasn't going home yet. He came to the Bay of Beket, to the ship graveyard where his father's old fishing boat had been left unattended for the past eleven years. He swerved the truck off the highway onto the rough sandy terrain, stopping beside *Kari qaiyk*. From the beach where some seven fishing boats were left in different stages of decay, the blue gray water of the Aral could be seen in the distance. This was one of the nearest places within driving distance from Aralsk where one could hope to see the sea. He needed a quiet moment to spend with his "Avay," his first baby word for the Aral.

He had just heard over the radio that the Aral Sea had split in two, the North Aral, in Kazakhstan, and the South Aral, mostly in the neighboring Republic of Uzbekistan. Never had the world seen such a drastic phenomenon. The Aral had given up, it seemed, and accepted its death sentence. Unlike the two times it had dried up in the past, this time it would never come back again in its entirety. The world—Ayan's world—had been forever changed.

Later that evening, when Ayan arrived home in Balta, he broke down and said to his father, "Ake, the Aral will never come back as before."

Nurzhan took the disastrous news of the Aral's splitting stoically, gallantly. "It may never be whole again, but we still have hope for the North Aral," he said to Ayan, his face firmly set, no doubt hiding the intense heaviness in his heart. His voice vibrating with emotion, he continued, "I will not rest till I have seen the day the Aral Sea comes back to Kazakhstan!"

———

More bad news came on a different front the following year. In May 1988, about half a million saiga antelope grazing in the Turgay Steppes northeast of Aralsk all died within an hour. At the time, Ayan was in Moscow teaching. He was not aware of the shocking tragedy until he received his father's letter informing him of it. According to official reports, Nurzhan wrote, the cause of death of those endangered animals was undetermined.

Ayan was totally stunned. Disease and death with unexplained causes had occurred one too many times in the region of the Aral Sea, starting with the smallpox epidemic in 1971. The cause of half a million saiga antelope dropping dead within an hour in nearby Turgay Steppes could not be brushed off so easily. Ayan had his own ideas of what could have killed so many antelope within such a short time. Their sudden death could not have been caused by poison residues from pesticides carried by ground water to the grazing steppes or blown in dust storms over the Aral region. Their deaths were too sudden and simultaneous—in short, too dramatic—to be caused by long-term effects from exposure to these toxins. Ayan thought, more likely, their deaths were caused by a disease like the plague. If that was the case, the disease must have come from somewhere. The mysterious Voz Island came to mind.

That summer when Ayan visited his grandparents in Kyzylorda, as was his custom every time he was home, he brought up to Grandpa Arystan the possible connection between the death of the saiga antelope and suspected germ warfare research on Voz Island.

"Ayan, your fears are not unreasonable. I share your suspicions. But we will keep them to ourselves. Remember, we can't talk about this in public. It will get us into deep trouble."

—

Just a couple days before he was due to return to Moscow at the end of that summer, Ayan saw his friend Darkhan when he dropped his brother Arsen off at the Aralsk train station.

"So, what's been going on with your life since the last time we met?" Ayan asked as the two sat together briefly during Darkhan's break.

"Nothing exciting. Still a bachelor! At least Aldiyar has a family to go home to. Not me. Same old job loading and unloading heavy cargoes. Who would want to marry me?" He was quiet for a moment, then his face lit up. "Except recently I got paid a nice sum for helping to unload and reload some special cargoes."

"Oh? What were these cargoes?"

"They were big, round, stainless steel drums, all wrapped in plastic. I don't know what's inside. Must be something valuable."

"Where did they come from and where were they going?" Ayan grew curious.

"The train came in from Sverdlovsk. We loaded the drums onto three army trucks, all driven by soldiers, and there was a fourth truck with armed soldiers probably to guard the cargoes, so they must have contained something very important. We weren't told where they were going, but I think they were heading for Moynaq."

"Moynaq? Uzbekistan? Why?" Ayan's ears and interest perked up.

"Well, we used to load a lot of cargoes onto ships from here when we still had a harbor and later the dug canal. But ever since the canal project dried up, we've been loading heavy cargoes onto trucks heading for Moynaq, which still has a bit of a harbor. I've heard that from there, cargoes continue on by boat to Voz Island."

"Voz Island . . ." Ayan turned the thought over in his mind. "Are there a lot of deliveries going to Voz Island?"

"We all know there is a military base there. Soldiers and people living there need supplies, equipment, even water—things that can't be flown out on military planes." Darkhan took a few sips of the beer Ayan had bought at a kiosk. He looked around him as if to make sure no one was nearby, then leaned in and whispered, "But there's something unusual this time with the cargoes."

"What do you mean?"

"We were told by the military personnel that the merchandise needed extra careful handling. And then I overheard one soldier telling another, 'The pits are ready once they get to the island.' They even lied, telling us those vats were not going to Moynaq, so we wouldn't suspect their final destination to be Voz Island. What's more, we had never been paid so well for loading anything from train to truck! There were four of us loaders, and we all got huge bonuses. In exchange, we were ordered not to talk about those cargoes to anyone. Those drums had to be holding something important." Darkhan whispered quickly, spilling everything to Ayan as if in one long breath.

It was Ayan's turn to lean over to him and speak into his ear. "Whatever those containers held, it must be something the government wanted to hide. Do not tell anyone about those vats and where you think they were going, for your own safety. I agree with you, the authorities don't want anyone to know they were going to Voz Island. Be smart, Darkhan, keep your lips shut."

19

END OF AN ERA

1987–1991

By the summer of 1987, Ayan and Valeria had been together for over six years, ever since 1981 when Ayan was in his fourth year of his diploma and Valeria her third. Upon graduation with a diploma in history in 1983, Valeria received an appointment in the State Historical Museum in Moscow. She enjoyed her work researching and preparing exhibits at the Museum, although she had long dreamed of working at the world-renowned Hermitage Museum in Leningrad, her hometown. Her parents were disappointed that their daughter had chosen Ayan, whom they regarded as a poor fisherman's son from some remote, less-than-developed Asian border outpost of the Soviet Union. They had hoped she would be placed in Leningrad to work after graduation and find a decent Russian husband there. But Valeria remained in Moscow, and she was happy as she could be with Ayan. They had talked of getting married, but Valeria had her parents to contend with on that issue. Rather than inciting their further displeasure, Valeria and Ayan discreetly carried on their relationship while she still lived at her aunt's house in Moscow. The arrangement was far from ideal, but at least they still had each other.

The summer of 1988, the night before they left for home, Ayan to his village of Balta and Valeria to her parents' dacha outside Leningrad, Valeria cooked Ayan a nice, cozy dinner at his apartment and shared some news.

"My love, I found out recently that the Hermitage will need more historians next year, including a specialist in Scythian art and history." She paused and looked at him intently. He knew that was her special field.

"Are you thinking of applying?" Ayan felt a heavy weight had just landed on his heart.

"I really want to." She looked at him with a pleading expression in her eyes. After a moment, she asked, "Would you go to Leningrad with me if I got the job?"

"I don't know . . . I need time to think it over. I am happy with my work here. It lets me work toward my candidate degree. And I love you and I want to be with you." Ayan shifted uncomfortably in his seat. "Let's both think it over carefully before we make any decision of this kind. I want to marry you and have a family with you."

If that was a marriage proposal, he meant every word. Valeria, on the other hand, must not have considered it much of a proposal. They both let the subject drop and continued eating in silence.

At the end of that August, when Ayan returned to Moscow after a two-day and two-night train ride from Aralsk, he was physically exhausted and emotionally drained, but anxious to see Valeria and have her in his arms again. That evening, she gave him the dreaded news: she had been offered a post at the Hermitage. They had asked her to start in two weeks.

"Are you going?" Ayan asked, his heart sinking, for he knew what her answer would be.

"You know working as a historian at the Hermitage has been the dream job of my life. This may be my best opportunity, perhaps my only opportunity."

"You are going then." Ayan looked over to Valeria, speaking her answer for her.

Valeria went over to where Ayan was sitting at the table, crouched down beside him, her hands on his knees, and, looking up at him, said in earnest, "Ayan, please come with me. I want so much for you to be there too. I love you."

Placing his hands on her shoulders while she remained crouching before him, Ayan was silent for a long moment. Ever since Valeria told him about the job opening at the Hermitage at the beginning of the summer, he had thought of giving up his teaching post and leaving Moscow to be with her should she get the job. He could try to find another position in Leningrad, although it might not be as ideal as his job at the Institute of International Languages. However, after days of ennui and disinterest in everything, including his teaching, reason took over. He could either let her ambition run his future or be his own person and make a life for himself without her. Plus, political times were changing in the Soviet Union. Trouble was brewing in the Baltic republics. Throughout the spring and summer of 1988, Estonia, Latvia, and Lithuania were pressing for governing rights and liberties within their own territories, and it seemed Moscow was giving in to their demands. Ayan was worried that his future in Moscow, and more broadly in Russia, might be undermined should the Union disintegrate. To start life anew in Leningrad in that political climate would not be a wise move. Finally he said softly in a voice charged with emotion, "Valeria, I have given this a lot of serious thought. I love you and I will miss you very much. Go, the Hermitage is waiting for you."

They embraced and kissed, washing each other's faces with their tears.

After Valeria left for Leningrad, Ayan decided to put his heart and soul into his work. He stayed on in Moscow and continued teaching at the Institute.

Ayan missed Valeria very much, but he was gradually able to cope with her absence. They had parted on amicable terms and remained friends. They still called each other from time to time, on each other's birthdays and in the New Year. In the first two years of their separation, they had met for meals a few times when she was in Moscow for seminars, talking mainly about their work, asking about each other's health and well-being while avoiding the subject of possible new love interests. For Ayan, there was none. But neither did they bring up the likelihood of their getting back together again. He was married to his job, and so was she to hers, at least for the moment.

———

Then in the spring of 1991, with increasing political unrest in the republics and Valeria no longer a part of his life, Ayan decided to leave Moscow for good and return home to Kazakhstan. He turned in his resignation to the Institute of International Languages and applied for a position teaching English at Kyzylorda Pedagogical Institute. He got the job. He stayed on in Moscow that summer, his last summer since he first stepped foot into Moscow State University fourteen years ago.

On August 21, 1991, Ayan and the world were shaken by the failed August coup against Mikhail Gorbachev by Communist Party senior officials, hard-liners who wanted to take over control of the Soviet Union from Gorbachev. They were furious over his loss of control of the Eastern European republics, and apprehensive of his decentralization reforms within the Union, which would compromise the power of the central government. Ayan knew it would be a matter of months, perhaps weeks, before the world order he was born into and grew up with would change drastically. The Union would disintegrate, collapse, like the once bounteous Aral Sea, shrinking, desiccating, dying . . .

Two days after the attempted coup, on August 23, Victor Luganov surprised Ayan with his brief re-entry into his life after nine years' absence. What was left of that meeting of the two friends was a note Ayan could make no sense of at the time, but had stowed away as a keepsake all these years.

Two days after that rendezvous, Ayan boarded his train at Moscow's Kazansky Railway Station, bound for Aralsk, on a one-way ticket home to Kazakhstan, bidding Moscow a silent goodbye. Ayan was finally returning to his own country, to do what he did best where it would count most. He rented an apartment not far from the Pedagogical Institute in Kyzylorda. Grandpa Arystan and Grandma Aliya had offered Ayan their home to stay, but this time he wanted to have his own place and space since he would most likely be working and living in Kyzylorda for a long time. He was not too far from his parents in Balta and he could go home every time he had a break from classes. He was living a life of peace and security at last. Or so he thought.

In November 1991, he returned to Aralsk on a Friday afternoon train from Kyzylorda to celebrate his father's seventy-first birthday. On arrival, he noticed an unusual influx of travelers, soldiers in uniform, and civilian men and women with children arriving at the Aralsk rail station. He sought out Darkhan to ask what was going on.

"Where are all these people coming from?" he asked Darkhan.

"Voz Island. They took a boat from the island to Moynaq, and from Moynaq they arrived by train here, on the way to their final destinations."

"Why? What's happening on Voz Island?"

"All the people on Voz are being evacuated. The whole place is being shut down. It's a pity. Some women who had worked there before as cooks and maids were talking about what a nice town they had for the families of the soldiers and scientists working there. There were shops, cafes, a park, a school, even a recreation center and a ball field! But you know what?"

"What?" Ayan asked warily.

"There must be lots of good stuff left on the island that people couldn't take with them. The place must be a gold mine! When the island is all abandoned, that's when I'll go out there and harvest the leftover crops."

Ayan frowned, looking at Darkhan with great unease. "I have no idea what Voz Island is like. Personally, I wouldn't go to that place. Darkhan, please don't go there."

"Our situations are different, Ayan," Darkhan said. "You don't know what it means to be working as a loader at the train station day in, day out, with no hope of breaking out of this dump I am in." Darkhan looked frustrated.

Ayan lowered his head. After a long pause, he said, "I didn't mean to be insensitive, Darkhan. I always have your interest at heart. I'm just very uneasy about that island. You must ask people coming back from there about the layout of the island and find out where the town is. If you really have to go, don't go alone, and stick to the town only."

"Don't worry. I'll be careful."

Ayan looked Darkhan in the eye. "You have to listen to me. There may be labs on the island where scientists used to work. Who knows what could be in those labs, diseases, toxic chemicals, dangerous substances. Avoid any building that looks like a lab at all costs. This is for your safety." His voice was urgent. His years of conjecture that Voz Island might be a site of biological weapon research had nurtured his fear of health hazards there. He knew money was tight for Darkhan, but the last thing he wanted was for anything to happen to his friend.

"I told you I'll be careful. I'll ask Aldiyar to go with me, and we will only stick to the town, okay?"

Ayan wondered for a moment if he was being too cautious, but if the rumors about Voz Island were real, the danger there might live on after the Soviet Union was no more.

—

On December 16, 1991, Ayan was on the phone with Valeria to wish her a happy birthday when news came over the radio that Kazakhstan had declared its separation from the Soviet Union.

"Did you hear that? Kazakhstan is now officially independent!" Ayan said to Valeria. "We are the last member republic to leave."

"Congratulations, Kazakhstan," Valeria said. Ayan could not detect any enthusiasm in her voice.

"Aren't you excited?" Ayan asked.

"Why yes, of course. Aren't you?"

"Yes, this is a promising beginning of a new age for my country, a fresh start to democracy."

"I am happy for Kazakhstan." She paused. "But from now on, we are no longer one nation, Ayan. You and I are separated by a political boundary." There was a slight tremor in her voice.

"That's not going to change anything between us, Val. Border or not, I will always care about you. Happy birthday, my dear!"

"Thank you, my dearest. And happy birthday, Kazakhstan!"

Later that day, Ayan and his family drove into Aralsk to watch news of Kazakhstan's Declaration of Independence broadcasted on the town's big-screen television. It was a moving experience for them and the whole republic. Feelings were mixed. From then on, they would have to fend for themselves without the protection of Big Brother in Moscow. How they would fare was uncertain. It promised to be a long, strenuous climb ahead for the young nation. While Ayan considered independence a fresh start to democracy, he knew that many challenges would confront the nation in years to come.

On a personal level, in spite of his reassurance to Valeria that nothing would change between them, he could hear her words echoing in his head: " . . . we are no longer one nation . . . separated by a political boundary." It seemed the chance of their getting back together was becoming slimmer and slimmer.

Ten days later, on December 26, 1991, the Soviet Union collapsed.

20

SCAVENGERS

1991–1996

F act was a more bitter pill to swallow than suspicion. Ayan's fearful nightmare surrounding Voz Island had turned into a real-life horror even more frightening than the monster of his childhood imagination. Since the island's evacuation from late 1991 to April 1992, and with the collapse of the Soviet Union, the clandestine activities that took place on Voz Island were finally brought into the light.

The dangerous research Ayan and Grandpa Arystan speculated about was openly confirmed in April 1992 when Russian President Boris Yeltsin declared the shutdown of all biological weapon programs on Voz Island. Biological weapon research and testing on the island during the Soviet era, which had previously been only a silent fear and a whispered rumor among sections of the general public in and around the Aral region, became a confirmed fact. According to the news, a Kazakh government commission had visited the island earlier in the year, and a non-government organization commission had just paid the island a visit as well. Russia assured them there were no offensive biological weapons tested, and all research and testing during Soviet time was for defense in case of a biological war. Russia had agreed to decontaminate the island within three years, which meant by 1995.

"Something else about Voz Island bothers me," Ayan said to Grandpa Arystan on one of his visits. "I heard on the news recently that the area of the island has grown from two hundred square kilometers to two thousand as the Aral Sea keeps receding. That's ten times its original size!"

"I heard that too. People predict the island will be connected to the mainland in Uzbekistan within a few short years. There's already only a channel between its southern tip and Uzbekistan," Grandpa Arystan said.

"That is worrisome," Ayan said. "As long as Voz is an island, animals cannot cross over and carry germs to the mainland. Once it becomes a part of the mainland, who knows what diseases might be carried over."

By 1995, the island was reportedly cleansed of biological agents of mass destruction and all facilities decontaminated, in accordance with the 1992 pledge from Russia.

One day in the summer of 1996, Ayan met up with Darkhan and Aldiyar for a meal at one of the cafes in town. By then, Aldiyar had taken over the shop from the cobbler who retired a few years earlier and had become the father of three sons. Ayan had met his wife Raushan and their boys once before Independence. A robust and stout woman she was, whose handsome features seemed to have hardened with the test of motherhood and hard times. At lunch that day, Aldiyar said proudly to Ayan, "Today, your plate of manti is our treat."

"What do you mean?"

"We are becoming rich men, my friend. We have a new source of income these days," Darkhan said. Ayan looked surprised. He explained, "Remember when I told you once that island was abandoned I'd go there and salvage the good stuff folks left behind? Well, the island is deserted now, not a soul there!"

"You've been to the island?" Ayan asked in alarm, then regretted his raised voice.

"Always with Aldiyar," Darkhan said. "I remember you said I shouldn't go alone. Wish we had gone out sooner though."

"We were out three times last year, just a day on the island each time. Well, three days total each trip if you include getting there and back," Aldiyar explained.

"We can take you out there if you like," Darkhan readily offered.

"No, thank you," Ayan said without hesitation, and rather brusquely too. "How do you get there? Aralsk is too far from the sea."

Darkhan explained, "We drive in my truck about three hundred kilometers west of here to Kulandy. I have a friend in Kulandy, Sairan. He takes us across the Kulandy Strait in his motorboat to Voz. He got the boat secondhand for a good price. It's a good size too with ample room for four, plus bulky items we take back from the island. Takes about three hours to get to the dock on the island's north coast from Kulandy. After we land, we still have to drive another thirty kilometers from the coast to the town."

"Drive?"

"Yeah, some guys from Aralsk went out there soon after Russia shut everything down and found a few abandoned trucks near the coast. They were automotive mechanics, and they got those trucks running. Since then, they've gone out there at the beginning of every summer to check the trucks, make sure they are in running condition, and bring out a few barrels of petrol for the trucks. They make good money renting them to people like us to drive to the town," Darkhan said.

"Since we are mostly bringing back bulky things like furniture and anything we can rip up and sell, those trucks really come in handy," Aldiyar pitched in. "We simply pay the people in Kulandy who are running that business and they give us keys to get into a shed and take out a truck."

"They certainly sound like good businessmen. I suppose there are many ways to make money, if one is enterprising enough," Ayan remarked dryly.

"The money we get from selling what we bring back, we divide three ways, between us two and Sairan because he takes us out there in his boat," Darkhan said.

"Have you been going only to the town?" Ayan asked, anxious to ask that question and still worried about what they might find in the areas outside the town.

"We stick to Kantubek, the town in the north. That side of the island also had a seaport, an airport, and a military base. The soldiers stationed there had cleaned out most of the military base, at least all the important and valuable stuff, so there isn't much to take from there," Darkhan replied.

"When people lived there, the town must have been very nice," Aldiyar added. "Seems like it had everything for a good life, buildings three or four stories high, a park, a playground for children."

"There were lots of things people who lived there couldn't take with them, pretty much anything big or bulky. We've made good money off furniture, floorboards, tiles, copper pipes, wirings, ceiling lights. Unfortunately other looters had been out there before us," Darkhan said with some bitterness.

"I heard there were even some TVs! My boys would have loved one of those, but they were long gone by the time we got there. The whole place is in bad shape now, broken windows, holes in the walls, collapsed roofs." Then Aldiyar volunteered, "On one of our trips, we went about three kilometers south and found the lab buildings where scientists must have worked."

"You went to the labs?" Ayan shouted in alarm. Turning to Darkhan, he said in frustration, "I told you not to go anywhere except the town!"

"The place seemed pretty deserted and harmless," Darkhan said with a wave of his hand. "We explored the labs for two hours, and were fine afterwards, not even a single scratch! All we took were light fixtures, clocks, some floor tiles, a few empty shelves, things we could sell."

"We didn't stay long because there was a bad smell inside," Aldiyar said.

"Even though the place is supposed to be decontaminated, you don't know for sure how safe those labs are. You two are risking your lives going there, and you're putting everyone at risk if you bring back some disease from the island!" Ayan yelled, infuriated with them. Then, recollecting himself, he said in a more controlled voice, "I'm sorry. I didn't mean to get mad, I'm just concerned."

"Don't worry, Ayan. We were careful. There were lots of broken glass dishes, mugs, and tubes on the floor of the labs, but we didn't touch them. We even left the good glass tubes and dishes on the shelves. No idea what scientists used those for before, right?" Aldiyar sounded like he knew what he was doing.

Ayan could visualize petri dishes, beakers, pipettes, and test tubes that had once contained virile germs broken on the floors of the labs as scientists scampered to remove evidence of biological weapon research and testing during their last days on the island. "If only I could persuade you two not to go there anymore and convince you that it's very dangerous going there! You could get very sick and bring back diseases to others too," he said at a normal pitch, looking from Darkhan to Aldiyar almost pleadingly. "I really don't think you should go back."

"This is good money for us. You wouldn't understand. You have a good education and good pay." Darkhan's words filled Ayan with guilt again despite his well-meaning concern, making him feel that he had been insensitive to the hardships his two childhood friends were facing with the sea and money both drying up. Darkhan was quiet for a moment, then continued, "If it makes you feel better, I assure you we will never get within ten kilometers of the south part of the island. There is a huge piece of open land there, over a hundred square kilometers. Folks call it the Field of Death."

21

A PART OF THE MAIN

2001–2002

Ayan's nightmare of Voz Island eventually joining the mainland became reality when, in June 2001, the channel separating the southern tip of the island from the mainland of Uzbekistan completely dried up. Ayan's heart was heavy as he took a stroll along the former harbor front of Aralsk in his first week home for the summer from Kyzylorda, thinking of the dreaded news he just picked up of the island-turned-peninsula. The Aral Sea was the epitome of good, Voz Island the embodiment of evil, he reasoned. As the good diminished, the evil magnified. That fact of life troubled Ayan acutely.

One April morning the following year, 2002, Ayan heard in the news that the United States, with the cooperation of the Kazakh government, had sent a team of specialists to the former Voz Island. Their mission was to decontaminate the sites of buried drums of anthrax spores that had been detected by United States intelligence through satellite imagery. It was reported that soil samples had been taken from those sites and brought back to labs in the United States for testing and found to contain living and lethal anthrax spores. Again, Ayan's worst fears had been confirmed: there were indeed still potent cultivated germs on the island after Russia had completed its decontamination job in 1995. The American team worked for two months and by June of 2002 had thoroughly decontaminated the sites, according to related articles on the internet. The vats containing the anthrax spores were properly and carefully re-buried in deeply dug pits. Tests on multiple samples of earth from the burial sites afterwards all came back negative. The report was reassuring.

The question that roused Ayan's curiosity was why there were vats of anthrax spores buried on Voz Island to begin with. With the internet at his fingertips at the Pedagogical Institute, Ayan spent hours at the Institute library searching for an answer. His effort was rewarded when he found in a monthly journal that, according to intelligence sources, live anthrax spores were transported in big stainless-steel drums in 1988 from Sverdlovsk to Voz Island where they were then buried in the ground. This was done by the Soviet government to avoid detection should there be an international inspection of the research center in Sverdlovsk for possible violation of an agreement signed at the Biological Weapons Convention of 1972, which banned the production of biological weapons as agents of mass destruction.

Immediately Ayan's thoughts raced to the mysterious metal drums Darkhan helped to unload from the train and reload onto military trucks to Moynaq, suspected final destination Voz Island. The precious cargo Darkhan had handled was none other than live anthrax spores. Voz Island was not only a secret site for the research and culture of biological weapons during Soviet time; it had also become an anthrax burial ground, a cursed legacy left by the Soviets on Kazakh and Uzbek soil.

Ayan brought up the subject of the buried anthrax drums to Grandpa Arystan. "It's good that the burial sites of those drums are now free of live anthrax spores, but I am still not fully convinced the island is completely safe."

Arystan took a deep sigh. "When the Soviet government ordered the entire operation on Voz Island to be shut down, scientists and lab workers probably rushed to bury all the cultivated bacteria and viruses under testing in a limited short period. You just wonder if they did a proper job."

Ayan nodded. "Most germs would die with time, heat, or exposure to the elements, but some are more resilient and can survive adverse conditions." Ayan frowned, looking worried and helpless. "Remember I brought up the point that as long as Voz was an island, animals could not cross over and carry germs to the mainland? Now the danger is more imminent with the island becoming a part of the mainland. Small animals of any kind can carry germs over."

Grandpa Arystan said, "But that shouldn't be the case indefinitely. Our government needs to do a careful inspection of the whole island, inch by inch, in cooperation with the Uzbek government, with foreign aid in terms of expertise and funding from international governments and organizations, and thoroughly clean up any and all contaminated areas." He added, "Until then, I wouldn't step foot on the island, or peninsula, I should say."

Ayan's thoughts wandered to Aldiyar and Darkhan scavenging on the island. He could only wish them well.

22

THE FIELD OF DEATH

2003

"**F**olks called it the Field of Death because that was where animals were brought out to have germs showered on them," Darkhan said. "It was a place of no return for those poor creatures."

Darkhan and Aldiyar confessed to Ayan in the summer of 2003 that they had recently gone to the Field of Death. Ayan was both livid and horrified. But his two friends had apparently survived the excursion unscathed. Darkhan rationalized that since the anthrax burial sites had been decontaminated by the U.S. specialist team and they had deemed the soil clear, it would be safe to make a trip to the Field of Death to salvage anything that might still be of value.

"The testing field was enormous. We couldn't see the end of it," Darkhan said. "There were lots of cages stacked up in sheds, probably to hold the smaller animals like monkeys and hamsters and other rodents. We went there with a guy who had worked as a lab cleaner on the island. He had been to the testing sites only a few times and never when the testing was taking place, but he said he could tell how the testing took place from the evidence of equipment left in the test range. The stuff he told us was horrifying, but it all made sense. I could see it happening."

"What did he tell you?" Ayan could feel his heart suddenly weighed down to the point of breaking.

"He said small animals would be taken out in cages to the open field. Then whatever biological weapons they were testing would be released, sprayed on the animals from a tower above." Darkhan dramatized the spraying with his fingers.

"The tower is still there," Aldiyar added.

"We saw iron poles planted in the fields, with iron bars sticking out from either side making a T shape, and chains dangling down from them over feed troughs," Darkhan said, using his outstretched arms and hands for visual effect. "The chains were for tying big animals like horses and donkeys for testing."

"Horses?" Ayan immediately asked in a grating whisper.

Aldiyar nodded. "Yeah, they used horses. The guy told us the feed troughs would be full of good things to eat—fresh fodder, apples, bananas. Horses and donkeys were fed well; that last meal especially was a feast to them."

"They fed them well and kept them healthy before testing to see how long they could survive the germ attack," Darkhan added.

"Where did they get the horses?" Ayan could barely get the question out as he felt his throat constricting.

"I suppose they were raised on farms in the area. After all, we are a horse country," Aldiyar conjectured.

"I heard there was a band of horse thieves living outside Aralsk," Darkhan said, not sensing Ayan's sudden intensity or observing his face turning bleached white. "They roamed the hills and steppes, stealing horses and donkeys. Then they sold them to the Soviet government for very good money."

Aldiyar looked at Ayan. "You okay, Ayan? You look like you're about to throw up!"

"No. I'm not okay. This makes me sick." Without another word to his friends, he left them at the cafe. His tears gushed forth uncontrollably, blurring his sight such that he could hardly see where he was going, a forty-three-year-old man crying like a child as he made his way out to the open air.

Ayan found his father by the defunct harbor chatting with a few friends. Nurzhan must have noticed something was wrong with his son, but when he asked, Ayan was mute. All the way back to Balta, Ayan sat in the passenger seat numb and not responding to his father's concern, to the point that Nurzhan stopped asking him questions. No matter where Ayan turned, with eyes open or shut, he saw Sarzhal snorting in fear, teeth showing and breathing hard as strange men came toward him with halters and ropes. He saw Sarzhal, along with other horses, lassoed and herded onto barges for their journey of no return to Voz Island. He saw Sarzhal chained to a pole in the Field of Death, happily eating treats from the feed trough, not knowing it would be his last supper. At that, Ayan broke down in uncontrollable sobs. Nurzhan turned to him and asked again what was wrong.

"Ake, I know what happened to Sarzhal," he finally replied. "I know how he died!" Ayan cried like he was losing his beloved horse all over again. He refused to be consoled.

That night, Ayan could not sleep. His wakeful mind saw only his loyal, docile, affectionate Sarzhal, his best friend, chained with the other horses and donkeys like a prison gang awaiting the unknown. As they indulged in the good food and thought themselves lucky, sprays of invisible deadly bacteria descended on Sarzhal and his companions. Yet, they felt nothing. Not an itch. No pain. Not yet. Then, Sarzhal would have been led back to the stables where his condition would be monitored carefully day by day as symptoms surfaced, the bacteria eating his insides, his organs, every part of him, torturing him for days, weeks, or longer, until merciful death liberated him from his suffering. Ayan saw all this. He was beyond consolation.

The rest of that summer, images of Sarzhal and conjectures of his sufferings filled Ayan's mind day and night, robbing him of sleep and all appetite for food. His mother was worried, as he was noticeably becoming thinner, looking listless, and draining away.

When he returned to Kyzylorda in late August that summer, in spite of himself, he researched on the internet the death of animals caused by inhaling anthrax spores. He focused on anthrax, because it was one of the most potent and horrifying bacteria—he felt the compulsion to know how bad it could have been. He read how the spores attached themselves to the lymph nodes and multiplied and grew inside the body, how they ate into the internal organs and rotted the flesh, causing victims profuse internal bleeding. He had no idea how long Sarzhal had lasted after exposure to the germ, most likely anthrax, they tested on him; he could not imagine what sufferings his beloved horse had gone through. He hoped his death came on fast, but he read it could take months before a victim of airborne anthrax poisoning died. Reading the subject matter was agonizing, yet Ayan couldn't help himself, as if he wanted to feel the torment alongside his beloved horse, as if he wanted to experience his pain, or even take his place.

That autumn, more disheartening news about the Aral arrived. The South Aral Sea had split further, into east and west, becoming the Southeastern Aral and the Southwestern Aral. Voz Island, which had joined with the mainland of Uzbekistan on the island's southern end in 2001, had become the causeway between the Southeastern and Southwestern Aral Seas. Much of the Southeastern Aral Sea was evaporating fast. Ayan knew it was only a matter of time before Voz Island and the evaporating Southeastern Aral would become one continuous piece of land, a part of the existing Aralkum Desert.

23

ALDIYAR AND DARKHAN

2007

On April 1, 2007, Ayan sat at the Float Restaurant by the old harbor in full view of the two cranky old cranes on the high embankment above the slough of mud, sand, rusty cans, and broken glass. He was waiting for Aldiyar and Darkhan, having driven into town early with his father who was having supper at a friend's house. Ayan was home on a sabbatical, taking time off that spring as he would be in charge of a program for foreign and local students that summer.

Not long after he sat down, Aldiyar and Darkhan arrived. They seemed more excited than ever, as though fortune had finally found them.

"How is life?" Ayan asked in Russian, one of his two languages of communication except when at home in Balta, where spoken Kazakh was enforced.

"Speak Kazakh," Darkhan reminded, looking around him, then continued in their native tongue, "You'll never believe this. A fellow came looking for me at the train station. He said he and his friend had a job for me and would pay extremely well," Darkhan said.

"What kind of job?" Ayan was curious, but wary.

"I knew you'd ask. I'm not supposed to talk about their mission to anyone."

"Sounds suspicious to me. Who are these people?"

Darkhan leaned over the table and spoke excitedly, but barely above a whisper. "Okay, okay, I'll tell you, but keep this to yourself. They're scouts for a major foreign film company. They want to make a movie about Voz Island. The fellow who approached me asked if I would take them out there."

"How come he asked you?"

"He said he stopped at the junk shop where we sell our stuff from Voz and asked for a good guy to take him and his friend out. The shopkeeper told him to find me at the train station."

"That's fine, but why the secrecy?"

"The film company doesn't want competitors to know. Not yet. It's going to be a major production. They are not filming on the island of course, that's why the producers need to send scouts out, to take pictures and videos for a set they are going to build," Darkhan explained.

"And Aldiyar is going with you too?" Ayan asked, glancing over to Aldiyar who had so far remained silent. Aldiyar nodded but let Darkhan enjoy the telling of this exciting news.

"You told me never to go to the island alone, and those guys are strangers, so I called on Aldiyar," said Darkhan. "So far I have only met one of them. His name is Timur. The other guy, I believe, is named Nikolai because that's what I heard Timur calling him on the phone, telling him I would only take them out if my friend could come along to help me with the boat."

"And?"

"He agreed. It seems this Nikolai is the one who makes the decisions."

"Are they foreigners? Where are they from?"

"Timur, the one I met, is Kazakh. Not sure where in Kazakhstan he is from. I don't know anything about Nikolai. I haven't met him. They speak Russian, but that doesn't necessarily mean Nikolai is Russian," Darkhan explained.

"Why can't they get to Voz from Uzbekistan? In fact, they can just drive over from the mainland there."

"That would be easier, but, according to Timur, there's some problem with Uzbek visas."

"And what about the film company? Did he give you a name? You know where it's based?"

"It's European but he did not give a name or country. It's confidential, because other film producers are fighting to make a movie about Voz Island too. It's a hot topic, you know. Germ warfare, research labs, Soviet intrigue."

"When are you taking them to the island?"

"In two days. They need more time on the island. They will bring camping gear to spend a night there, for us too. We have to be there with them. First time sleeping on the island. People call Kantubek a ghost town, and it may really be, with all the happenings on the island before Independence. A bit nervous about that, but there will be four of us. Should be okay." Darkhan laughed, sounding a bit nervous. "We will drive with them to Kulandy to rent Sairan's boat. Sairan will not be coming with us. We will go back the next day to Kulandy and return the boat in the late afternoon."

"So you leave on April 3, spend that night on the island, and return to Kulandy the next day, April 4." Ayan calculated the dates.

"Yes. And we will spend the night of April 4 in Kulandy, since it'll be too late to drive back here. Darkhan and I will sleep at Sairan's house, and those two at a guesthouse. Then we drive back to Aralsk with them the next day," Aldiyar said.

"Timur gave us a down payment the other day when he met with me, and the rest will be paid when the job is done," Darkhan said.

"I don't know, Darkhan . . . The deal sounds shady. How much are they paying you altogether?"

"Two thousand American for the two of us, plus two hundred for renting Sairan's boat and a hundred for renting a truck on the island. I couldn't believe how much they were offering, but movie companies have lots of money," Darkhan said. "Aldiyar and I will split the two thousand. They've already given us four hundred as down payment, two hundred for me, two hundred for Aldiyar."

Ayan raised his eyebrows. "It's a lot of money for taking them out to the island."

"Yes, but this one is a big venture! We need to drive them from Aralsk to Kulandy, stay overnight on the island with them, give them time to explore the place and take pictures, and return to Kulandy before sundown the next day, and drive them back to Aralsk the day after," Darkhan said.

"That money could do a lot for Raushan and me," Aldiyar spoke up.

"I'm not comfortable about the deal, though I can also understand why the job is so attractive," Ayan said. After pondering, he continued, "Ask them to pay you everything upfront. Tell them you want full payment before you will go with them. This way, they can't go back on their word after you have fulfilled your part of the bargain. Can you call this Timur?"

"We don't have his phone number. But he is going to call me tonight to tell us where to meet on Tuesday, the day we are driving to Kulandy," Darkhan said.

"When he calls, tell him you need all the money upfront. No money, no go!" Ayan said with finality.

Before they parted that day, Ayan asked one of the cafe attendants to take a photo of the three of them with his film camera, which his father Nurzhan gave him when he graduated from his diploma program at Moscow State years ago. It still worked very well, and Ayan had kept it for sentimental reasons. In all the times he and Aldiyar and

Darkhan had gotten together in the past since he moved to Moscow and back, and even before when they were kids growing up, they had never taken a photo together. Ayan thought they ought to have at least one. He would have three copies of the photo developed and give one to each of his two friends when they returned from the trip to Voz Island with the two strangers.

That night, Ayan and his father did not go back to Balta, as it was late when Nurzhan left his friend's home after dinner, and he had had a few drinks too many. They would spend the night in their house on March 8th Street, which was still occupied by Ayan's Uncle Kairat and his unmarried daughter Nurgul. Kairat's wife had passed away several years ago, and their other daughter had moved out when she married. At about ten that night, Ayan received a call from Darkhan telling him that Timur had called and agreed to pay him the rest of the money upfront, and that he would bring it to the train station the following day, Monday, at noon. Darkhan would meet Timur in the main hall by the front entrance.

"Can you meet me tomorrow afternoon after I get the money, Ayan?" Darkhan asked. "I want you to take Aldiyar's portion to him at his shop. I'm working late tomorrow, and we are driving to Kulandy early Tuesday morning."

"Of course. And this way I'll see both of you before you leave to wish you good luck on the trip."

Shortly before noon the next day, Ayan placed himself in a corner of the train station close enough to the main entrance to command a clear view of it. As the station clock approached noon, he saw Darkhan walk out from the back of the station to the main entrance, stopping by the wall about ten paces left of the swinging doors. Minutes later, a man in his late twenties or early thirties, a bit taller than Ayan and Kazakh by the look of him, walked through the main entrance. He was wearing jeans, a black t-shirt, and sneakers. He glanced to the left, then to the right, spotted Darkhan, and walked up to him. That had to be Timur. They talked for a few minutes. From where Ayan was watching them, he got a fairly clear look at Timur, who handed Darkhan a white envelope. Darkhan opened it and looked carefully inside without taking the contents out. He nodded, and the man then left the same way he'd come.

Ayan waited for a couple of minutes in case the man returned for any reason, then walked out to the designated loading dock beside the tracks. Darkhan soon joined him.

"We are going to meet them at the corner of Abulkhair Khan and Baktibai Batyr Streets tomorrow at 5 a.m. From there, I will be driving them with Aldiyar to Kulandy in my truck," Darkhan said. Handing Ayan the envelope Timur had just given him, he continued, "Please give eight hundred to Aldiyar at his shop. He already has the two hundred from the down payment." Then taking two more crisp, new American hundred-dollar bills out of his pocket and adding them to the stack in the envelope, he said, "Keep my share till I return. Don't want to leave so much money in my room. My landlady is trustworthy but there are other tenants in the house."

"Darkhan, good luck, and be very careful," Ayan said.

"I will. This is not the first time we are going to the island. We know our way there very well. See you when we get back, my good friend, and we'll celebrate."

They shook hands, gave each other a spontaneous pat on the back, and each went his own way.

Ayan stopped at Aldiyar's shoe repair shop next and gave him the money due to him. "Raushan will be very happy with this," Aldiyar beamed. "First, two hundred, and now eight hundred! Easy money!"

"Take good care when you go out to the island with those men. You and Darkhan look out for each other, okay?"

"Okay, old man!" Aldiyar laughed. "You talk as if we will be in any kind of danger! The island is as safe as anywhere as long as we don't touch the stuff in the labs."

"Will those two guys be going to the Field of Death?"

"I don't know where they want to take pictures, but they can go anywhere they want on the island in the truck we are renting. We won't even go with them. They can drive around, and we can wait for them at a good spot to camp for the night, or we may do some more scavenging on our own."

"Aldiyar, I wish you and Darkhan the best of luck. I only hope this will be the last time you guys go out though."

Aldiyar looked at Ayan. "I won't get rich mending shoes."

———

It was not until four days later, April 6, that Raushan called Ayan. "Ayan, Aldiyar has not come home! He hasn't called either. He told me to expect him back yesterday. I called Darkhan's phone, no reply. I'm beginning to worry." She sounded anxious.

Ayan assured her he would do his best to locate Aldiyar and Darkhan. Raushan gave him the phone number for Sairan, their friend in Kulandy, and Ayan immediately called him. Sairan told Ayan that Aldiyar and Darkhan had arrived at Kulandy about mid-morning on April 3 and had rented his boat for that day and the next. They were supposed to bring the boat back by sundown the next day, Wednesday. He had not seen them or the boat since. Ayan asked if he had seen anyone else with them. Sairan said there were two fellows waiting off to the side while Darkhan was talking to him. One looked Kazakh, medium height, and the other was a stout blond Caucasian. They had backpacks and some camping gear with them. Ayan got from Sairan the phone number of the truck rental agent, Gabit, and called him next. Gabit said he had not seen anyone else with Darkhan and Aldiyar when they paid for the use of a truck on the island, and so far they had not returned the keys to the truck or the shack in which it was parked.

Ayan went to the police station in Aralsk and reported the case of his two missing friends. He told the police everything he knew about Darkhan and Aldiyar's voyage to Voz Island and their taking along two strangers who claimed to be working for a movie company. The police chief, a man by the name of Aibek Nurmanbetov, was the grandson of a friend of Ayan's paternal grandfather, Aidar Kazbekov. He listened in courteous silence as Ayan told the details of the case, nodding sympathetically, and assured Ayan of police assistance. Aralsk being a small town, a good number of the policemen knew Darkhan as a porter at the train station, and many had brought shoes that needed mending to Aldiyar, the cobbler on Toke Esetov Street. The police documented the case of the two missing Aralsk residents, but it was not their intention to go out to Voz Island in a speedboat looking for them.

Regarding the two strangers who hired Darkhan and Aldiyar to take them out to the island, the police had no record. Ayan told Chief Nurmanbetov that he had no knowledge of them, except he saw the one who was Kazakh, known as Timur, from a reasonable distance when Darkhan met him at the train station. About the other, a stout blond Caucasian as described by Sairan, he knew nothing. The next morning, Chief Nurmanbetov himself drove out to Kulandy to check out the area and question Sairan and Gabit in person. They both gave him the same information they had given Ayan on the phone. Chief Nurmanbetov then reported the case to the oblast police in Kyzylorda.

Three days went by with no news of Aldiyar and Darkhan. The chance of Ayan seeing his two childhood friends ever again was growing slimmer by the day. Darkhan had no immediate family in Aralsk. They had all moved out east following the death of the fishing industry. Looking up a distant cousin of his in Aralsk, Ayan was able to get the phone number of Darkhan's brother in Almaty and call him about Darkhan's disappearance. As for Aldiyar's wife, Raushan, she was beside herself with anxiety, living day to day with uncertainties and fearing the worst. Meanwhile, Sairan's motorboat was found afloat west of the Bay of Kulandy on April 8. No one was on it.

The dreaded news came on April 10, four days after Aldiyar and Darkhan were reported missing. The body of a man matching Aldiyar's height had been recovered off the coast of the North Aral Sea in the Bay of Kulandy. It was taken back to Aralsk. Ayan accompanied Raushan and her youngest son to the town morgue for what was the hardest ordeal for all of them. Fear and anguish as Ayan had never experienced before gnawed at his gut at the prospect of identifying the dead body of his friend. He could not imagine how Raushan and her son must feel. The agony and pain when they saw the bloated and partially mangled face of Aldiyar were beyond words. Raushan immediately fainted in the arms of her son.

As expected, more tragedy awaited. A day later, on April 11, the partially decomposed body of Darkhan was also recovered in the waters of the North Aral Sea further east of the Bay of Kulandy. Ayan notified Darkhan's brother, who immediately made plans to travel to Aralsk with his elderly father. No coroner's report was published. The causes of Aldiyar's and Darkhan's deaths were stated as drowning. Chief Nurmanbetov called Raushan, and then Ayan, to convey his condolences.

"I wish we could trace those two men they took out to the island and get them here for questioning. They must know the circumstances that led to the two victims' drowning," Chief Nurmanbetov said to Ayan over the phone.

"You really think it's drowning?" Ayan asked.

Chief Nurmanbetov was quiet for a few good seconds, then said in a low voice, "I can't be sure. But that's what the oblast coroner's official report stated."

"I think they were killed by those two fellows they took to the island." Ayan was too grief stricken to mince words.

"There is no proof." After a moment's pause during which Ayan could hear Chief Nurmanbetov's sighing, the police chief said, "Let me give you my after-hours telephone number in case you wish to contact me further about the case." Sometimes, a little family connection goes a long way.

On April 12, Ayan attended the funeral of Aldiyar, followed by Darkhan's funeral two days later, on April 14, upon the arrival of the latter's father and brother. As he bid his friends farewell, Ayan could see the three of them as kids running on the beaches of Balta, and hiking up with his brother Arsen to the top of Sea Cliff to watch the waves rush home. From that windy vantage point on Sea Cliff, they had strained their eyes to look for the mystery island where the horrid monster lived. The night following Darkhan's funeral, after all fell quiet, Ayan let the tears flow freely down his cheeks. As a young boy, little had he known the fearsome island of his childhood would turn out to be a living horror in his adult years.

On April 16, two days after Darkhan's funeral, Ayan took the train to Kyzylorda, then flew to Astana, to attend the fundraising event for victims of the Gulag. As he looked out the plane window, he imagined seeing the faces of his two childhood friends in the clouds. It gave him solace to think they were high up in the sky, far above that hellish place that was once Voz Island.

BOOK IX

GRACE AND AYAN

24

A VERY DISTURBING DISCOVERY

May 13, 2007, Aralsk, Kazakhstan

A ralsk comes into view in the near horizon. The train carrying Grace and Ainur rolls slowly into Aralsk railway station. The time is 5:10 p.m. As Grace steps down to the platform with her two bags, Ayan is there to greet her.

"Welcome to Aralsk!" Ayan says, shaking her hand firmly. "You must be exhausted after a flight from Almaty and then such a long train ride here!"

"It wasn't that bad. I met a young woman on the plane to Kyzylorda and she was also coming to Aralsk on the same train. We had a long chat in the dining car. The journey didn't feel so tedious with someone to talk to."

"Glad you had a good journey. We have a very nice place for you to stay in Aralsk, and interesting and unique things to see!" Ayan says. "But before we leave here, I want you to see something in the waiting room—the glory and pride of Aralsk."

Picking up Grace's shoulder bag, Ayan leads the way to the escalator while Grace wheels her carry-on suitcase after him. Down on street level, they enter the waiting room, which is quite occupied at that late afternoon hour even though Aralsk is not exactly a bustling hub with heavy rail traffic. Grace notices the white-washed walls, the arched windows, the metal linked chairs; the room is spartan, cold. Then her eyes come to rest on the mosaic centerpiece on the wall facing the door, and she is gripped by its dominating presence.

"That's some picture," she comments.

"That's what I want you to see." Ayan is about to explain the story behind the image when an old man, presumably noticing they are studying the mosaic, comes up to him and says in Kazakh, "Do you know what this picture is about? It commemorates one of the proudest moments in the history of Aralsk."

"Yes, I grew up around here, so I know the history," Ayan replies politely.

The old man continues nonetheless, pointing a thick, coarse finger at the wall, "It shows Lenin sending a letter to the people of Aralsk asking them to help the starving population of the Soviet Union. In answer to his call, the town of Aralsk sent fourteen railway wagons of fish to aid the hungry people in the young Union in 1921. *Fourteen railway wagons of fish.*" His proud voice rings across the waiting room, as though he wants the whole world to hear. "Who would think that eighty years later, our sea would be drying up, and all our fish dead?" His words resound with bitterness.

Ayan politely acknowledges the old man's words. He turns to Grace and translates for her.

"Aralsk did Moscow a great service back then." Grace nods appreciatively toward the old man.

She follows Ayan out of the railway station, but not without glancing back once more at the famous mosaic celebrating the generous giving of the mighty Aral. Outside, Ayan leads the way to where he has parked his father's old truck by the roadside. At 5:30 p.m., the sun has not set. Daylight will linger till 8 p.m. this time of year.

"We'll go to your guesthouse directly to deposit the luggage. It's

the best guesthouse in town," Ayan tells her. "Local residents call it
Alikhan's House, but I have nicknamed it Noble House, for what it used
to be in better times, a grand mansion, perhaps the best house in town.
But even now, it is the best guesthouse in town."

Nurzhan's cranky old truck, like many in Almaty, has a cracked
windshield and threadbare seats. As Ayan drives along the main
street of Aralsk, buildings assume many shapes and colors, but most
are dilapidated bungalows along with a few whitewashed two-story
houses on paved and dusty graveled streets. At a street intersection,
their car stops to allow a pair of camels to cross, apparently on their
own without a guide, as though camels are regular pedestrians of that
town. At another crossing, a man wearing a taqiya herds three goats
across, the scene quietly but blatantly clashing with the giant billboard
above them showing a young woman in a smart white blouse typing
at a computer keyboard. Such incongruity! They pass a sandy playground with a couple of tired-looking swings and a rusty slide. Cars
are parked along street curbs, wherever there is space.

They soon come to a big two-story corner house at a quiet intersection. Ayan stops in front of the yard guarded by a wrought iron fence
with opened double gates, more to impress than for security; the black
paint on the fence is sorely chipped and fading. Ayan parks his truck
on the dirt sidewalk near the gate, alights with Grace, takes her luggage from the back, and leads her to a side door. He rings the bell. A
thirtyish man, slight in stature and wearing an *I Love New York* t-shirt
and blue jeans, opens the door. Ayan shakes his hand, addressing him
in Kazakh, then turns to Grace and says, "This is Alikhan, owner and
manager of the guesthouse."

"Welcome to Aralsk!" Alikhan greets Grace in English. "We
are happy you are here." His English is stiff but correct. He ushers
Grace and Ayan into the house and down the hallway dominated by
a wide wooden staircase, presumably stained a dark red at one time,
although its color has faded into a pale maroon. They are soon joined
by Alikhan's wife Dinara, a pretty, reserved young woman, wearing a

floral house dress and black leggings. While Grace follows Dinara to her guest room on the second floor, Ayan waits for her downstairs and chats with Alikhan.

Grace's room is a decent size, furnished with a double bed, a night-stand, a wooden wardrobe, and a small desk and chair. Like the rest of the house, the furniture has seen better times, but every item is still serviceable. Best of all, the place looks clean.

"*Rakhmet!*" Grace says one of few Kazakh words she has picked up to thank Dinara, who smiles and bows her head slightly before leaving her to refresh herself.

Alone in the room, Grace plops onto the bed, her arms outstretched, and looks up at the stucco ceiling. She notices the pattern of a ship's helm in the center. The house was probably built by one of Aralsk's rich residents in the golden era of the town, when it was the biggest port on the Aral's northern shore. Grace gets up and walks to the window to look outside. She spots the children's park they passed earlier. Then her eyes wander to the far distance, to two dark skeletal structures with long protruding necks. Those must be the abandoned cranes at the old harbor she has seen in stock photos of the town. Grace feels a lump in her throat at the sight of them, and what seems like an extensive flat of mud and sludge below them that must have once been the sea.

After calling Glen on her mobile phone to let him know she has safely arrived in Aralsk and to make sure he too has arrived safely in Baku, Grace refreshes herself and goes downstairs to join Ayan. Dinner is a home-cooked meal of Kazakh cuisine, smoked and thinly sliced horse meat, stuffed cabbage, baked fish, and a tomato and cucumber salad, all prepared by Alikhan's mother. Grace helps herself generously to the Kazakh fried bread *baursak,* which reminds her of doughnut holes back home. Fresh fruit and dried apricot and raisins complement the scrumptious meal. The dining room they eat in is an extravagant, well-kept, oval-shaped room furnished with a dark wood dining table that seats ten and two full-length china cabinets. No other guests join them that evening. Perhaps there is no other guest staying there that day. After dinner, Ayan takes Grace on a leisurely walk around the town while they still have some daylight so she can get a better feel of it.

"They must have a big family to be living in such a big house," Grace remarks as they walk along Tokey Esetov Street in the direction of the former harbor.

"Four generations are living there. Alikhan and Dinara just had a baby girl last month. Alikhan's mother and grandmother live there too, plus some of their extended family, uncles, aunts and cousins."

"I gather it is the custom here for younger generations to live with family even after marriage?" Grace looks enquiringly at Ayan.

"It's Kazakh custom for the youngest son to live with his parents and grandparents after marriage. It is also our custom to welcome relatives under our roof, if they need help. Alikhan is the youngest. His grandfather built that house in the 1950s. They had a big share of the fish canning business in Aralsk back then."

"How do they manage to support such a big household now?"

"In addition to running the guesthouse, Alikhan is the manager of the local historical museum. The family also owns a cafe in town, which they have managed to keep open even through bad times. They also own a camel farm not far from here that brings in income from the milk and meat."

"They are a very enterprising family," Grace observes.

Ayan nods. "One has to be in order to survive here. And the good news is fish are starting to come back after the completion of the Kokaral Dam just two years ago."

"I was reading about that dam before coming. It sounds like a huge project," Grace says.

"For sure," Ayan bobs his head in agreement. "It was built across the strait separating the North and South Aral Seas."

"Bet the residents here are hopeful of better times now."

Ayan's face lights up as he nods. "Fishermen around here, including my father, have been going out to fish again, though the catch is not as plentiful as before. Still, it is a good start," he says.

They have come to the former shores where the old harbor was. The two old cranes look even more forlorn and pitiful close-up, with long stooping necks straining over the once bustling harbor, as if waiting futilely for the next boat to come in with its big haul. Patches of wet mud and scrap metal from rotten ships lie across the cracked seabed, as well as rust-covered segments of anchors, pipes, and broken bottles, cruel remnants of the Aral's heyday. Not far from the cranes are the abandoned canneries, run-down warehouses with broken windows.

"You can tell the Kokaral Dam hasn't yet made too much of a visible improvement to Aralsk," Ayan says. "Where we are is by the seashore forty years ago. I never saw the sea from here, but my father said that when he was little, the waves came all the way up to our house on March 8th Street. Ships sailed into the harbor from Uzbekistan and Turkmenistan, bringing goods and food to Aralsk, to be sent to different parts of the Soviet Union."

"So this was like an *entrepôt*," Grace says.

"Something like that. My Uncle Kairat and his family have lived in our house for many years. He still lives there with one of his daughters. Whenever we come to Aralsk, we stay there. In fact, I'm staying there now, while you are here visiting. It's more convenient this way."

"Just walking around town with you has been an eye-opener," Grace says to Ayan as they head back toward Noble House by another route. "You're a knowledgeable guide! I'm lucky you're on sabbatical this semester."

"I'm glad to have the chance to show you around. It's good that you will keep me busy with your visit the next few days. We have so few foreign visitors to our town. We are an invisible dot on the map of the world. How many people have even heard of us?"

"It's true not many people have heard of Aralsk or the Aral Sea. And not many people come to visit. I suppose those who do have a special reason to."

"Like you, looking for a story for your novel," Ayan says.

"Exactly. But I still do not know what my story is. I'm going to let time and opportunity steer their course, and see how the plot unfolds," Grace replies.

"So this trip to Aralsk is your story and you are living your novel! You get to make your own ending!" Ayan says, smiling at Grace.

"That sounds exciting when you put it that way! To be a part of my own novel . . . "

"Make sure my character has an important part," Ayan says, laughing.

"Definitely!"

By then they have reached Noble House. "Want to come inside for a cup of tea before you head back?" Grace asks.

"Sure. I'm in no hurry to go anywhere, and home tonight is just our old house on March 8th Street in town. I'm on vacation like you."

Dinara brings out tea, cookies, and dried fruit for them as they sit at the dining table. Taking a sip of the fruity tea, Grace asks, "I know you're not married, Ayan, but do you have a girlfriend?" She finally voices her curiosity about Ayan's private life.

"I did, a lovely Russian girl. We met at university. Unfortunately, we were not meant to be, as you would say."

"What happened?"

"Well, we were happy together in Moscow for eight years. We wanted to get married but her parents were not happy to have me, a small-town boy, for their son-in-law. They wanted her to move back to Leningrad—that's what St. Petersburg was called during Soviet time— and marry a Russian man. When she finally got her dream job at the Hermitage in Leningrad, she decided to go back."

"You must have been heartbroken when she left."

"I was. She asked me to go with her and get another teaching post in Leningrad, but it would have been difficult, especially at a time when the Soviet Union was on the brink of falling apart. Besides, I was happy teaching English at the Institute of International Languages in Moscow."

"I'm sorry it didn't work out between you two. Is she married now?"

"No. We are still good friends, and we email occasionally." Ayan takes in a deep breath. "Nothing is changed as far as our relationship is concerned though. Valeria seems happy and contented with her job as a research historian at the Hermitage. As for me, I strongly feel my place is here with my family, my people, and my sea. I'm finding much fulfillment teaching English at the university. I do care deeply about her though, and I still carry a picture of her."

So saying, Ayan takes out his wallet. As he pulls out a few small photos to find the one of Valeria, they all fall to the floor. One by one he picks them up. There are four pictures. He hands them all to Grace, saying, "You may be interested in seeing the others as well; these people all mean a lot to me."

Grace eagerly takes the photos. The first one is a beautiful woman with the sunniest smile, and a full cascade of long golden curls. Valeria in the sunshine. "She's beautiful," Grace says with admiration. "No chance of a reconciliation?"

"Not at present, and I don't see a way for us to be together so long as I am here and she is there. Besides, we are both in our forties now."

"You never know," Grace says. "I wish the best for you both. I can see you still have feelings for her." Ayan remains quiet. Grace looks at the next photo. "And this black-and-white one must be your father in front of his fishing boat."

"Yes. That was taken in the summer of 1977, a year after he abandoned it in the Bay of Beket after the Aral stopped yielding fish."

"That must have been heartbreaking."

"Yes, every time I think of the day my father abandoned his boat, I feel very sad."

"Can we visit it while I'm here?"

"I plan to take you there tomorrow."

Grace flips to the third picture. "And who are you with in this one?"

Ayan looks at the photo and replies, "That's my good Russian friend from Moscow State University, Victor. We look so young there . . . This was taken at the Ploschad Revolyutsii Station, one of the busiest metro stations in Moscow, where we used to go after a few beers in town. That statue of the dog with the guard—see how shiny the dog's nose is? Commuters rub it for good luck!"

"What a handsome boy!" Grace exclaims.

"Sure is. You like dogs?" Ayan asks.

"Yes, I do, but I was referring to your Russian friend!" They both laugh and Grace pursues with some embarrassment, "Where is he now?"

"Good question. I have no idea. After he finished his aspiranture and started working, we didn't have news of each other for nine years. Then one day in 1991, not long before the collapse of the Soviet Union, he suddenly called me, and we met for beers that evening, and then he was gone again. I haven't heard from him since. I don't even know if he's still alive. I guess I'll never know for sure." Ayan looks sober, a dark cloud hovering over his countenance.

"I pray he's alive and well, and that he'll turn up again one of these days," she consoles. She turns to the last photo. "And who are these two guys with you?"

"Aldiyar and Darkhan, my best childhood friends from Balta," Ayan says, a tremor in his voice. "That's the first and last photo we took together. This was at a cafe in Aralsk, shortly before their deaths." The last few words are uttered under his breath, as if he is in deep pain. He looks away.

Grace stares at Ayan in disbelief, shocked beyond words. "Their deaths?" she asks, as if hoping she has heard wrong.

Ayan swallows hard. "They were found drowned recently." He heaves a deep sigh and continues, "Months before, I had planned to attend the Karlag memorial events to pay respects to my grandfather and the victims of the Gulag, but I had no idea I would be going with such a very heavy heart. This happened just days before I left for Astana."

Suddenly, Grace's mind reels. "When did they drown? I mean, what was the actual date?" Grace asks in a rush, her nerves on edge.

Ayan gives her a strange look. "Either April 3 or 4. Presumably they were drowned while taking two strangers out to Voz Island. But Aldiyar's body was recovered in the Aral Sea on April 10 and Darkhan's on April 11. I fear foul play, but the police have no proof and the two fellows they took out there are nowhere to be found."

"April 10 and 11 . . . the dates your two friends' bodies were found." Grace mumbles the dates. "They must be the two men from the newspaper clipping I received." Grace can hardly believe her own shocking deduction.

"What newspaper clipping?"

"Someone left a newspaper clipping with a magazine vendor near our apartment building in Almaty with directions to pass it on to me. It was just a headline, and it was in Kazakh, but a passerby translated it for me." Grace pauses, anticipating Ayan's next question.

"What did the headline say?"

"'Bodies of Two Missing Aralsk Residents Found in Aral Sea.' It was dated April 12, the day after your second friend was found. That article must be referring to their deaths. But why would someone give me that article? To freak me out?"

"It sounds like a warning or threat of some sort." Ayan looks worried.

"But why me?" Grace frowns. Recollecting herself, she says, "I am very sorry about your loss, Ayan. I had no idea these were your friends, or that you had gone through such a terrible personal tragedy just before I met you. I wish the police would do more to figure out the real cause of their deaths."

"Aralsk is a small town. Our police have limited resources."

After a moment of silence, Grace asks, "Care to talk about it?"

For the next hour, Grace listens to an account of events leading up to the recovery of the bodies of Aldiyar and Darkhan in the waters of the North Aral.

"God rest their souls," Grace finds her voice when Ayan finishes, her tone reduced to a hollow whisper.

"How could they rest in peace with whoever murdered them at large?" Ayan asks in frustration. "Our police seem powerless!"

"They were most likely killed by those two strangers they took out to the island. It seems to me the motivation of the two men was questionable from the start. I don't believe in that crap about scouting for a movie set," Grace says, switching into detective mode.

"I agree, the movie story sounds like a lie to cover up their real motive. The murders might only be skimming the surface of a deeper, more intricate plot." Ayan looks thoughtful.

"It seems to me those two men might be looking for something on the island," Grace says, "and I don't mean settings for a movie."

"If you're correct, then whether or not those two men found what they were looking for that day, they would still kill Darkhan and Aldiyar to keep them quiet," Ayan voices his conjecture aloud. "From the moment my friends agreed to take them out to the island, they had sealed their fates. This seems like something much bigger than what our local police could handle."

Grace takes one last look at the photo of Ayan with Aldiyar and Darkhan, these two good men whom fortune had not favored. Grace studies the faces of the three friends and their happy, unsuspecting smiles. She is about to return the photo to Ayan when something catches her eye. She stares at the photo, freezes, then looks over to Ayan and in a shaky voice asks, "Who is that man in the background, behind you and your friends?"

"What man? You look like you've seen a ghost!" Ayan says.

"The man in the background, behind you," Grace reiterates in a hollow voice, passing the photo back to Ayan. Her hand shakes so badly that she accidentally drops it on the floor.

Ayan bends to retrieve it, then studies it. "The man sitting alone at the table behind us? No idea. Why? Should I know him?"

"That's the guy I first saw in the Palace of Peace and Reconciliation, the one who walked in while you and I were talking in the conference room at the top. I know you hardly looked at him that time, but I remembered his face because we passed each other on the stairs as I was going up to the top, and then, when we were at the Kasteev Museum, he came up to me while you were in the restroom. I told you about him, remember? In fact, he came up to me twice in Almaty, the first time at the Kasteev Museum, the second time on Kok Tobe when I went up there with Glen. This was a couple weeks ago, after you had left Almaty."

"Are you sure that's the same guy in the photo?" It was Ayan's turn to freak out.

"I am positive."

"This photo shows he was here in Aralsk just days before you saw him in Astana!" Ayan says, looking concerned.

"I meant to warn you about this blond fellow, but I was too excited once I got here, it slipped my mind. I think he is stalking you. At first I thought he was following me in Almaty, maybe even in Astana, for what reason I had no idea, but when he confronted me on Kok Tobe after you had left Almaty, I realized it was you he was tailing the whole time."

"That's disturbing." Ayan looks worried. "What makes you think that?"

"When he accosted me on Kok Tobe, he asked for some information he thought you had given me. He said he saw you giving me a book at Panfilov Park and seemed convinced there was some secret information in there. He must have been tailing you in Astana and Almaty, and this photo shows that he was stalking you even before, in Aralsk." Grace is talking fast, her adrenaline flowing, tripping over her words, as though she cannot get across to Ayan quickly enough all she wants to. She stops to catch her breath. "Wait a minute. Now that I think of it, he probably followed us to Karlag as well! Remember I told you I saw a dummy scientist in the lab move? You said it might have been a ghost, and I thought it could be a live person. Maybe it was him! The moving mannequin with the blond hair!"

"Yes, I remember that incident," Ayan recollects.

"When he saw you giving me a book at Panfilov Park, he thought you were passing me the information he was looking for, and so he decided to get it from me, after you left Almaty."

"That's really worrying," Ayan says, looking his words.

"What's more, both times he talked to me, at the Kasteev Museum and on Kok Tobe, he mentioned the Aral Sea and Voz Island. He seemed interested in the region, and especially Voz Island. He told me at the museum that he had been to the Aral Sea region but not the island, that he'd like to go to the island the next time."

Ayan is thoughtful for a good minute, looking at the telltale photo. "He might be tailing me, but he could also have been watching Aldiyar and Darkhan. This picture was taken just days before they were drowned. I saw one of the two strangers they took to the island, the Kazakh named Timur who dealt directly with Darkhan, but I haven't seen the other one. I heard from Sairan, the guy who rented the boat to them, that the other one was a stout blond Caucasian, like this man in the photo here. If my intuition is correct, then this man in the photo could well be the other stranger Aldiyar and Darkhan took to Voz Island. He could well be one of their murderers!"

"This is getting super disturbing. I have a strong suspicion he was the one who left me that newspaper clipping—and the note I got at the hotel in Astana telling me to ask you about Voz Island."

"You may be right. He could be the one who sent you both messages."

"What could he be after? What's the important secret information he is looking for?" Grace asks, surprising herself that she has waited this long to ask Ayan about it.

"I have no idea, Grace. Honestly, I have no secret that would warrant someone tracking me all the way across Kazakhstan!" Ayan shrugs, looking as baffled as Grace. Then slowly, in an ominous tone of voice, Ayan says, "He's probably back here in Aralsk, even as we speak."

25

LONG DAY'S EXCURSION INTO NIGHT OF FEAR

May 14, 2007, Bay of Beket, Kazakhstan

In solemn silence, Grace follows Ayan as they walk over sand, salt, and vagrant grass, as if they were a funeral procession, paying respects to a beloved dead. Ayan has driven her in his father's truck to the ship graveyard in the Bay of Beket.

"It doesn't seem like it, but thirty years have passed since my father left *Kari qaiyk* here," Ayan says, looking over to the far horizon where the sky meets the diminished sea.

"Has it been that long?"

"July 17, 1976. It'll be thirty-one years this July. I was sixteen then. I'm now forty-seven," Ayan says with a sad smile. "Time doesn't wait."

Their feet make crunching sounds as they walk in the direction of the stranded, decaying vessels. Grace looks down and notices the shells. Seashells by the millions on the desiccated seabed of the Aral. She has read about the Aral's ship graveyards on the internet, and now

she's here in one of them, bearing witness to the humiliating down-
fall of a fleet of once able-bodied work vessels. This cemetery for the
deserted fishing boats of the Aral Sea generates a morbid interest in
its visitors, taking tourism to a new sordid level. Instinctively, Grace
scoops up a handful of the shells, small but with beautiful serrated
edges in shades of pastels, orange, red, purple, blue. "A souvenir from
the Aral Sea," she says, looking up at Ayan hesitantly, as if asking for
his permission or approval.

He smiles. "Help yourself. You won't find another opportunity like
this. How many people in the world can say they have touched the
bottom of a sea?"

"I wish I never had this opportunity. I'm sorry for behaving like
an indulgent tourist." In spite of her apology, Grace carefully wraps
several of the shells in a tissue and stores them in the sunglass case
in her backpack.

A little farther out are seven rotting fishing boats spaced some three
to five hundred meters apart, stranded on the endless shore of sand,
slush, and salt.

"Ships of the desert," Ayan says, pointing with his chin toward the
broken vessels. "The camels had competition for the title here and lost."

As they near the abandoned boats, Grace looks on with incredu-
lous dismay at the rusty metal corpses the vessels have become in the
thirty years since their abandonment.

"Looters had come to take everything worth anything—doors,
window frames, wheels, nuts and bolts, every scrap of metal and good
wood that they could sell. Some of the boats just collapsed and rotted
away in the mud and salt," Ayan explains.

"Which one is *Kari qaiyk*?" Ayan points to the boat about two
hundred meters away. "She looks small compared to the others,"
Grace remarks.

"She's big enough to hold a crew of eight, but my father and his
helper were the only ones taking her out every day."

Even from a distance, Grace can see evidence of the atrocities brought upon *Kari qaiyk* by vandals and the elements. However, despite all the indignities she has endured, *Kari qaiyk* has retained her shape and more or less her position. She is somewhat tilted but still miraculously holding up better than the other boats in that graveyard. Like an old loyal servant waiting for her master to come back and take her out to sail the mighty Aral again, she refuses to give up her fight. So silently, stoically, indefinitely, she waits. If she were human, she would have withered away from a broken heart. Grace weeps silently for her.

They walk up to *Kari qaiyk* and circle her counterclockwise. Grace climbs the deck with Ayan's help, the boarding ladders having been removed by looters long ago. They enter the wheelhouse through a long rectangular opening where the door once was. The helm is missing, as expected. Through a starboard window in the wheelhouse, Grace looks out across a rugged beach scattered with yellow grass to the horizon where the sea meets the sky just a few kilometers away. The Aral hasn't receded too far from the original shoreline at the Bay of Beket.

Ayan heaves a deep sigh and shakes his head as his eyes span the vast concave space of land, sea, and sky. "Growing up beside the Aral Sea, I never dreamed that I would lose it one day because of mankind's senseless actions. There were hundreds of these abandoned boats all around the dying sea, from here to Uzbekistan. And one by one, they just rust, rot, and fall apart."

Through an opened hatch on the deck in the bow section, Grace peers into the hull below. Just a deep, dark void extending about two-thirds the length of the boat and reeking of putrefaction and urine.

"What's down below?" Grace asks.

"All kinds of rubbish you can think of. You can imagine from the smell. I haven't been down there since my father left her here."

"How did people get down? It's pretty deep."

"There used to be a metal ladder. That had to be one of the first things the looters took. When my brother Arsen and I were kids, our father would take us on the boat sometimes when he wasn't working.

Our favorite hideout was the hull. We loved climbing down there and closing the hatch above us so Father couldn't find us when it was time to leave."

"That sounds like fun," Grace remarks, eyeing the opening. "Not so much now."

Ayan laughs. "It's certainly a pretty long way down!"

—

As they drive back to town, Grace asks, "Now that the new Kokaral Dam has brought back some fish and fishermen are going out again, there ought to be some working fishing boats around. Where *are* they?"

"They don't use big vessels like *Kari qaiyk* anymore. Mostly they go out in small boats with outboard motors. My village is still twenty-five kilometers from the shoreline, but there has already been an increase in fishing since the dam was completed. These days, my father and other fishermen drive to the shore at dusk, take their motorboats out to cast their nets, and leave the nets in the sea overnight. The next day before dawn, they go out again to haul in the nets, which usually have a decent quantity of fish in them."

"Your father and the other fishermen must be glad to be out on the water again," Grace says.

"They sure are. These days, my father leaves his boat on the shore, but the motor he stores in his truck when the boat is not in use, because it's very expensive. He can't afford to lose it."

"It makes sense to use smaller motorboats, I guess. But seeing *Kari qaiyk* like this makes me sad that she will never get to go out with your father again, even if she could be repaired," Grace says. "If she had feelings, she'd be very jealous of that little upstart, your father's motorboat."

Ayan laughs at the analogy. "My father still has strong feelings for *Kari qaiyk*. But sometimes, we have to do what reason guides us to do, when following our feelings may not be in our best interest."

Their truck passes a couple of abandoned mud huts that were once used by fishermen of old for shelter and rest. Ayan veers the truck away from the rough terrain onto a paved road carved out of the desert wasteland, in the direction of Aralsk.

Ayan looks over to Grace. "We are only thirty kilometers from Balta. I would like very much to take you to meet my family, but if I'm being followed by one of those guys who might have something to do with Aldiyar's and Darkhan's deaths, I shouldn't be leading them to Balta of all places!"

"You are right," Grace says. "In fact, I'm not sure if you should return to the house where your uncle and cousin live."

"I've thought of that too after your discovery in that photo last night, but if that man was following me around in Aralsk even before he followed me to Astana, he would already know I have family living there. I have warned Uncle Kairat and Nurgul to be careful, and not to be out alone in the dark or let strangers into the house."

Back at Noble House that evening, at Dinara's invitation Ayan again stays for dinner. When he bids goodnight to Grace, it is about 8:30 p.m. He will pick her up at 7 a.m. the next day to go to Kokaral Dam.

———

As Ayan walks to his truck parked at the curb around the corner from Noble House, two men approach him. By the glow of the streetlight, Ayan recognizes Timur, the one he saw at the train station. The other, Caucasian with light hair, about his own height but a bigger man, in all likelihood is the one Grace recognized in the photo. Ayan's pulse immediately accelerates.

"Good evening, sir." Timur steps in front of Ayan, speaking in Russian, while the blond guy stands behind Ayan, trapping him in a vulnerable position.

"Yes?" Ayan lowers his chin in an attempt to steady his voice.

The blond man takes over from behind in Muscovite Russian.

"You look nervous. We are looking for a friend of yours. Perhaps you can help us. We'd like to ask you a couple questions."

"Who are you?" Ayan manages to ask, as he turns to face him.

Ignoring Ayan's question, and wasting no time, the blond guy takes a photograph from out of the breast pocket of his khaki jacket. Timur, meanwhile, flips out a flashlight and shines it on the photo. By its light, Ayan sees himself with Victor at the bar in Moscow in 1991. The picture must have been taken by that KGB agent, Andrei. It shows Victor putting some bank notes into Ayan's hand. Ayan's heart is now thumping so hard that he fears the two fellows can hear it. He answers, trying to sound as casual as he can, "That's a friend from Moscow State University. I haven't seen him in years."

The blond man continues, "We know. His name is Victor Luganov. This picture was taken in 1991. That evening, did Victor tell you anything about his work on Voz Island?"

"Voz Island?" There was that cursed name again. "No! In fact, I didn't even know he worked there. You seem to know more about him than I do! That meeting was the first time I saw him after he graduated and left Moscow. He never wrote and we had lost touch for nine years until he called me that day out of the blue." Ayan is almost yelling, his initial nervousness and fear giving way to a sense of betrayal and absolute disappointment in Victor for doing work on Voz Island, if indeed this man is telling the truth. As well, Ayan is overcome with feelings of hurt that Victor had kept him in the dark all those years.

"So, he did not tell you anything about his research work on Voz Island?" the blond man continues to press.

"No! I know nothing!"

"Something he had produced, something he had buried on Voz Island?" Timur squeezes in a question.

"I have no idea what you are talking about!"

"This photo was enlarged using a micro focus finder with high magnification. Take a careful look at what I saw in Victor Luganov's hand as he gave you the money." So saying, the blond man produces another photo from his jacket's inner pocket. Timur again shines the flashlight on it, showing Ayan a magnified segment of the same photo. Zoomed in on Victor's and Ayan's hands, the enlarged image betrays some minuscule white edges on the small stack of banknotes. "We know he passed you a note that night. We believe Victor Luganov entrusted you with the knowledge of the secret hiding place of something very important, something he had developed on the island. You will tell us where it is." The blond guy scrutinizes Ayan's facial reaction with an icy, penetrating gaze.

"What are you talking about? He gave me rubles to pay for the beer and food, and that was all!" Ayan is obviously losing his cool. "I didn't even know he had worked on Voz Island until you told me just now!"

"For your own good, you'd better tell us what the note says." The blond man fixes his eyes on Ayan with an intimidating glare, then edges close enough to Ayan that he can smell his vodka breath as he drawls, "Tell us what the note says, and you will walk away unharmed."

In that moment, as if by a stroke of luck, a white patrol car pulls into view, approaching from up the street at cruising speed. Without a moment's hesitation, Ayan suddenly pushes his way onto the street before his two potential assailants have a chance to stop him, waving his arms and shouting, "Help!" in Kazakh. It works; the driver of the patrol car heads toward him and his potential assailants, who, sensing the danger, melt back into the darkness behind Noble House. By the time the cruiser reaches the shaken and confused Ayan, Timur and his companion are nowhere in sight.

"Sir, is everything alright?" the police officer asks.

"I was accosted just now by two men I believe Chief Nurmanbetov wants to question in connection with the drowning of Aldiyar Rymov and Darkhan Baizhanov last month," Ayan says with urgency.

After getting a general description of the two men from Ayan, the officer phones for backup and asks Ayan to wait in his parked truck with the doors locked, while the police search for the suspects. Ayan would need to identify them should they be found and caught.

The streets are quite deserted by that time. Alone in the truck, the dark quietude gives Ayan the jitters. The lights are still on from some second-floor windows of Noble House facing the street where he's parked. Perhaps one of the lit windows is Grace's, and she is still up. He'll have a lot to tell her when he sees her in the morning. He looks at his watch. 8:57 p.m.

Every minute Ayan waits in his truck before the police cruiser returns seems like an eternity. And it is an excruciating eternity, as he tries to process what he has just learned from the blond fellow about Victor's connection to Voz Island. Victor's ambition for the future floats back to mind: *Short term, I plan to stay on as an aspirant in microbiology. Long term, I want to be one of the best in my field. Make a mark as a scientist and make a difference. Maybe even discover something that will be a contribution to my country and to science.*

Had he indeed discovered something to contribute to his country and to science, something so big these men are after it now? Was researching biological weapons of mass destruction his idea of making a difference?

Twenty-five minutes later, the police car pulls up. "No luck," the patrol officer says to Ayan. "They have probably driven away. I will record this incident and talk to the Chief tomorrow." He takes down Ayan's personal information for the record.

Thanking him, Ayan drives back to the house on March 8th Street. Uncle Kairat is home, as is his daughter Nurgul. Exchanging a brief greeting with them, he quickly disappears into his room, flustered by his ordeal. Who are these men who know Victor had worked on Voz Island when Victor had kept that information from him, his most trusted friend? And what are they looking for that Victor had presumably buried on the island before it was shut down? Whatever it is, they think Victor had told him its hiding place, and there is no convincing them otherwise. Ayan feels threatened and agitated, even desperate.

Ayan calls Chief Nurmanbetov on his private line even though it is late. He gets the Chief on the phone and tells him he has just been confronted by two men outside Alikhan's House. He tells the Chief that he recognizes one of them, a Kazakh by the name of Timur, to be one of the men Darkhan Rymov and Aldiyar Baizhanov took to Voz Island, and that the other one, a Russian by the look of him, could well be the second man who hired them. Chief Nurmanbetov is very excited about the news. He is adamant about finding Aldiyar's and Darkhan's killers. But why did those two men accost Ayan that night as he was walking to his car, he wants to know. Ayan says the reason is not related to the deaths of Aldiyar and Darkhan, but that those two men are looking for his friend from Moscow State University, Victor Luganov, with whom he long ago lost contact. Apparently they have some serious issue with Victor and know he and Ayan were close friends at the University. Ayan decides not to tell the police chief the true reason the two men confronted him—whatever those two are looking for on Voz Island must be of much graver consequence than what a small-town police department can handle.

Chief Nurmanbetov reiterates his intention to get those two men to the police station for interrogation in connection with the deaths of Darkhan and Aldiyar. Not knowing about the real reason for the two men to confront Ayan that night, the Chief must not realize the grave danger to Ayan. He asks Ayan to immediately alert him should he sense they are following him or about to confront him again. Meanwhile, Ayan is to be careful with his own safety, he warns, and not to go to deserted places, especially at night.

26

THE NOTE

May 15, 2007

"**S**o let's get this straight. According to Timur and the blond guy I met in Astana and Almaty who accosted you last night, Victor was working on Voz Island, presumably researching biological weapons. Timur and the blond guy are looking for something they think Victor had hidden on the island." Grace summarizes the case leading up to Ayan's nerve-racking ordeal the previous night as she sits in the truck with Ayan on their way to Kokaral Dam, two hundred kilometers from Aralsk.

Ayan has relayed to Grace the entire incident of the previous night, including his reporting the case to the local police chief who is determined to get these men in for questioning. He has also told her about his meeting with Victor at the bar in Moscow in 1991, at which Victor passed him the note sandwiched between two money bills. Ayan has told her the content of the note, to the best of his recollection, the original note being still in his cigar box back in his apartment in Kyzylorda.

"Let's call the blond guy Nikolai, assuming he was the one Darkhan heard Timur call by that name on the phone, and let's assume he was also the one going to the island with Timur," Grace says. "Timur and Nikolai hired Aldiyar and Darkhan to take them out to the island to hunt for something Victor had hidden there, most likely some biological weapon Victor had a part in developing," Grace conjectures.

"If a biological weapon is what they are looking for, it has to be something they believe has survived. I have a hunch it's anthrax because the spores can be revitalized even after hundreds of years," Ayan deduces.

Grace shifts in the passenger seat to face him, baffled yet excited. "Yes, anthrax! And even though the United States had decontaminated all the known anthrax burial sites on the island, those guys think there could still be some Victor had developed and buried on the island yet undetected, and they are after it."

"Exactly. But why are these guys so keen on finding Victor's secret, and how did they find out about Victor and his work there in the first place?" Ayan wonders aloud.

"To answer your second question, I think someone who worked on the island and knew Victor must have told them about him," Grace reasons. "Victor himself wouldn't tell anyone about his work on Voz Island. He hadn't even told you!"

"When I learned about his work on Voz Island from Nikolai last night, I felt so hurt and betrayed. Reflecting back on how evasive Victor was when I brought up his work or asked where he had lived all those years he was away, I think what Nikolai said about Victor was probably true. I'm very disappointed in Victor. I don't think I can ever forgive him for choosing to turn his mind to such senseless, destructive work that could cause deaths of terrible proportions. I thought I knew him to be better than that, but apparently not. I am sorry I had ever called him a good friend." Ayan's face is flushed.

"But wait," Grace reasons. "You shouldn't judge Victor until you have proof that he did what Nikolai implied he did."

"I suppose you're right. I shouldn't condemn him before I know the truth." Ayan calms down a bit. "You've answered my second question, but what about the first: Why are those men so interested in finding the biological weapon Victor might have developed?"

"The answer to that is more worrisome." Grace swallows and continues, "Assuming Victor did develop some new bacterium for use as a weapon of biological warfare, I think those guys are interested in it because they or whoever sent them may want to use it for their own evil purposes."

After that far-from-comforting brainstorming session, Grace is quiet for a while, deep in thought as the truck bumps along a dirt road before joining up with the paved road that would take them to Kokaral Dam. After a good ten minutes, she speaks her mind slowly. "Ayan, I've been thinking about that secret note Victor gave you in the Moscow bar."

"What about it?"

"A photo was presumably taken by the KGB guy of Victor handing you some money with a note tucked between the bank notes."

"Well, actually I wasn't sure Andrei was a KGB guy, but I would assume he was, considering he was keeping a close eye on Victor the whole time we were there."

"It doesn't matter. We'll just assume he took the picture. If the Soviet authorities had seen the blown-up segment of it soon after that photo was taken, they would have been after you in no time. They would have wrung the secret out of you at all costs. Think you could still come home to your Aral Sea if the Soviet government suspected you of holding secrets affecting national security? Going back to Victor, he probably had something to hide from the government at the time, otherwise why would they assign Andrei to watch every step he took? But the fact that the Soviets were not interested in you in 1991 meant they were not aware Victor passed anything to you other than money. In other words, that photo was not blown up till possibly sixteen years later, but by whom? We don't know."

Grace looks out to the barren expanse of steppe country. After a while, she says, "What could be the hidden meaning in Victor's note? He was trying to tell you something. Can you run that by me again?"

"I don't remember the exact words, but more or less it said, 'Go back to visit the girl across the street from your best friend before leaving Moscow and give her a good feel.' What does it mean? I'll leave it to your imagination!" Ayan snickers.

"Who do you think your best friend might be?"

"My first thought was Victor himself! You know, soon after I read the note that night, I thought the girl across the street from my best friend was Valeria, because he lived across the street from her in the last year of his aspiranture, assuming he meant my best friend to be himself."

"Did you bring that matter up with Valeria? You said you two still talked on the phone sometimes."

"I didn't mention the note of course, but I did ask her if Victor had been in touch with her since he left Moscow. All I got was 'No,' with a bit of uneasiness from her that I should ask such a question."

"We should leave Valeria out," Grace says. "I don't think Victor meant himself as your best friend, at least in the note. There was obviously more to it than what it literally said."

"I realized the note was coded from the start. I just couldn't figure out what Victor meant. Who did Victor mean to be my best friend?"

Grace repeats the content of the note as Ayan remembers it, meticulously chewing every bit of the message. "Quite a riddle! There are three questions to ponder. Since you don't know who Victor meant to be your best friend, let's start with the place as the first question. He didn't specify a place to go back to, but just to go 'back,' assuming you would know. It must be somewhere you and Victor have been before, somewhere the two of you hung out. Question two, your best friend at that place. Finally, a female neighbor across the street. You must be very familiar with this female neighbor, as was

Victor probably, since you were supposed to go to her and touch her before you left Moscow. You have to solve all three questions before you can crack the riddle."

"Our common hangout, as you call it, could be Gorky Park where we jogged, or one of the bars in Sverdlov Square where we went for drinks. But that night we were already in one of our regular spots, the Russian Bear. I really don't know what he had in mind." Ayan shrugs, then says slowly as an afterthought, "There were also the Moscow subway stations. Those were also places we frequented."

"The Moscow subway stations would be a good place to hide a secret. Now we go to question two. Your best friend. Assuming the place was a metro station in Moscow, you need a best friend there. Was there a certain beggar sitting in a particular corner of a station you guys always gave change to? Or a favorite conductor selling train tickets?" Grace is obviously enjoying trying to fit different pieces to the puzzle, looking for prompts to break the riddle.

"Even if there was someone I could call a good friend in a metro station—leave out the best friend—how could I possibly find the girl? People come and go every day! This is silly." Ayan is beginning to show exasperation.

"Forget the note. I'm just curious how Nikolai even got a hold of the photo of you at the bar. Andrei the KGB guy could have given a copy to Nikolai," Grace says, "but under what circumstance I have no clue. Maybe Nikolai worked for the KGB at the time? Then it wouldn't be hard for him to get a copy of that photo. But I still think the picture was not magnified until recently."

They soon came to the bank of the Syr Darya. For the first time, Grace sets eyes on the once lifeblood of the Aral Sea. How grand, imposing, nurturing, and calm she looks, rippling gently in her downstream flow, oblivious to the man-made obstacles awaiting her downstream that would prevent her from feeding her starving sea, and instead divert her waters to the chemical-infested cotton fields.

About eighty kilometers south of Aralsk, they come to a detour with a signpost pointing to Lake Kambash and its beach. They decide they need a break.

There isn't much at Lake Kambash, just water, sky, sand, and a few shacks. Dinara has prepared some sandwiches for them, knowing they are going to the Kokaral Dam, a good three hours' drive from Aralsk. They sit on the sand under the shade of a run-down shed, eating egg sandwiches washed down with bottled water. As they rest, a Caucasian man runs past on the beach with a handsome, gaunt German Shepherd.

"You like dogs?" Grace asks Ayan casually.

"Yeah, I do, but I can't keep a dog in my apartment in Kyzylorda."

"I love dogs too." Grace smiles. "Glen had a Golden Retriever in Chicago years before we were married. He became my dog too afterwards. Vernon died two years ago. Glen was totally devastated, and I was heartbroken too."

"I am sorry for your loss. Dogs truly are man's best friends," Ayan remarks, his eyes following the man and his dog as they fade into the distance.

There is silence after that as they both look out to Lake Kambash, munching on their sandwiches. After a few good, long minutes, Grace abruptly looks over with widened eyes at Ayan sitting on the sand beside her, as though a lightbulb has just popped to brightness in her head.

"I think I've got it! I've got it, Ayan!" she says gripping his right forearm and looking at him with overwhelming excitement.

"Got what?"

"The riddle! In the note! Victor's note!"

"What do you mean?" Ayan looks at Grace in total astonishment.

"Your best friend. He wasn't talking about a person. He was referring to man's best friend, a dog!"

"What dog?" Ayan asks. "Neither of us had a dog in Moscow."

"Not a real dog! The bronze dog in the subway station in

Moscow! I saw it in the photo of Victor you had in your wallet the other night, remember?"

"Ploschad Revolyutsii Station!" Ayan claps his hands together. "You are a genius and a natural detective! I remember now. That night at the bar, Victor and I talked about our student days, including our patrol of the metro stations late at night. And we brought up Ploschad Revolyutsii Station and the statue of the dog!"

"Wait, the riddle doesn't stop there. Victor's note says to go see the girl across the street from your best friend. Who could that be?" Grace knits her brows.

"That must be Old Maid!" Now it's Ayan's turn to shout with excitement. "There was a statue of a female soldier near the guard and the dog! Victor called her Old Maid because hardly anyone noticed her, all the attention was on the dog! In fact, that night at the bar, Victor brought up Old Maid too!" Ayan scores that time. "What do you think Victor wanted me to do?"

"Go see Old Maid and feel her up!" Grace laughs with the ecstasy of sudden revelation. "You have to go to that subway station and feel her up!" she repeats.

"Ploschad Revolyutsii Station!" Ayan calls out. "Revolution Square Station!"

"Yes, go to Revolution Square Station in Moscow, not to the statue of the dog but the one of the female soldier across from it, and look for something presumably on her person," Grace concludes.

"But you think whatever he wanted me to find sixteen years ago is still there? Wouldn't someone have taken it? And even if I do find it, you think it'd still be relevant today?"

"After what those men said to you last night, do you think Victor's message, whatever it is, is not relevant today?" Grace rebuts in triumph. Tingling all over with eagerness, she continues breathlessly, "Ayan, we will not go to Kokaral Dam today. We'll drive to Kyzylorda and you will take the next flight out to Moscow. Go to Revolution Square Station. Rub the dog's nose for all I care, but find whatever

Victor wanted you to find sixteen years ago on the statue of the woman soldier. After your ordeal last night, I think Victor's message is very much alive, and I bet it's waiting for you in Moscow." Grace blurts out her plan for Ayan in an excited volley of words. Then she immediately gets up from her sitting position on the beach.

"I should get some cash and stop by my apartment in Kyzylorda on the way to the airport to pack an overnight bag," Ayan says, standing up too.

"No, you should go directly to the airport and get on the first available flight to Moscow. Just forget overnight necessities for once. I'll give you some cash for the journey." Grace is insistent. "So far, we haven't seen any suspicious-looking car behind us. I bet they are leaving you alone while you are taking me around on day trips as your guest. Still, to be safe, we should not go back to your apartment in Kyzylorda. We can't take a chance of them following you to the airport. They must not tail you to Moscow."

27

PLOSCHAD REVOLYUTSII

May 15-16, 2007, Moscow, Russia

There is no direct flight from Kyzylorda to Moscow. Ayan will have to fly east to Almaty, then from there west to Moscow. Without hesitation he buys a plane ticket for the 2:30 p.m. flight from Kyzylorda scheduled to arrive in Almaty at 5 p.m., with a connecting flight at 6:20 p.m. from there to Moscow. Ayan barely makes it to the gate before the doors close for the first segment of his journey. As much as Grace wants to go with him, on her American passport and without a visa to Russia, she cannot go to Moscow but will wait for him in Kyzylorda at a hotel near the airport.

That evening, Ayan's plane from Almaty touches down in Moscow at 9:12 p.m. local time. The two-hour time difference between Almaty and Moscow is in Ayan's favor. He immediately takes a taxi to Ploschad Revolyutsii, arriving at the underground station about 10:10 p.m. Ayan has almost three hours before the metro closes at 1 a.m. to find what Victor had hidden for him, provided it is still there.

Ploschad Revolyutsii Station, situated below the Square of the same name in the heart of Moscow, remains as haunting and mysterious as Ayan remembers, that somber and sinister atmosphere, the same dim passageways, the same creepy bronze statues.

Ayan's heart beats faster at the sight of his favorite pair. The guard in a squatting position but erect in posture, his right hand holding on to his rifle, left arm around his dog, whose shiny nose is luminous as ever, polished to a high gleam by commuters rubbing it for luck. Intuitively, Ayan raises a hand to rub its nose, more out of affection for an old friend than any belief in superstition. He follows the dog's gaze to the other side of the arch entrance, where his eyes come to rest on the bronze casting of a young female sailor. Stealthily, as if afraid to be seen lingering on the platform even though he is quite confident he has left his stalkers back in Aralsk, Ayan walks across to Old Maid.

She sits on a bronze block, her head held high, with rifle in hand, her straight hair touching the nape of her neck. She is wearing a female sailor's skirt uniform that reaches down to her mid-calf boots. Among the troupe of bronze actors, each representing an occupation that contributed to the making of the USSR, she is a sailor fighting for the cause of the Revolution. Ayan notices that her right boot is stepping on a nautical chart of some sort. Only the right side of her back is exposed, the left side being too close to the wall for him to see or touch. He looks left and right of him, up and down the platform which, though not crowded, still has moderate traffic at 10:20 p.m. Even though most commuters only seem interested in getting on a train at that late hour, Ayan decides to wait, lest people notice him feeling up the bronze statue of a woman and wonder at his mental state or, worse, gawk at his perversion. His return flight back to Almaty is scheduled for 7:35 the next morning, the earliest he could get. He has time. He paces the platform for a good long while, until it is relatively vacant and quiet, with only occasional commuters trickling in and out. His watch registers 11:20 p.m. Time to carry out his plan to find whatever he has come for.

Taking a deep breath, he walks up to the statue of Old Maid. He crouches down to run his hand over every centimeter of the woman's back and dress from her waist down to the trapezoidal block on which she sits. He feels every fold of her skirt, every nook and cranny where her rear touches the seat. He feels the entire surface of the block she sits on. All is solid. Not a hairline crack anywhere. Frustrated, he lets his hand roam down the back of her thigh, the creases of her skirt covering her thigh. Nothing. There's got to be something. He makes another go at it, retracing the statue, feeling centimeter by centimeter. The triumph of breaking the code with Grace that morning, followed by the excitement of catching the flights, the gratification of making it to Ploschad Revolyutsii in good time all dwindle down to this anti-climax of not finding whatever he has been so hopeful to find. The sense of defeat is excruciating. All that trouble getting to Moscow in the span of twelve hours for nothing, just a waste of Ayan's time and Grace's money, for she has insisted on financing his trip and would not hear otherwise from him. With the hope of finding Victor's secret message for him crushed, Ayan sits down on a bench to ponder what to do next.

The time is 12:08 a.m. It's now May 16. Not knowing what he is looking for adds to his frustration. Has he missed something? Or could he and Grace be barking up the wrong tree in the first place? Time is running out. It's now or never. He will do one last check before leaving the station. Then forever will he hold his peace. His eyes scan the statue from head to boot. He gives her back one last rub from neck to posterior, then the block on which she sits, its flat surface and its one side that is exposed and facing out. All is smooth, no crack, no secret compartment to hold a message or anything else. There is not the slightest fissure where the woman's buttocks meet her seat even though the two are separate pieces of bronze. The only thin gap visible to Ayan is where the block touches the arched wall at the back of the statue. That is the only fissure, easily undetectable to the human eye, as if anything could have been hidden in it. In a last-ditch attempt, thinking it likely fruitless yet pushed as though by an inner will, Ayan takes out his penknife and slides the blade down into the tiny gap. As Ayan inserts the blade, he feels something move. Carefully, Ayan maneuvers the knife handle to position the blade beneath the object, then gently slides it up to the top of the block. When the blade emerges, it brings with it what looks like a small, squarish, silver tape-wrapped envelope, flat enough to fit into the tiny cleft between block and wall.

Breathless, with no time for thoughts, Ayan picks up the little silvery envelope, pockets it and his penknife into the inner breast pocket of his windbreaker, and checks that no one has witnessed his discovery before turning to go. As he passes the dog and guard, he rubs the dog's nose endearingly one more time, as if to say, "Thank you."

In minutes he is out on the street, which is still bustling with traffic even though it is after midnight. He takes in deep breaths of the cool evening air. He would love a beer at one of the pubs, but not tonight. He makes his way to a street corner and hails a city taxi to take him to Hotel Voskhod near Sheremetyevo Airport. In the taxi, he calls Grace from his mobile phone to tell her he has "found something near where the lady sits" but doesn't know yet what it is. Grace is delirious with excitement, and Ayan can hear her squealing on the other end of the line. Ayan promises to call her again after he gets to the hotel.

Ayan has several hours to rest before his flight to Almaty at 7:35 a.m. the next morning, that is if sleep can come to him. But first, as soon as he checks into his room, he takes out the little packet and sets it on the nightstand by his bed gently, as though it was a sacred relic. Then he calls Grace, who picks up on the first ring.

"Well? What is it?"

"It's a small flat envelope, about three-inch square, wrapped in some sort of waterproof silver tape. I haven't opened it yet. I wanted to wait until you were on the phone."

With trembling hands, he carefully removes the tape. He can hear Grace's tense breathing on the phone. He then picks up the little envelope, tipping its contents out gently onto his palm.

"It's a 35-millimeter black-and-white film negative sealed in a miniature zipper baggy, like the ones attached to new sweaters containing spare buttons," he relays to Grace. "Let me see if I can make out what the negative is."

"Yes, what is it?" More audible breathing on Grace's end.

With great caution, almost reverence, Ayan takes the negative between his thumb and index finger and holds it daintily to the light.

"It's a big room with two rows of seats, facing what looks like part of a huge TV screen."

"You see people?" Grace prompts.

"Yes, a few sitting in the seats."

"Maybe it's an art museum."

"There may be more seats, but the negative shows only part of the two front rows, and part of the big painting in front of them if it's really an art museum."

"It could also be a theater with a big screen, but partially cut off. You have to get it developed, Ayan."

"I am flying out of Moscow in the morning, arriving in Almaty shortly after 3 p.m. Then there is no flight to Kyzylorda until Thursday afternoon, so I'll have almost a whole day in Almaty to get the negative developed."

"Yes, get it developed in Almaty. The developed photo should give us a better idea what Victor wanted to tell you," Grace says. "I'll meet you at Kyzylorda Airport on Thursday. And good night, Ayan. It's been a most long and eventful day and night. You did amazing!"

28

COMMEMORATING LENIN'S REQUEST

May 17, 2007, 3:30 p.m., The road from Kyzylorda to Aralsk

"**T**his is closer to home than I thought!" Grace exclaims, staring at the photo as Ayan drives his father's truck from Kyzylorda back to Aralsk after she has met up with him at the airport. He has refrained from showing Grace the developed photo until they are safely in the truck. "Notice the photo is of only a part of the mural, about a third of the entire piece, meaning Victor wants you to focus only on this section," Grace says, studying the black-and-white photo of the famous mural in the Aralsk train station. Victor had photographed just the segment dominated by the profile of Lenin's head, above some fishermen at sea.

"I still don't get it. I've seen this mural hundreds of times. What's so significant about this part of it?" Ayan wonders.

"Why would Victor intentionally take a shot of Lenin's head above the fishermen?" Grace ponders. "Wonder if there's some underlying meaning to these subjects in the mural, implying something he wanted to convey to you."

"Another coded message?" Ayan raises his brows with a hint of cynicism.

"Or," Graces says slowly, "since Victor had a message for you, and since he only showed you this segment of the mural, he could be literally hiding the message either inside this part of the mural or somewhere close to it." Grace pauses in thought. "It would be very hard to hide anything inside the mural without damaging the artwork. Besides, he wouldn't have the time or opportunity to do so. If he went this route, the logical thing for him to do would be to hide the message in whatever physical format somewhere in that segment of the wall displayed in the photo."

"That means behind the chair guard or the wood paneling below that segment of the mosaic," Ayan concludes.

"Good thinking! Those areas would be easiest to pry open to hide something," Grace says. "Now the question is, how are we going to break down the wall below that segment of the mural without anyone stopping us? The station manager, the office staff, the cleaning crew, they're not going to just let you knock down part of a wall without some sort of explanation. You'll have your Chief Nurmanbetov on you in no time!"

"How indeed? It's an impossible mission!" Ayan bites his lips as his truck speeds on to Aralsk.

—

May 17, 2007, 9:00 p.m., The Train Station, Aralsk

Ayan parks his truck at the back of the Aralsk train station. He dares not go back to the house on March 8th Street. Five minutes later, a van pulls up beside them. Immediately Ayan gets into the van while Grace stays in the parked truck.

"Thank you, Uncle Kairat. I'll explain everything to you later. Take a look at this photo while I change into these overalls."

Kairat looks at the picture. "You say you want to remove the paneling to get to something hidden behind it?"

"Yes. I don't know what I'm looking for, but I'll know it when I see it," Ayan says, as he removes his shirt and pants to don the white workman's overalls.

Kairat drives his van around the corner to the left side of the station and parks at the curb. The two promptly alight and haul out a collapsible aluminum ladder, a folded floor cloth, and a huge toolbox from the back of the van. They walk to the main entrance of the station and enter, Ayan carrying the ladder, Kairat the toolbox and cloth. There are only a handful of people sitting on the metal link chairs in the waiting room. Without hesitation, as if with full authorization from the train station management, Ayan and Kairat approach the mosaic on the wall. They lay the large cloth at the foot of the wall, preparing their work area. Taking out a crowbar, Kairat proceeds to pry loose the long horizontal piece of the wooden chair guard that extends half the length of the wall. Ayan helps him remove the loosened chair guard, exposing the brick wall behind. Then, one by one, they pry the vertical panels from the wall with the crowbar, starting from the right and working toward the center. They work around a big radiator, careful not to damage any piece of paneling. To their surprise and relief, the panels come off easily. They lay each piece of wood on the floor, then continue on to the next. All the while, Lenin watches them with a constant side-glance from the mosaic's upper right.

The people in the waiting room pay little attention to the two construction workers who are keeping the noise level of their work to a minimum, as though afraid to disturb the dull, cold tranquility of that space. Still, the disruption eventually attracts the attention of the night manager, who enters the waiting room to see what the commotion is all about. A distinctly audible conversation in Kazakh ensues, the loudest coming from the older workman who looks annoyed with the interruption to his work, while the night manager, thirtyish, perhaps fairly new to his position, looking somewhat insecure and unsettled, speaks to the two workmen with quiet and controlled courtesy. The younger workman produces a work order, with the company name "Kairat Building Repair" at the top.

"We got orders to come at night when there are fewer people at the station," the younger fellow explains. "Water leakage in the wall, very dangerous to the electrical wiring. May cause a serious fire. That's why your management called us earlier today to come fix the problem this evening."

The night manager takes the work order, studies it for a good minute, then peeks at the wall behind the removed panels. He presses a hand against it as if to test for moisture, while the older workman stands close by, checking his watch, then rolling his eyes, puffing with impatience.

The manager then fumbles in his pocket and fishes out his mobile phone. "I'll just give my superior a call about this, and I'll get out of your way," he says politely.

The workmen stand in silence, the older one with an air of impatience, the younger wearing a serious and tense expression on his face, as all three men wait for the manager's call to be picked up. The waiting is eternal until after a full minute the manager gives up and turns off his phone.

"Well, I guess it's after hours and nobody happens to be on call. I'll just leave you to your work," the manager says. "Sorry for the interruption. I wish management had alerted me about your coming tonight." He then exits the waiting room.

Ayan and Kairat waste no time in removing the panels till they reach the one right below the uniformed emissary with outstretched arms in the mural. About ten panels have been removed. The job so far has taken an hour and twenty minutes, including the interruption from the night manager. Ayan proceeds to touch the brick wall behind the removed panels, from right to left, top to bottom, feeling it carefully, meticulously, bit by bit, brick by brick, as though assessing the construction of the wall. The job is easy compared to what he had to do at

Moscow's Ploschad Revolyutsii Station. He doesn't have to go far—his hand stops directly below Lenin's profile. Ayan notices a fair amount of grouting missing from between two stacked bricks. Inserting the blade of his indispensable pocketknife into the gap between the two bricks, he is able to push out a thin, dark blue plastic bag, about four-inch square, tightly closed with silver duct tape.

As quickly as they can, Kairat and Ayan hammer the panels back in place. Next, they reinstall the chair guard. They gather their tools into the toolbox, wrap the debris from their work in the floor cloth, pick up the ladder, which is mainly for show, and are out of the station by 11:20 p.m.

—

Kairat drops Ayan off at his truck parked at the back of the train station, where an overly anxious Grace is waiting. Ayan thanks Uncle Kairat profusely, saying he has saved the day, and promises he will explain the reason for the night's shenanigans as soon as he has a chance. As Kairat drives away, Grace notices by the light of the streetlamp the words painted on the side of his van: Kairat Building Repair.

"The van makes you look like real professionals," observes Grace, while holding in her anxious question about the evening's outcome.

"Yes, before he retired, my uncle drove that van around Aralsk to do building and home repair. This was after the canning factory closed down. He had been a construction worker in his hometown before he came to Aralsk. Good thing he has kept the van and all the tools and the ladder, and even his old company notepad. You never know when these things will come in handy," Ayan laughs.

Then comes Grace's burning question, "How was it?"

"You really want to know?" Ayan teases. Unzipping the top of his overalls, he fishes out the small dark plastic bag from an inside pocket and hands it to Grace.

"Whatever is inside feels thin and hard, like a floppy disk," Grace says, slipping it into the interior pocket of her padded jacket. "The only problem is my laptop doesn't have a floppy disk drive."

"Mine does, but it's at the house on March 8th. We'll ask Alikhan. He probably has an older computer, which should have a floppy disk drive," Ayan says.

"You were smart to drive directly to the train station and ask your uncle to meet you there. But more than likely, those crooks may be staked out near Noble House even as we speak, waiting for you to show up. They must wonder about your absence," Grace conjectures.

"And yours," Ayan smiles. "In case they are waiting for me outside Noble House, let me call Alikhan and ask him to turn the front porch light on and wait outside the door for our truck."

Ten minutes later, Ayan parks the truck at the curb in front of Noble House where Alikhan is waiting under the porch light. As they enter the house, Alikhan gawks at Ayan in his painter's overalls.

"Long story," Ayan says with a chuckle. "I'll explain another day."

They enter the dining room. The time is ten minutes before midnight. Ayan asks Alikhan to close the curtains at the bow window. Dinara soon brings in hot tea, cake, and dried fruit, which they welcome. Grace takes out the blue plastic bag and opens it. Her guess is correct: it contains a blue three-and-a-half inch floppy disk.

As predicted, Alikhan's grand-daddy computer has a floppy disk drive. They ask to borrow it, and Alikhan readily brings it into the dining room, then leaves them alone to tend to their business. Grace looks breathless as she watches Ayan insert the diskette. She and Ayan are on the verge of finally unraveling Victor's secret that had been buried for sixteen years.

Together Grace and Ayan scan its contents. It consists of two files. The first one is entitled *QA90*, the second entitled *Letter to my friend,* as Ayan translates from Russian. The file *QA90* contains multiple pages of what appear to be molecular formulas and chemical structures, accompanied by charts and tables. The *Letter to my friend* written in Russian is presumably from Victor to Ayan though no name is specified. Ayan decides to stay up in the dining room of Noble House to translate Victor's letter into English for Grace.

Meanwhile, Grace returns to her room to call Glen, who is on his business trip in Baku. Four days have elapsed since Nikolai and Timur's confrontation with Ayan outside Noble House, although it seems an eternity considering all that has happened in that time. Ever since boarding the plane out of Almaty, Grace has been keeping her promise to Glen, calling him every night before going to bed with an update on her trip. She would never keep anything from him, even if it would make him worry for her personal safety.

"You should fly back to Almaty tomorrow, Grace," Glen says after Grace has relayed to him the events of the day, ending with the success of the scheme Ayan and his uncle pulled at the Aralsk train station. "Something is happening in Aralsk. You've only been there for a few days, and look how much has already happened. Stalkers, murderers, secret messages hidden away for sixteen years! Sounds great for a movie, but not in real life when my wife is personally involved. Too bad I have these meetings in Baku right now or I'd come out there to bring you home myself." Glen has never sounded as insistent as he does about her leaving Aralsk the next day.

"I'll go home as soon as I can, Glen."

"Tomorrow," Glen says assertively. Then softening, he adds, "I love you. I don't want anything to happen to you."

"I love you too. I'll try to go home tomorrow. But first let me find out what's in Victor's letter. Ayan is downstairs translating it into English as we speak and I'm dying to know."

A pause. Then Glen says, "It's already 1:30 a.m. Ayan is staying at your guesthouse for the night?"

"I suppose so. He is staying up to translate the letter in the dining room. No knowing how long it will take him to translate it. He knows the owner here well. He will probably stay here for the night."

"They have ample guest rooms?"

"This is a mansion, Glen! It has seen better times. They have many guest rooms. It seems I'm the only guest here at the moment," Grace says. "Besides, it's not safe for Ayan to go back in the dead of night to the house where his uncle and cousin live, after those two fellows threatened him a few nights ago." Moments elapse while Glen remains silent. Then Grace asks, "Why are you so silent? Are you worried, Glen? About him staying for the night here, under the same roof as I?"

"I just miss you very much," Glen finally says.

"Are you jealous of Ayan, Glen?" Grace asks teasingly.

"Of course I'm not! You know I trust you," Glen rebuts, a tad too seriously.

"Yes, you are jealous even though you have no reason to be, but I love you all the more for it."

29

THE LETTER

May 18, 2007, 6 a.m., Aralsk, Kazakhstan

Ayan is waiting for Grace in the dining room when she goes downstairs at six the next morning. She takes the seat across from him at the dining table. Ayan hands her the translated letter.

April 20, 1991
My dear friend,

I hope you are the first person to open this diskette. My heart is full, but I will let its silence speak for me. I will get right down to urgent, practical matters. This letter will also satisfy any curiosity you may have concerning my whereabouts in the past nine years since we last parted in Moscow in 1982.

At the end of my aspiranture, at the invitation of a classified government institute for the research and advancement of biological weapons as agents for national defense, I left in the autumn of 1982 for Voz Island in the Aral Sea to join the research team there, at a test site known to insiders as Aralsk 7, codenamed

A-7. *I was honored to be asked to take up that position, fulfilling my aspiration to serve my country and the Union well. One of the hardest things for me at the time was to keep the location of my work from you, knowing how you love your homeland and the Aral Sea. But I could not tell you that I was going to work in Kazakhstan because of the clandestine nature of the work on Voz Island. The research there was connected to national security at the highest levels.*

At first, I was happy living and working on the island alongside so many distinguished scientists, whose high caliber in their fields had earned my deepest respect. The town, Kantubek, had everything I needed to live comfortably. Families of scientists lived there too. We were well taken care of. Above all, I considered my work patriotic and meaningful, researching biological weapons as defensive measures should any part of the Union be threatened by a biological weapon attack. I was doing what I did best and making a difference.

I was assigned to a team dealing specifically with anthrax, one of the deadliest diseases we studied there. And I was paid very well for the work I loved to do. However, things were too good to last.

In my second year there, I realized all the research on the island was for an ulterior motive: to produce offensive biological weapons as agents of mass destruction. My patriotic ideal was crushed. I felt trapped. I felt terrible about the work I was doing, but leaving was not an option. My team consisted of three scientists, myself included. I will only identify them by pseudonyms, for their protection should this letter fall into the wrong hands. The most senior team member I call Egor, a Russian bacteriologist who was assigned to Voz Island in 1972 after a year of research work at Sverdlovsk. When I met him in 1982, he was already in his late thirties. I heard from fellow scientists on the island that he had had a very sad history; his wife and baby were killed in a train accident while they were on their way back to the island after visiting his wife's family somewhere near Aralsk. It took him a long time to recover from his great loss. After that, he decided to devote his entire life to biological weapon research to serve his country. He once told me that he had nothing to live for, with no family, except to serve his country well. He was a Russian patriot, his allegiance to the Soviet Union. He was determined to do his part in helping to establish the USSR as the greatest power in the world at whatever cost to human life, with the development of an offensive biological weapon of mass destruction that would bring all other countries to their knees before the Soviet Union.

The other member of our team, whom I will call Anton here, was a young, brilliant, ambitious biologist who completed his aspiranture at Leningrad State University. He joined the team two years after I did, in 1984. Anton would work, in his own words, where there were the brightest prospects for him. To him, a job was a job, even though the nature of the work might not be the most glorious.

Anton and I were assigned to help Egor in his research and development of a deadly strain of Bacillus anthracis, a lethal pathogen genetically modified and designed to be resistant to known anthrax vaccines and to antibiotics used for treatments of those infected.

In the summer of 1988, during the testing period of our strain, when success was in sight, Anton was reassigned to work at the Stepnogorsk biological weapon research site in northeastern Kazakhstan. I remember he was extremely disappointed and frustrated. The reason for his transfer was never made known. Ours was a society where we followed orders without asking questions. Not long after Anton left, the results of tests on numerous primates, horses, and donkeys proved the strain exceeded Egor's expectations in its virulence and capability to withstand vaccines and antibiotic treatments. We had created a monster, code name 5942.

About that time, August 1988, Voz Island received a big shipment of anthrax spores contained in metal drums from Sverdlovsk, not as virulent as 5942, but any strain of anthrax mass produced would be a terrible weapon and threat if turned against other nations in a biological weapon war. Our workers buried these metal drums *in eleven pits somewhere on the island. We heard that the sudden transfer of those pathogens to Voz Island was because of an impending inspection by a United Nations commission to investigate if the research work at Sverdlovsk was breaking the disarmament agreement made at the 1972 United Nations Biological Weapons Convention banning the development, production, and stockpiling of biological weapons as agents of mass destruction. Meanwhile, Voz Island remained safe from the scrutiny of the international community, a secret hideout in the Aral Sea.*

Following the success in developing the deadly anthrax strain 5942, Egor became depressed, partly from physical and mental exhaustion—he had been getting only three or four hours of sleep every night for several years—and partly from a dilemma of conscience. He was torn between his invaluable contribution to the Soviet government and the knowledge that the use of 5942 on human targets would result in mass destruction of human life beyond imagination. With that dilemma biting into his conscience, Egor lost his will to continue with his research work, which was a never-ending process. But if you ask me, I sensed that he had never truly recovered from the loss of his wife and child. I felt very sorry for him and kept him company as much as I could in my spare time, to make sure he wasn't alone.

By December 1988, Egor's mental state was deteriorating, his depression getting worse. He was relieved of his service by the Department of Defense and instructed to return to his home near Moscow to recuperate from what was diagnosed as mental exhaustion. The news came as a shock to me, but I felt it could be for the best for Egor. Perhaps being home among family and friends would help him recover from his depression. But I was also sad to see my brilliant mentor go. When we said goodbye before he boarded a military plane leaving Voz Island, we both knew we would not be seeing each other again. Egor's parting words to me were: "Do what you can, Victor, for humanity."

Since realizing that my work in the research and development of 5942 was not in fact for the defense of the Union but intended

for use as a weapon of aggression, I had struggled with the same
dilemma and remorse for a long time. But instead of letting heavy
guilt drag me down into the abyss of despair, I set my mind to
find reparation for the monster that I had helped create. Only
by developing an antidote for 5942 would I ever be able to sleep
easy again. Day and night, other than taking a few hours of
sleep and short breaks when my body needed it to keep going, I
buried myself in researching an antidote. I had two assistants, but
while they thought I was doing more research into the resistance
of 5942 to vaccines and antibiotics, they had no idea that I was
also researching antibodies to fight it. Throughout 1989, I worked
at it. To cut it short in layman's terms, I came to the conclusion
that antitoxins could be developed to fight 5942 or any strain of
anthrax. If administered on subjects soon after exposure to an
anthrax attack, they can neutralize it before infection takes hold,
or they can be used for treatment in conjunction with antibiotics to
fight and kill the anthrax bacteria. By late 1990, I had developed
an antitoxin that had tested well on primates as a protective and
fighting agent against anthrax bacteria, including 5942.

The file QA90 accompanying this letter has the molecular
formula and chemical structure for the antitoxin I developed.
No one knew about my secret research and development of this
antidote. Egor had informed Moscow of the successful cultivation
of 5942 as the deadliest strain of Bacillus anthracis known to
date soon after our final tests proved that it was working. At
Stepnogorsk, Anton might also have talked about its early stages of
development although he did not stay on Voz Island long enough
to see it fully developed and tested successfully.

You must wonder what happened to the batch of live anthrax
spores 5942 that Egor and I developed. I have buried them in a safe
place, knowing the research center here will soon be shut down.
Moscow has asked me for the burial location of 5942. I have not
disclosed it to the government, nor will I to any government or
person in my lifetime. I know the Soviet government will pressure
me more and more, perhaps try to coerce me in unimaginable

*ways, but the secret of its burial place that only I know will go with
me to my grave. I am determined that the buried 5942 spores Egor
and I cultivated never be found and resurrected for use as weapons
of mass destruction in biological warfare or acts of bioterrorism.
In days to come, I will be watched and every move I make will
most likely be monitored by the KGB, lest 5942 lands in the hands
of a foreign enemy. It is my ultimate intention that those anthrax
spores will remain forever in their grave, and the knowledge of the
burial location will die with me.*

*As for the antidote, I will take the diskette containing this letter
and File QA90 with me to Aralsk on my way to Novosibirsk next
week to see my mother, who is quite ill. You might recall my parents
moved back there from Moscow when my father retired in 1982.
I want to give the diskette to you because you are the only person
I can trust to pass the antidote formula to the right authority, for
protection of the world on the chance the buried 5942 spores get
resurrected. You may think giving the diskette to your father or
uncle when I am in Aralsk would be the simplest way for it to
reach you, but I will not involve your family in any way, for their
safety and protection. Believe it or not, I am beginning to trust in
a Providence, and I will find a way to leave this diskette in a safe
place for you in Aralsk before I board the train to Novosibirsk.*

*In all the years I have been working on Voz Island, I go home
to see my family in Novosibirsk once a year. Each time, I take a
military plane from the island to Aralsk, then a train from Aralsk
to Novosibirsk. I know you spend your summers in Aralsk and
your father's fishing village, but I usually go home in the spring or
autumn, as I need to be back on the island during bacteria testing
time in the summer, and so we have never run into each other in
Aralsk. It is better that way for both of us even though I have often
thought of you and wondered how you are doing now.*

*With the research center on Voz Island closing in the near future,
I should be leaving the island for the last time later this year. Where
I will go after that, I have no idea, but I believe my first stop should
be Moscow. My dear friend, I hope to see you one more time in*

Moscow then, to see you and to pass on to you the information of where to find this diskette.

When you read this letter, we will have parted for the last time. Moscow does not believe in tears, so my friend, be happy the rest of your life, doing what you do best where it counts most.

Ever your faithful friend,
Victor

30

WAITING

May 18, 2007, 7 a.m., Aralsk, Kazakhstan

When Grace comes to the end of Victor's letter, she is lost for words. In silence she mourns Victor. In silence, she pays tribute to the selfless, incorruptible soul that he was.

"He was right here in the Aral region, and I never knew. He had frequented Aralsk so many times, and I never ran into him," Ayan says in a hoarse voice. "Soon after our meeting at the bar in Moscow in 1991, they probably arrested him, tortured him, trying to make him tell where he had hidden the anthrax spores 5942. They must have killed him for not talking." Ayan puts words to Grace's fears as he covers his face with his hand, weeping into it.

"I can only have full respect for him," Grace finally manages to say. "Assuming they had arrested him and killed him for not disclosing the location of the anthrax spores, he died a martyr. He made the ultimate sacrifice for humanity. Ayan, you should have every reason to be proud of him, proud of your friendship. And now, it's up to you to carry out what he wanted you to do with the secret antidote formula, so that . . . " Grace stops in the middle of her sentence, lost for words.

"So that he won't have died in vain," Ayan completes her sentence in a broken voice.

Grace gives an affirmative nod. "Just know that Victor is at peace now. He has earned his forgiveness from the Providence he acknowledged near the end of his letter."

"Thank you, that is a comforting thought," Ayan murmurs. "Besides, as long as we don't know the truth of his fate, there's always hope that he may call some day from out of the blue. It wouldn't be the first time."

—

Dinara enters the dining room with a breakfast tray of fried eggs and toast, fresh sliced melon, and steaming milk tea.

"Let's tackle the present," Grace says, sipping the warm and soothing milk tea. "First, Timur and Nikolai are still lurking around. I think it's safe to say they are involved in the murder of your two friends and in trying to dig up Victor's research. We don't have any direct proof yet that they killed Aldiyar and Darkhan, but circumstantial evidence points that way. Second, they know about Victor and the anthrax he helped develop on Voz Island, although they don't know where he had hidden it on the island, and they are after it."

"Pretty hard to find anything on that island if you're not familiar with its layout and terrain. That must be why they needed scavengers to take them out there and show them around," Ayan surmises.

"Scavengers are of no help to them. That anthrax is probably in some deep recess in the earth's crust close to the labs and research areas, or even the testing fields."

"The earth's crust?" Ayan laughs. "Remember, Victor had to dig and hide all that himself! He couldn't have buried it more than a few meters down."

Grace sobers up. "Okay, not that deep down then. Still, Victor must have hidden it where no one would easily find it. Assuming he is dead, it may never ever be found. Back to the immediate danger, you need to call the police again. They will have to plan a way to grab those two men as suspects in the murders of Aldiyar and Darkhan before those two guys spring out of nowhere at you again."

"You must have watched too many crime movies," Ayan chuckles nervously.

"Ayan, I'm just worried that the next time Timur and Nikolai accost you, they will make you talk, and whether you tell them what they want to know or not, they will kill you, just like they did your friends."

"What you are saying is that anyone they approach regarding the hidden site of the anthrax is already marked for disposal," Ayan says, a cloud of doom hanging over him, like a man awaiting his execution.

"That's what I'm afraid of. The only way out for you is to get them first, before they have a chance to kill you."

"How? With the help of the little police regiment here?" Ayan asks in a cynical voice.

"I have an idea," Grace says. "I believe the police suspect that Aldiyar and Darkhan were killed by the two strangers they took out to Voz Island. We know Timur was one of the two. You saw him at the railway station giving Darkhan the money. We suspect our blond stalker whom we call Nikolai to be the other one. The guy who rented the boat to Aldiyar and Darkhan saw both of them. You just have to show him your picture with Nikolai in the background to know for sure."

"True, Sairan, the boat owner, can identify from the photo if Nikolai was the other one Aldiyar and Darkhan took to the island."

"If Sairan recognizes Nikolai to be the other one, you can ask the police chief to have 'Wanted' posters of both of them circulated all over the Aral region and beyond, based on that photo of Nikolai you have, and a facial composite of Timur from your impression of him!" Grace is all excited.

"I have a film negative of that photo with Nikolai in the background since I took that picture with my film camera. I will just give the negative to the police and they can blow up the face of Nikolai!" Ayan says, as excited as Grace.

"Perfect! Call the police chief immediately about this idea. Then drive to Kulandy to show Sairan the photo. You've got to do whatever you can to get those crooks before they get you. We cannot be sure if manhunt posters will work, but at least you are trying to get them, and not being a passive sitting duck waiting to be shot." Grace pauses and continues, "As a double precaution, I think you should go into hiding for a while until Timur and Nikolai are apprehended. You can't let them confront you again. Aralsk is not a safe place."

"You may be my lifesaver yet, Grace," Ayan says, his tense demeanor somewhat relaxing. "I'll take the telltale photo this afternoon to Kulandy to show Sairan, and stay down there for a while. Good thing I am on sabbatical at the moment. By the way, have you spoken with your husband these few days?"

"Yes, I've been updating him on all the happenings here. Last night I told him how you recovered the diskette Victor left for you in the Aralsk train station. He was so engrossed in the story, like he was listening to an audio thriller, except he doesn't love that his wife is caught in the intrigue." Grace hesitates before continuing. "He is worried about me. In fact, he wants me to go home this minute."

"Maybe you should, Grace. Don't put yourself in danger. Those two fellows mean business. They are not gentlemen from a peaceful nation."

"I want to see this to the end. It's like reading the denouement to a mystery-thriller. Remember you said I was living my story? I think I have finally found my story, and it's going to be a mystery-thriller."

"Forget about your mystery-thriller; this is too dangerous. You really should go home, Grace. Think of Glen, if not yourself."

"He's worried about me, I know. But seriously, I'm more worried about you. I feel like I'd be leaving you in the lurch if I go now."

"Don't worry about me. I'm going to call Chief Nurmanbetov about your excellent idea of the manhunt posters right away." Ayan pauses. "There's another reason for you to go."

"What is that?"

"You have to take the formula for the antidote to the right authorities, or else mass destruction of human life would result if the buried 5942 spores are ever uncovered and used for biological war or bioterrorism."

"I know," Grace says grimly. "We can't risk sending the antidote formula through the internet. Make a copy of it to keep here in a safe place with you, and I will take the diskette back to Glen. He will make sure the formula gets into the right hands."

"The sooner the better, Grace."

31

ARMAGEDDON

May 18, 2007, midmorning, Aralsk, Kazakhstan

Following his brainstorming with Grace that morning, Ayan calls Chief Nurmanbetov to discuss the plan of circulating manhunt posters of the two suspects in the murders of Aldiyar and Darkhan. The police chief is all supportive—any move that may help catch the two murder suspects is worth the effort. As well, Ayan tells the police chief of his intention to drive to Kulandy that afternoon and stay down there until the two murder suspects are apprehended, as he feels unsafe to stay on in Aralsk after they accosted him a few nights ago. He will show Sairan the telltale photo for identification of the blond suspect soon as he reaches Kulandy that evening.

Right after Ayan's call to Chief Nurmanbetov that morning, the police chief drives over to Alikhan's House to pick up the film negative of the photo with Nikolai in the background. Once Sairan can confirm the blond man in Ayan's photo to be one of the two strangers Aldiyar and Darkhan took to Voz Island, Chief Nurmanbetov will have "Wanted" posters of him printed using Ayan's film negative. As well,

Chief Nurmanbetov will send for a police artist to go to Kulandy in a day or so to work with Ayan and Sairan on a facial composite of Timur for a "Wanted" poster of him, since they both have seen Timur on separate occasions from a fair distance.

Grace's initiative that Ayan should try to get those crooks before they get him is underway. The wheel has started to turn.

—

May 18, 2007, noon to midafternoon

Ayan has just dropped Grace off at the train station to take the train to Kyzylorda, from where she will board a flight back to Almaty. While Grace takes the noonday train out of Aralsk, Ayan will drive to Kulandy to Sairan's house.

"This is not goodbye. I'll just say do svidaniya," Grace says to Ayan on the platform, her voice faltering. She then gives him a spontaneous, warm embrace before boarding her noon-time train for Kyzylorda. "Promise you'll be very careful."

"I promise. And yes, Grace, we'll meet again. Thank you for bringing Victor's message where it needs to go."

After trying to hold up a brave face as he waves to Grace through the train window, Ayan heads downstairs to the station's main hall. The station is quite congested that day, and the waiting room is full too. His watch registers 11:47 a.m. as he leaves the train station. He has calculated that it will take about six to seven hours to drive the three hundred kilometers to Kulandy, parts of the way along unpaved gravel roads. Sairan is expecting him to arrive at his home in Kulandy before sundown. If all goes well, he should arrive at Kulandy about 6:30 p.m. He should have daylight in his favor all the way there.

Timur and Nikolai haven't made an appearance since the night they confronted him outside Noble House. Six days have elapsed since then. Ayan has the premonition that his assailants are near, and like vipers lurking in their scrubby, rocky desert hideouts, they may strike any time. He just hopes the manhunt posters once circulated will get them apprehended before they confront him again. Besides, if he stays in hiding in Kulandy, those two suspected killers should not find him. His biggest consolation is that Grace is safe, on her journey home to Almaty, and with her is the invaluable information crucial for the protection of humanity.

Leaving the station, Ayan walks to his parked truck and gets in. He starts his truck without delay and proceeds down the main road toward the town's west gate, which marks the Aralsk town limit.

He drives roughly parallel to the Aral shoreline, although now he cannot see the sea except sporadically at certain areas along the two-lane motor road. The day is overcast but so far there is no portent of rain. Soon he comes to the arched west gate. He drives through the archway and continues on the paved road, westward bound. About five kilometers beyond the gateway, traffic thins, and he notices a blue car behind him. No cause for alarm. However, for the next ten kilometers, the blue car keeps the same distance behind his truck. That tailing makes him nervous. He takes out his mobile phone to dial the police. Then to his utter alarm, he realizes he has lost signal on his mobile phone as his car speeds away from Aralsk on the country road. By then, he is only thirty-some kilometers from Balta. But even if he makes it to Balta without incident, he cannot stop at the village. Implicating his parents and the villagers is the last thing he wants.

He has reached a stretch of endless beach scattered with saxaul bushes where camels straddle here and there on the seaward side of the motor road, with some undulating hills and plateaus on the landward side. From the road, he can see the waters of the Aral beyond the beach. Meanwhile, the blue car is picking up speed, closing in to about thirty car-lengths behind. A herd of five or six camels of varying heights and sizes step out onto the roadway soon after his truck passes, blocking the road for a few good minutes, giving Ayan time to put distance between his truck and the blue car, which has to stop for the animals. Seizing the sudden break, Ayan speeds forward, and before long the blue car is out of his rear mirror view as the road follows the bend of a hill on his right. On his left, he sees the Bay of Beket and the ship graveyard. From his truck, he observes the battered fishing boats on the beach, his father's *Kari qaiyk* still standing though a bit slanted among them. The sight of her boosts his heart especially in that critical moment. She seems to beckon. Ayan knows the blue car will catch up soon. There is no way his truck can outrun it. The camels only buy him a little time—time enough to make that split second decision to swerve his truck to his left, off the paved road into the ship cemetery where *Kari qaiyk* seems to inexplicably call like a beacon of comfort in his moment of dire distress. He maneuvers his truck over the bumpy, sandy steppe until he is about forty meters from the broken vessel, and there he brings the truck to a standstill on the far side of a clump of tall saxaul bushes where it is not easily noticeable from the road. He turns off the engine.

Without a moment's hesitation, he runs toward *Kari qaiyk*. He climbs up to the deck, stepping on any foothold his sneakers can find. Once on the deck, he scampers for a place to hide. A quick glance toward the paved road is unsettling: the blue car is in sight again, having just turned the bend. Not far from him on the deck is the opened hatch to the hollow interior of the hull, its trap door having been ripped off by looters long ago. With no time to ponder his next move, Ayan lowers himself through the opening into the dark void below and lands on his buttocks at the bottom with a heavy, painful thud. At least no bones are broken. He looks up to the square of daylight through the opening. It will be impossible for him to climb back up with the old ladder gone, but at that moment that is the least of his concerns. The putrid smell inside the hull is nauseating, but to Ayan nothing matters as long as he can be saved from his impending assailants. He looks about for a weapon of sorts to defend himself and finds a wooden dowel, thick and about a meter and a half long, leaning against a wall of the hull interior. He picks it up and goes to a far corner of the hull away from the hatch opening, where he crouches down, breathing as silently as he can.

It seems an eternity as Ayan waits in the dark emptiness of the hull, inhaling the foul, stale air and roasting in the enclosed heat. After a while, he wonders if it is only his paranoia causing him to imagine he is being followed. Perhaps the blue car has passed the Bay of Beket and is not tailing him. He is beginning to relax a bit. All of a sudden, he hears faint footsteps of someone walking on the crunchy seashells. The footsteps draw nearer. His heart races, his mind reels. His stalkers must have seen his truck behind the bushes and figured he is hiding inside *Kari qaiyk*, the boat closest to the truck. The footsteps stop. Ayan crouches in the deep, dark corner of the hull, gripping the dowel with his hands, his fingers interlocking as if in prayer. He hears voices, then scratching and scraping sounds on the boat's outside walls. Then footsteps above him. They are on the deck. Ayan can hear them checking the wheelhouse, the fish hold. They finally stop at the opening into the hull. Someone squats over the opening and peeks in, casting a shadow and blocking the daylight. Ayan is thankful he is out of sight, crouched in his far corner below.

"We know you are down there. Come up or we'll set this garbage dump of a boat on fire and smoke you out." The words are in Russian, the voice familiar. It is Nikolai. Should he respond? Those two fellows will kill him regardless. If he remains in the hull, they will smoke him out or burn down *Kari qaiyk* with him inside it. He is between the devil and the deep sea, except that while the devil is close to him, the sea is far away and no longer deep.

Then Nikolai's accomplice Timur speaks, also in Russian. "There are lots of dry bushes around here. Easy to light and start a fire. I'll go cut some branches and bring them back," he pauses, giving Ayan time to think of the worst scenario, then adds, "unless you come up and tell us what we want to know."

Ayan takes a deep breath and shouts his response, thus

acknowledging his presence in the hull, but remains out of sight. "What do you want to know?"

A pause. Then Nikolai gives a direct, no-nonsense answer, "So you are down there. We want to know where Victor Luganov hid his anthrax spores on Voz Island."

"He did not tell me anything about anthrax."

"We know he gave you a note. What did he write?" Nikolai shouts his question down to Ayan.

"If I answer your question, you'll let me go?"

"For sure we'll let you go!" Timur shouts without hesitation. "We'll throw you a rope so you can climb up."

"I'm not coming up. I have a gun," Ayan says in as menacing a tone as he can muster, all the while clutching the wood dowel for dear life.

Some discussion between Timur and Nikolai ensues. Then Nikolai calls down. "I have a better idea. Since you will not come up, and we are not coming down, we will talk where we are."

"Tell us what your scientist friend wrote to you in the note!" Timur shouts.

"There was nothing important. He didn't mention anthrax. He never even told me he was a scientist on Vox Island—you told me that!"

Nikolai takes over again. "When I was initially shown photos of you with Victor Luganov at a bar in Moscow, I believed in your innocence. A harmless teacher in Moscow. But then I saw that magnified segment of the photo of Victor Luganov handing money to you at the bar! You know more than you say you do. That note. What did it say?"

"Nothing important! Nothing about anthrax or Voz Island! Why would anybody take pictures of us at the bar anyway? We did nothing wrong!" Ayan interjects, trying to side-track.

"There were spies everywhere in those days. The Soviet government was mindful of Victor Luganov, watching and recording his every move," Nikolai says. "That photo of you two was taken by someone who is now working with me."

That person must be Andrei, Ayan thinks. "Before I tell you anything, tell me why you want to know where Victor had buried the
anthrax," Ayan says as confidently and steadily as he can, trying to
sound as though he indeed has something invaluable to impart.

"I will tell you why if you will tell me where that anthrax is."

"Fine, but you answer my question first," Ayan insists.

A long moment, then Nikolai answers, "I was a scientist who
worked with Victor Luganov and another scientist on the development of that deadly anthrax strain on Voz."

"You were?" Ayan blurts out, then kicks himself for betraying
his surprise at Nikolai's self-revelation, not that it matters under the
circumstance.

"But I got reassigned to another project and left Voz Island before
I could see the anthrax culture past its development stage. I found out
later that the new strain had finally tested successfully. Don't you see?
I was one of its makers! It was as much *my* intellectual property as
theirs!" His voice rises. So Nikolai is the third scientist, the one Victor
code-named Anton in his letter.

"But why do you want it so badly now?" Ayan asks.

"Why? Because it's mine! It belongs to me, and I'll do whatever I
want with it!" Nikolai shouts. He sounds fiercely angry. "I gave the
Soviet Union my life, my knowledge, my expertise in scientific research,
and since its breakup, what recognition have I received? These last
sixteen years since Independence, what have I gained? Was I ever recognized or appreciated for all my contributions? I am now my own
master. I don't work for anyone anymore, and I will find those anthrax
spores at all costs and take them for my own purpose."

Ayan stays quiet, terrified at the burst of frustration and antago-
nism from Nikolai.

"But never mind. All that is now history. I know those anthrax
spores are buried somewhere on Voz Island. Those two who took all
the laurels for producing them are now out of the picture. That strain

belongs to me. As for you, you will tell me where the spores are buried, and I'll let you live."

"You still haven't told me why you want those spores so much!" Ayan persists.

"This is wasting my time. Just tell me where the spores are if you don't want to die with the boat!"

"I threw away the note long ago. But I still remember vaguely what it said and can tell you, if you think it bears clues to where the anthrax spores are buried. The note contained a riddle. I've never been to Voz Island. Maybe it will make more sense to you than to me, since you had worked there."

"Spit it out then!" Nikolai is losing patience.

"It said, 'When you are on the island, pay the maid across the street from your best friend a visit. Give her a good feel and a playful pinch on her butt.'" Whatever version of the note he gave Grace with a little more variation sounds good enough.

"What kind of nonsense is this?" Nikolai's impatience gives way to wrath. "You know your life is in our hands. Do you take me for a fool?"

"Truly, that's all I recall of the note, and I threw it out long ago."

"Then you are of no more use to me. We're going to kill you now!" Nikolai gives the death sentence.

"I have a gun, and I'll shoot anyone who comes down here," Ayan threatens again, his fingers tingling, still holding on to the wood dowel, wishing it were a magic wand.

Ayan hears murmurings between Nikolai and Timur but cannot make out what they are discussing. His fear is building up as he hears quick steps on the deck, followed by more scraping noises on the exterior of the hull. One of them must have left the boat and gone to fetch something, a ladder or rope, or a weapon to kill him, or dry branches to light a fire.

Armageddon is at hand. No matter what he tells them, truth or otherwise, he is going to die, right there with *Kari qaiyk*. In no uncertain voice he cries out with vehemence, echoing his father's words, "I was born by the Aral Sea. I grew up with the Aral Sea, and I will die with my beloved Aral Sea!"

"I admire your loyalty to the Aral," Nikolai says from above, as though he means his words.

The moment is an eternity to Ayan, as he braces himself for the end, knowing the sort of agonizing death that awaits him. His thoughts wander to his parents and siblings. He will never see them again. The image of Valeria floats into his mind's eye, Valeria in the sunshine with the long golden hair, Valeria whom Victor nicknamed Lady Godiva, Valeria whom he still loves. He will never see her again. In his anguish, he also thinks of Grace, relieved that she has left safely on the train, and with her the diskette. Victor will not have died in vain. He hears more scraping and scratching sounds, louder and closer this time. He smells burning. A few tense moments pass. Then, like flashes of lightning, he sees branches on fire coming down through the hatch opening, lots of them, impossible to put out. Smoke fills the hull. Heat sears his skin. Still crouched in his far corner, he closes his eyes and waits for the inevitable. In his delirious state, he hears a ringing in his ears, his summon bell to eternity.

At least he will die cradled in the bosom of *Kari qaiyk*, as she ferries him to eternity. This then is her last mission in the service of his father, her captain.

32

MEANWHILE...

May 18, 2007, Aralsk, Kazakhstan

After a fond and somewhat emotional farewell to Ayan on the train platform, Grace boards the train. She waves to Ayan from an aisle window. She has specifically asked him not to wait, but to start on his journey to Kulandy as early as he can. She fears for his safety. In the silence of her heart, she says a prayer that somehow the dire danger confronting him will be abated and the two suspects apprehended. She walks along the aisle, looking for her compartment. She finds it and enters. It is much like the one she had on her train journey from Kyzylorda to Aralsk. Putting down her bags, with still fifteen minutes to her train departure, she goes out again to use the washroom. She is careful to keep her mobile phone and the diskette on her at every moment, the phone in a side pocket of her hiking pants, the diskette in the inner zippered pocket of her thin down jacket.

Glancing toward a window along the train corridor, in case Ayan is still there, what she sees strikes a bolt of alarm in her heart. The flaxen-haired fellow Nikolai and a Kazakh guy, presumably Timur, are weaving their way along the platform toward the stairs leading down to the main hall. They must have followed her and Ayan to the train station and know she is leaving Aralsk. They will go after Ayan in no time, perhaps already moving in. She must alert Ayan and the police. With a shaky hand, she takes out her mobile phone to call Ayan, only to find it dead. She had forgotten to charge it the night before. She curses under her breath, but there's nothing she can do about the dead phone now. With not a minute to waste, she walks to the end of her carriage, alights from the train, and makes her way on the platform, zigzagging through the crowd till she gets to the stairs at the far end of the platform, away from where she has just seen Nikolai and Timur. Back in the main hall, she stops a young man and asks to use his phone but to no avail. She then asks a middle-aged woman who also fails to respond. Nobody seems to understand English. Rather than wasting time and taking the risk of Nikolai and his companion seeing her in the hall, Grace exits the station through a side door.

Once outside, she finds herself at a crossroad from which she can see in the distance the giant billboard of the young woman typing at the computer, which first caught her attention on her first ride to Noble House. If her sense of direction is correct, Noble House is not much further down the street from where the billboard is. Her best bet is to run back to Noble House to get the owner, Alikhan, to call Ayan and the police. He's the only person in Aralsk she is sure can speak English and whom she feels she can trust. At that moment, she sees Ayan driving his truck past her but on the opposite side of the street. He has not seen her. It is just as well that he hasn't, under the circumstance. She has expected Nikolai and Timur to be on Ayan's trail again soon after her leaving Aralsk, but she hasn't imagined those two would be after him even before her train leaves the station. The light turns green for pedestrians. As she is about to step off the curb to cross over to the street in the direction of Noble House, she sees an old blue sedan on the opposite side of the street slowing down to a halt at the lights,

Nikolai in the driver seat with Timur beside him. She ducks behind a group of pedestrians and turns away from the crossing to wait for the next change of lights. As soon as the lights turn in its favor, the blue sedan is off after Ayan.

Once the blue car has gone, Grace jaywalks to the other side of the street and breaks into a run. All her training for the Chicago marathon is paying off in a way she has never imagined. She passes the sandy playground with the creaky swings and exhales with relief, confident she is on the right track. She soon sees Noble House at a corner in the distance ahead and reaches it in a record thirteen minutes from the station. Praying Alikhan is at home, she runs through the open front gates and knocks with urgent loudness on the door. Her prayer is answered when Alikhan opens the door.

"Call police! Ayan in danger. Two men—killed Ayan's friends—are following him to Kulandy," Grace erupts, out of breath. "Ask for police chief! He knows Ayan."

Without a question, Alikhan calls the police station, his tone expressing urgency. Chief Nurmanbetov is not in. Grace senses that Alikhan is explaining the gravity of the situation to the police receptionist. The station immediately pages the police chief, coding high emergency, and gets him on the line. Though Grace cannot understand a word of what Alikhan is telling the police chief in Kazakh, she can guess he is getting across the urgency of the situation.

"Police is going on road to Kulandy," Alikhan says to Grace as soon as he hangs up the phone. "Ayan can't go very far. They will find Ayan and the two men soon."

"I hope it isn't too late," Grace says, squeezing her hands.

"Stay here. Police will call me about the situation," Alikhan says.

Grace has no other place to go. Looking down at her watch, she realizes it is only 12:30 p.m. although it seems like hours have elapsed since she spied Nikolai and Timur at the railway station. The train to Kyzylorda having left thirty minutes ago with her belongings on it, including her laptop, is the least of her worries. She is thankful she has

the most important item with her, Victor's diskette, and, secondary to
that, her dead phone, which she can probably charge at Noble House.
It is best that she remains here to await updates, and it is also a safe
place for her while still in Aralsk. All the while, she is anxious for
Ayan's safety.

Alikhan is hospitable and Dinara is attentive as ever. They serve her
a lunch of *plov* and salad, food which she would normally love, but
her appetite escapes her. Still, she takes a bit to be polite. They ask her
to rest in the room she vacated just that morning, although sleep is far
from her mind. She wants to call Glen, but refrains from doing so as
he is in the middle of an important meeting in Baku.

The minutes tick away, turning to hours. She tosses on the bed,
torturing herself with thoughts of Ayan's stalkers catching up to him
on the deserted and secluded highway to Kulandy. They will torture
him to make him disclose the burial place of the deadly anthrax, and
regardless of whether he makes up something to tell them or not, they
are going to kill him. Perhaps they have already killed him. Tears burn
her eyes as she thinks of the hopeless, worst-case scenario.

Sometime in the mid-afternoon, she finally succumbs to her mental
and physical exhaustion and dozes off until a knock at the door calls
her back to her anxiety. She sits up, taking a minute to re-orientate
herself. She walks to the bedroom door, dreading the news that awaits
her on the other side. As expected, Alikhan is there. His lips pinch
tight into a half smile.

"Chief Nurmanbetov phoned. Ayan is okay."

———

"From what the police chief told Alikhan, it was a head-on show-
down between cops and suspects," Grace tells Glen over the phone
that night from Noble House, where she is staying again. She has
already proudly and excitedly relayed to him her own experiences
from that morning up until her desperate marathon run from the

railway station to Noble House, and she has also told him about the content of Victor's letter to Ayan, though skipping the most crucial part about the antidote formula, as if she fears the walls have ears. "Three police cars with six cops went in the direction Ayan and his stalkers were going," she continues, recapping to Glen what Alikhan has heard from Chief Nurmanbetov. "They saw Ayan's truck and a blue car at the ship graveyard and drove toward them. There was smoke coming from the deck of one of the abandoned fishing boats and they saw the two men getting into the blue car. The police fired shots, hitting one of the tires. The men were armed and returned fire, and a shot by the police hit one of them. The other surrendered, knowing he was outnumbered."

"Is Ayan okay?" Glen asks immediately.

Instead of giving a simple answer, Grace continues, "Well, three of the cops went up on the deck of the smoking fishing boat with fire extinguishers and a rope ladder. The fire was coming from the hull. They put that out and found Ayan semi-conscious in a far corner of the hull. He was taken to a hospital in town and is being treated for smoke inhalation."

"Thank goodness. It sounds like he's going to be okay."

"Yes, that's a relief. However, the one the police hit isn't okay. He was shot in the stomach and is in semiserious condition at the hospital."

"The one who was stalking you in Almaty?"

"No, the other one, the Kazakh. My stalker, Nikolai, is in custody at the Aralsk police station now. If nothing else, they will both be charged for the attempted murder of Ayan."

Grace hears a sigh from Glen. He asks, "And when will you be coming home?"

"I'll come home as soon as I've seen Ayan."

"When will that be?"

"Probably the day after tomorrow, assuming I can visit Ayan at the hospital tomorrow."

"I'll be flying home tomorrow evening, so I'll pick you up at the airport when you arrive. I miss you very much, Grace."

"I miss you too. Can't wait to be home." After a slight pause, Grace adds, "I have a very important reason to be back as soon as I can."

"I think I know your reason," Glen says, sounding impish.

Grace laughs. "You are always my reason! I love you, Glen Curran!"

33

VICTOR'S MISSION

May 19, 2007

"Kudos to the Aralsk Police! They got there not a minute too soon!" Grace says to Ayan in his hospital room where he is recovering comfortably. He has just told her all that happened to him from the time he left the train station to his last moments of consciousness in the hull of *Kari qaiyk,* then waking in the safety of a police patrol vehicle.

"I should say kudos to you, Grace. I really thought I might never see you again when we parted at the station! The police did a great job saving my life at the end, no doubt about it. But you were the one who notified them, running back to Noble House to tell Alikhan."

"When I saw those two guys on the train platform, I knew you were in great danger, so I had to act quickly." Grace bubbles with excitement, not without a strong sense of incredulity at how things have turned out, as well as a good measure of self-satisfaction with her own part in the rescue.

"By the way, I have a surprise for you. Nikolai admitted to me that he was the third scientist, the one Victor code-named Anton in his letter."

"Really? Our blond stalker is in fact Anton the scientist from Victor's letter?" Grace would have never guessed.

"Yes, really! The pieces are all falling into place. But now the biggest mission is getting Victor's formula for the antidote to the right authority," Ayan says.

"Haven't we decided I am going to take the formula to Glen, who will take it to the right authority?" Grace asks rhetorically. "I've kept it close and safe the whole time, right here!" She pats her chest pocket. "I'll take it home with me tomorrow."

"Yes, that's your most important mission. The world will thank you for it. As for me, I am also thankful *Kari qaiyk* survived the fire. She was my savior too."

"Even in her broken condition, *Kari qaiyk* served you well. I'm glad she didn't suffer too much extra damage from the fire," Grace says.

"Grace, there is one more important matter I've wanted to tell you ever since I read Victor's letter. In that letter, you remember he talked about the senior scientist, the one he called Egor, and how he lost his wife and baby in a train accident?" Grace nods with full attention. "When I was a student in secondary school in Kyzylorda, I witnessed something terrible at the Aralsk train station. It was late August 1976. A woman holding her baby jumped in front of an approaching train. The train crushed her and her baby, killing them both. The image has haunted my mind ever since. After reading Victor's letter, I believe the woman I saw was Egor's wife. I can never forget talking to her just before her tragic death. She told me her name, Kulyash Krylova, and her baby's name was Dina." Ayan closes his eyes with a pained look as if reliving the tragedy of that day. "I wonder what happened to Egor."

"You witnessed the death of Kulyash and her baby?" Grace asks in a shaky voice. "When I read Victor's letter yesterday morning, the part about Egor touched me in a very special way. I had wanted to talk to you about him but by the time I finished reading Victor's letter, I was so moved by his own story that I forgot to tell you about Egor."

"You knew about him?" Ayan looks at Grace in disbelief.

Grace nods. "Egor's real first name was Vladimir, whose wife was Kulyash and their baby's name was Dina." Ayan stares in astonishment. Grace continues, "I think I mentioned to you I met a girl on my journey here. Her name is Ainur. We were on the same flight, and the same train, and she offered to tell me the sad story of Kulyash after she found out I was going to write a book about the Aral Sea. She heard the story from her mother, who knew Kulyash's family while growing up. She told me Kulyash was the wife of a scientist named Vladimir who worked on Voz Island during Soviet time. Kulyash was suffering from severe depression after the birth of their baby. At the end of her visit home in the summer of 1976, she jumped in front of a moving train with her child Dina at the Aralsk train station."

"No doubt then that the Egor in Victor's letter was Vladimir Krylov," Ayan concludes, still looking baffled by what Grace has just told him.

"Ainur said after many years working on Voz Island after the death of his wife and baby, Vladimir returned to Russia. He hung himself in 1989, exactly thirteen years to the day after his wife and baby daughter died in that train tragedy that you witnessed," Grace fills in the gaps in a broken voice charged with deep sadness.

"What a tragic ending for Vladimir," Ayan says, shaking his head sorrowfully. "And what a strange coincidence you heard about it from this girl you just met on the way here."

"I never dreamed when I heard about the tragedy of Kulyash from Ainur that Kulyash's husband Vladimir would turn out to be the senior scientist working with your friend Victor on Voz Island, along with our stalker and your potential killer Nikolai," Grace says, looking bewildered herself.

"Kulyash Krylova did not tell me her husband's name the day I met her at the train station before she plunged to her death. Now that we have a name for him, we will always remember Vladimir Krylov, his wife Kulyash Krylova, and their baby Dina as a family that became sacrificial victims of a cruel society controlled by greed and power, with no regard for human life," Ayan eulogizes.

"Very heartbreaking, but nonetheless a closure to their tragedy. I pray they are at peace now," Grace says.

———

Grace receives a call from Ayan a week after her return to Almaty. He has fully recovered from his physical ordeal. Timur has survived the gunshot wound and is recovering. Sairan, the friend who provided Aldiyar and Darkhan with a boat in Kulandy, was summoned to Aralsk to identify the two persons they took to Voz Island that fateful day of April 3, 2007. He confirmed Nikolai was Timur's companion. Furthermore, specimens of DNA taken from Nikolai and Timur have been sent to Almaty for crime testing. Another week goes by. Grace receives an email from Ayan with the news that Timur's DNA is found to match a couple strands of human hair taken from Aldiyar's remains, and Nikolai's DNA is a match for the blood encrusted under Darkhan's fingernails. It is obvious that a struggle took place between the two murdered men and their assailants. Nikolai and Timur, who have been taken to Kyzylorda and held without bail, are arraigned for the murders of Aldiyar Baizhanov and Darkhan Rymov, and the attempted murder of Ayan Kazbekov.

Grace is grateful Ayan no longer needs to fear Nikolai and Timur and that Aldiyar and Darkhan will have justice. She is happy to be back home with Glen, who is more than anxious to have her in his arms again.

Within ten days after her return to Almaty, Glen passes Victor's file containing the formula for the antidote for anthrax strain 5942 to the United Nations World Health Organization. The threat of the deadliest strain of anthrax to date, the cultivated spores of which are supposedly buried somewhere on Voz, once an island in the desiccated Aral Sea, has been neutralized. When Grace calls Ayan to notify him the formula for the antidote has been safely delivered to the WHO, Ayan says with deep emotion, "Victor has found his peace. He has fulfilled the mission his mentor, Vladimir Krylov, gave him before leaving Voz Island."

"Do what you can, Victor, for humanity," Grace quotes. "He did it."

—

Glen's one-year term in Kazakhstan turns into a five-year assignment, with his promotion from Senior Assistant to Chief of Party. Grace stays on in Almaty with Glen through his years of service in Kazakhstan. She finally has the time to dabble on her first novel, a mystery-thriller, and then another. A year after her return to Almaty from her hair-raising adventures in the Aral Sea region, she and Glen welcome their first child, a son, whom they name Victor.

AUTHOR'S NOTE

To avoid confusion, the author has retained the name Aralsk for the former harbor town on the northern shore of the Aral Sea in Kazakhstan throughout this novel, although the town's name has been changed to Aral since the end of the Soviet Union.

The name of Vozrozhdeniya Island in the Aral Sea has been shortened to Voz Island in this novel.

GLOSSARY

Ake—Father in Kazakh

Apa—Mother in Kazakh

Aspirant—Student studying for aspiranture program in preparation for doctorate degree in Soviet time

Aspiranture—Three-year studies beyond first diploma in university in Soviet time

Ata—Grandfather in Kazakh

Baursak—Kazakh fried bread

Belyashi—Deep-fried Central Asian pastry of meat and onion

Bulochka—Russian bun or pastry

Dacha—Summer cottage in the countryside

Do svidaniya—"Goodbye" or "Till we meet again" in Russian

Dobroe utro—"Good Morning" in Russian

Docent—Lecturer in university in Soviet time

Dombra—Kazakh two-string musical instrument

Manti—Central Asian dumplings

Oblast—Province or state in Soviet time

Pelmeni—Russian dumplings

Plov—Central Asian dish of rice, lamb, onion, carrot

Rakhmet—"Thank you" in Kazakh

Ruble—Soviet currency, also Russian currency

Samsa—Baked Central Asian pastry of meat and onion, usually triangular in shape

Shanyrak—Round wooden frame at the roof of a Kazakh yurt

Shashlik—Skewered grilled meat cubes, usually lamb or beef, originating from the Caucasus and Central Asia

Sovkhoz—State-owned farm in Soviet time

Taqiya—Kazakh hat worn by men

Tenge—Kazakh currency

USAID—United States Agency for International Development

Ya ne znayu—"I don't know" in Russian

Yurt—Kazakh tent house used by nomads

Zdravstvuyte—"Hello" in Russian

ACKNOWLEDGMENTS

I am deeply grateful to all the wonderful people I met in Kazakhstan who have been my inspiration, have offered me encouragement, and have acted as walking encyclopedias throughout the writing of this novel, including Kuralay Yeldesbay, Inessa Sze, Ainur Yerdaulet, Karlygash Baizhanova.

To Sam Sze, my son, who took time off his busy work schedule to produce the custom maps I requested with efficiency and promptness, a big and heartfelt thank you.

To Leanne Lieberman, my deep appreciation for reading early versions of *Sea Fever*, giving honest and constructive critiques of the former drafts, which led to what the novel is today.

I am thankful to Isabel Huggan, always my mentor, for her encouraging remarks and enthusiasm about *Sea Fever*.

Finally, *Sea Fever* would not have materialized if it weren't for my ever-supportive husband, Michael, who opened a new world for me the first time I accompanied him on a business trip to Kazakhstan over twenty years ago and has gone back with me countless times since to this fascinating country. I thank God for him as we count our blessings and continue to navigate life's multifaceted adventures.

ABOUT THE AUTHOR

 **B**orn and raised in Hong Kong, Elsie Sze has spent a good part of her adult life in Canada and the United States. Her first novel, *Hui Gui: A Chinese Story* was shortlisted for *ForeWord* Magazine's Fiction Book of the Year Award in 2005, followed by *The Heart of the Buddha*, a finalist in ForeWord Magazine's Book of the Year Award for Multicultural Fiction in 2009. Her third novel, *Ghost Cave: A Novel of Sarawak*, won the Saphira Prize inaugurated by the Women in Publishing Society, Hong Kong in 2012. *Ghost Cave* has been translated into French.

Elsie holds a master's degree in English from the University of Toronto and a master's degree in Library Science from the University of Chicago. She is an alumnus of a creative writing program with Toronto's Humber School for Writers.

Elsie lives with her husband and family in California.

Made in the USA
Las Vegas, NV
16 December 2022

62456233R00163